THE ANCHOR IS THE KEY

LINDA ANTHONY HILL

BLACK ROSE writing™

The final approval for this literary material is granted by the author.

First printing

This is a work of fiction. Names, characters, businesses, places, events and incidents
are either the products of the author's imagination or used in a fictitious manner.
Any resemblance to actual persons, living or dead, or actual events is purely
coincidental.

ISBN: 978-1-61296-960-2
PUBLISHED BY BLACK ROSE WRITING
www.blackrosewriting.com

Printed in the United States of America
Suggested Retail Price (SRP) $18.95

The Anchor is the Key is printed in Adobe Garamond Pro

This is dedicated to my mother who was in the process of reading it when she died from a tragic accident. She never found out what happened with Joe.

THE ANCHOR
IS THE KEY

CHAPTER ONE

The Crystal ball rolled slowly across the old hardwood floor until it stopped inches shy of Madam Celeste's right foot. Stooping down to pick it up with great care so as to maintain the exact aspect of where it had stopped caused her to utter a small sigh. She peered deeply into the purposely imperfect yellow citrine globe. Had it been clear and flawless there would be no point in maintaining the aspect. This was one of her favorite Crystal balls because of all it's interesting imperfections deep within the stone.

"What's this?" Celeste asked the universe in general. "Do you feel like I need a nudge today? Let's just have a look."

"Hmmm…. I see an adventure in store. And that some things are going to take me by surprise. Me? Madame Celeste? Really?"

As if to answer, one of her currently being read books fell to the floor with a loud crash. It landed with the pages up. Celeste glanced at the page and found a passage about the mysteries of the universe unveiling themselves in the mundane and ordinary routines of simple daily life.

"I see. You want me to read my own cards today. My days are never adventurous. Now you want me to believe there's an unpredictable adventure headed my way. Very well, let the personal reading begin."

Celeste walked to a large wooden box that was kept unobstructed near the bay window. It looked like a small steamer trunk from a time when Lords and Ladies traveled on tall ships and carried with them everything they owned not because they were moving, but because they were traveling in a world without banks. Lifting the curved lid revealed the tools of her trade laid out neatly in various compartments. The Oracle cards that were used every day, two sets of runes, several other versions of the Oracle cards (also known as Tarot cards), one set of Angel cards, candles for wax readings, at least ten pendulums for scrying and two crystal balls.

Reaching for the daily Oracle cards she carried them to the reading table and shuffled them until something told her to stop. Three cards were drawn and laid down in a row. It was an odd assortment. All were reversed and all were cups. This was something new that made no sense to her.

Back at the trunk a small bag of runes beckoned her. She drew one stone from the bag. There was no Rune on this stone. It was the one called Wyrd, oddly enough pronounced weird. It signified that whatever was coming was inevitable and must be accepted as such.

Celeste decided to take a short walk. Her first client wouldn't be there for another hour and this would allow her to think about the signs she had just received. Pulling a sweater from the closet and heading for the door brought, once again the Crystal ball rolling to her feet. It had been returned to its pedestal earlier, but here it was on the floor again. She lifted it carefully and took a seat studying it more closely this time. There was a flaw deep inside the ball that had eluded her before. It looked like a small anchor. What could that mean? Celeste placed the ball back on its pedestal in the center of the reading table. This changed nothing. "I'm still going for a walk."

Chaos walked between Celeste's legs and meowed softly. "I'll be back in plenty of time," said Celeste. "I just need to clear my head before my first reading. It will be fine."

Celeste walked down the street and breathed in the fresh morning air. Her intent was to walk across the tracks and down to the creek. There had been rain recently so it was possible there would actually be water in the creek. It did not disappoint.

The property next to the creek pastured two horses. They recognized Celeste and sauntered over to the fence. They were hoping for the usual carrots or apples. They nuzzled up to her outstretched hand. They quickly realized that there was nothing for them, but they stayed. Animals liked Celeste and the feeling was mutual. Celeste thought herself to be a heavy woman and would never subject such beautiful beings to carrying her weight, but suspected that they would if need be. In reality she was five ft. five inches and wore a size fourteen. This beautiful woman had been slender in her twenties and every pound gained since then made her feel grossly obese.

Celeste walked on down to the creek. This was no typical creek. Its hollow was taller than Celeste. Its width was easily twenty ft. at the base, but there was usually only a trickle of water, if that. There were no trees or brush growing alongside it. The creek had been dredged and widened to control flooding when the rains came too fast. Celeste remembered the old creek. It was wide and deep, yes, but there was growth on the side of the water. There were trees and bushes and sometimes flowers in the right season.

Today there was still water flowing from the recent rains. Celeste went to her special spot and moved a few rocks around in the water. They revealed a cache of beautiful crystals and precious stones she had placed there recently to be cleansed and energized by the rains and the full moon. Having hidden them in such a way that the water could reach them, but prying eyes wouldn't see them. Gathering them up in a silk scarf she then tied them securely to her belt.

Passersby might have mistaken her for a gypsy as they crossed over the bridge and glanced down, but the locals all knew her and paid her no mind.

As Celeste turned to leave something across the creek caught her eye. There was a small model boat on the rocks. Some child had no doubt left it for another day not realizing that the water could carry it far away if there was a rain. It reminded her of the new symbol in the crystal ball, wondering if the two were tied together. Gathering up her long ample skirt she waded across the few inches of water to the toy boat and picked it up. It revealed itself to her.

A young boy had been playing with it by the creek when the creek was swollen from the rains. It got away from him and he ran along the creek to try to reach it. He stumbled on the rocks and fell into the rushing water.

Celeste scanned the surrounding landscape. There was no child to be seen and no way to tell how old the vision was. The child could be washed up on the shore hurt. Something compelled her to search for him walking slowly down the creek searching with the boat still in hand. After walking all the way to the next bridge, which was only a short block, there was a need to stop.

"Where did you get that boat," called a man from the bridge. "It's my son's boat."

"I found it near the last bridge," called Celeste. "I'm looking for the boy now. I have seen no sign of him, but I had a vision that he fell into the creek chasing the boat when the water was much higher."

"He did," called the boy's father. "We have found him and he is safe. He is obsessed with finding the boat."

"Then this is your lucky day," said Celeste with a broad smile. "Here it is."

The man helped Celeste up the bank which was significantly steeper at this bridge than the one where she had entered. It would have been a challenge reaching the road if the man had not been there to help.

"My name is John Scott." The man introduced himself. "My son did fall into the high waters after the recent rains. How did you know?"

"I'm a psychic," Celeste reached into her pocket and withdrew a card with her information. "I live only a few blocks from here and I see clients in my home. In fact, I am expecting someone in the next few minutes and I need to hurry if I'm not to be late."

"Let me give you a ride," said Mr. Scott.

"Not ordinarily, but I am in a hurry now. Thank you."

Celeste was no further from her house here than at the other bridge, but she had spent more time than planned when the mission changed to looking for a drowned little boy. It was wonderful that the boy was safe, but for her there was nothing more offensive than being late for an appointment.

"How much do you charge for a reading?" asked John.

"I generally charge by the hour. But simple readings that only take a few minutes are usually fifteen dollars."

John reached in his pocket and pulled out a roll of cash. "Here is fifty for finding the boat." He said. "I will want to talk with you again later about how you did it. I cannot tell you how much I appreciate your help." He said as he dropped her off at her house.

"Thank you for the lift, Mr. Scott. I will hold this as a payment for future services."

"No. I insist. That is for your efforts today." He replied.

Celeste did not have time to stand there and argue. She put the cash in her pocket and said, "Thank you."

Celeste's client pulled up as John pulled away. "Come on in," called Celeste. "I'll only be a minute. Just have a seat at the reading table and I'll join you shortly."

Having forgotten to return her runes and cards to their proper places, Michelle was eyeing the runes as Celeste returned to the table.

"What are these for?" asked Michelle. "Are they magic?"

"They have a special energy, but they are not the kind of magic you are thinking of. We can use them today in place of the tarot if you'd like to see how they work."

"Oh, let's do. I'd like to see how you use them. Do I get to choose my own?" she said reaching for a stone.

"No," said Celeste quickly placing her hand in front of the stones effectively denying access. "The energy in these stones is mine and mine alone. If you or anyone else touches them then I have to do a cleansing ritual that would take a few days depending on the moon phase."

"Oh," said Michelle in a small disappointed voice.

"Let's get started, shall we?" said Celeste and proceeded to draw a complicated set of stones from the bag. This reading would take the better part of an hour which is what Michelle paid for.

The reading went well and there was no interference from the Crystal ball. Celeste was glad the rune stones had been "accidentally" left out. In her philosophy there were no such things as accidents. The runes had made for a very unusual reading and exactly what Michelle had needed. She scheduled an appointment for next month and left happy.

Celeste had had quite a morning. It made her uncomfortable having things so close together. It would have been nice to have a few minutes between John and Michelle, but it worked out. Wondering if the toy boat was what the anchor had been predicting there was little time to think about it as the phone rang.

"Hello, this is Madame Celeste. How can I help you fulfill your destiny today?"

"I, I uh, I"

"Would you like to schedule a reading, my dear?"

"Yes. Exactly! Can I come over now? Can you do this by phone? I need help right away," said the anxious woman at the other end of the line.

"I have an opening at one. Can you make that?"

"Where are you located?"

Celeste gave her the address and directions. Her house was in downtown just a few blocks from the square. Most people found it easily enough.

"I'll be there at one," said the distraught client.

Celeste could have seen the woman at noon, but wanted time for lunch.

"No sense working on an empty stomach and the hike this morning took a lot out of me,"

Walking to the kitchen to put on a pot of tea water and to make a sandwich was done slowly and mindfully. She made the act of creating the sandwich a process of meditation and cleansing. This was also part of her philosophy and was incorporated into every task. It helped her to stay in the moment and focused. There was also the knowledge that it made the food healthier as she poured her attention and her soul into it.

Spending quality time eating the food was equally important. She shared a bit with Chaos. It was a pleasant meal with pleasant company. Clean up was an act of meditation which led to a short trip back into the reading room.

"Chaos! What are you doing?" Celeste cried as she saw the cat standing on the reading table with her tail standing straight up. Chaos knew better than to ever be on the reading table. It was the only place in the house that was off limits to her. This day was just out of control.

Celeste walked over to the table where Chaos was still standing with her paw on the black velvet bag that held the psychic's most precious stones and a smaller bag of handmade silver runes. As our heroine picked up the bag Chaos jumped down from the table and rubbed her ankles. *Interesting*, thought Celeste.

"Is this what you wanted me to do? Am I now to be told by a cat and a crystal ball what tools I am to use?" she said smiling with a wink as the words left her mouth. She pulled out the stones that had been marked ages ago as to what energies they magnified.

First was a tiger's eye labeled "focus, NOW, business." Next was the pink quartz that was marked "heal, soothe, relax". Third was a double pointed quartz crystal with a piece of tape where it had been written "nature, garden". And finally a turquoise that said simply "notice details". There were also two homemade pendulums in the large bag. One was made from a nugget of wood and the other was made from a seashell. Last but not least was her most special sterling silver rune casting set. Each silver piece had been formed with a torch while concentrating on the rune she was creating thus letting the "stone" make itself. Since these were first made, no one had ever touched them except Celeste and they were saved for very special clients. She still called them stones, but they were more like fine silver jewelry.

"So, what were you trying to tell me, Chaos?"

Chaos responded with a soft "Meow." Jumping in Celeste's lap and pawing the bag of Crystals and stones.

"Wow! You really are trying to tell me something. I'll keep the stones on my person for the day and I'll use the divining tools for my clients this afternoon. Is that what you want?"

Chaos jumped down and walked to the window perch as if her job was complete.

Celeste looked at the clock and realized she had enough time to put a small Kielbasa in the crock pot with some potatoes and onion and carrots. If it started cooking now, it would be ready by dinnertime.

A car door closed outside just as the lid was placed on the crock pot. It was a little early for her emergency client. Looking out the window was a small very old Mercedes sportster on the street in front of the house. *This should be an interesting meeting*, she thought and went to the door to show the woman in.

"I'm early, I know. I just couldn't wait. I need help right away."

"Let's start with your name, shall we?" said Celeste, picking up a client book and a pen from the desk by the door.

"I'm so sorry. My name is Judy Wells. I live here in Gloryville. Well, not really here in town. I live out near Bella View. I need..."

Celeste held up her hand to stop the verbal deluge. "What is your exact address?"

Collecting the necessary information she then explained her fees and created the payment arrangement. Judy would be paying cash today.

Celeste showed her to the reading room and signaled her to take a seat at the reading table. Once seated Celeste asked, "Now what brings you here today?"

"I think my house has a ghost or a demon or something supernatural. A friend of mine, a neighbor actually, told me you could help. She said you talk to spirits a lot and you could tell me what's going on and maybe even fix it."

"What is your friend's name?" asked Celeste, hoping the reference would be an understanding client if Celeste decided she could not help this woman.

"Christy Baker."

Celeste opened a notebook and wrote Judy's name in it. If Christy had sent this woman then there was something going on at that house and Celeste would be duty bound to help.

"What makes you believe there is something supernatural happening? Be specific."

Judy began to list the things that had happened, "There are noises coming from the attic. It's like someone is walking around up there, but we don't even have any flooring up there."

"That could be squirrels or a raccoon or some other animal," smiled Celeste.

"It could be, but we've had it checked. It isn't. And that's not all. Someone calls my name when there is no one else around."

At this point Celeste was looking at an older woman. Well, a specter of an older woman who was nodding her head in agreement with Judy.

"Is your mother still living?" asked Celeste, knowing the answer before asking.

"No, my mother passed last year. It may sound crazy, but I often feel like Mom's still around. It comforts me to think she watches out for me," said Judy.

"That doesn't sound crazy at all," said Celeste looking at Judy's mother who was nodding in agreement. Mom wasn't smiling though. It occurred to Celeste that Judy's mother might be ready to get on with her afterlife. "What is your mother's name?"

"Judy, just like mine. I was named after her."

"Judy, are you ready to move on?"

The spirit nodded and smiled.

"No, she's not ready. I need her here. I need her watching over me especially now that there's something evil hanging around," cried Judy.

The spirit had stopped smiling again and was standing there with her hands akimbo tapping her foot.

"Judy, is there anything evil lurking around your daughter?" The spirit shook her head. "We need a sign that your daughter can see. Will you ring the bell if your daughter will be safe if you move on?"

The bell rang immediately. Judy gasped. This was not the right answer. There were things going on. Who was going to help with whatever was going on at the house?

"What about the shadow man?" Judy yelled in a panic. "Am I safe from that?"

The bell rang again. The spirit pointed at Celeste. Celeste could not hear her but saw her mouth the words, "You help her now." Judy Sr. faded slowly until Celeste could no longer see or feel her.

"Your mother is gone now, Judy. Her request was for me to look out for you and help you spiritually. Can you meet with me when things are worrying you?"

"I, I suppose so," said Judy.

"You should notice less things happening now. Your mother was trying to get you to call in someone like me, who could see or hear her. The intention was to say goodbye and then move on."

"Well that wasn't much of a goodbye. Tell her to come back. I still need her here. I'm not ready to let go."

"Let's make an appointment for next week and see how you are doing. Hopefully, there will be no supernatural phenomena in the next week," said Celeste. "What time and day would be good for you?" opening the appointment book to set it up. Judy went on her way.

That was almost too easy, thought Celeste preparing the space for her next client. This was a regular and would want her tea leaves read and the tarot cards cast. It was about time for a little normal in this house.

The next client came and went without incident. There was a forty five minute break until her final client of the day and that was a phone client. Phone clients were a little more difficult in some ways because things like what had happened this morning with Judy's mother couldn't happen as easily by phone. That's why Celeste required at least four face to face meetings before doing phone sessions. It was helpful to know what spirits were involved, if any. Also important was learning facial expressions along with speech. Celeste was as much a counselor as a fortune teller and needed all the clues available.

The phone rang half an hour before the appointment, so Celeste assumed it was not her client. "Hello, this is Madame Celeste. How can I help you fulfill your destiny today?"

"This is John. You found my son's boat this morning."

"Hello, Mr. Scott. Was he happy to see it?"

"Oh yes," said John. "Please call me John. I was hoping to schedule an hour of your time one day this week. Do you have an open appointment anytime?"

"Let me get my book. I'm sure I have some openings. I'm never appointed for the full week. How will tomorrow afternoon at one o'clock work?" One p.m. was almost always left open for emergencies.

"That will be fine. I'll see you then," he said and hung up.

So today's excitement is going to carry over to tomorrow. How wonderful! Came the sarcastic thought. *And I still haven't sorted all the messages I received this morning.*

Celeste decided to make a cup of tea for her phone session. Becky was always delightful to talk to. A lively young woman from New York City, arguably one of the most exciting cities on the planet always had some news to share. They would talk for at least ten or fifteen minutes before the session started. Becky's adventures would always transport Celeste to Manhattan and that was almost as good as being there in person..

Celeste was sipping her tea when the phone rang.

"Hello Becky. How are you today?" asked Celeste.

"Oh, Celeste! It's been a horrid week. My best friend died in a subway accident. I don't know what I'm going to do," cried Becky.

"I'm so sorry for your loss," said Celeste quietly.

"I know my reading last week said that it would be a difficult week, but I never expected anything this bad," said Becky.

"I understand, dear. Death is always a shock. Have you been to the service yet?"

"Yes, it was yesterday. Her mom and dad were there and a few friends and people from her office. I already miss her so much, Celeste," cried Becky.

"I'm so sorry, Becky," sympathized Celeste. Today would not be a regular session. Today would be a conversation between friends. Celeste had a degree in social work. There would be no charge for this session, but it would be a therapy session, none the less.

"I just don't know what to do," Becky repeated.

"Cry, my dear, you must let go of some of the grief by crying. Go ahead and let it out."

Becky cried for a time and Celeste listened and imagined herself holding Becky and comforting her. Then asked, "Will you tell me the things you liked most about your friend?"

Becky began listing the things she loved about her friend. It made her feel the loss a little more, but it also made her feel a little more light-hearted.

The session went on for over an hour. They made an appointment for the next week. This was actually one of Celeste's favorite kinds of sessions. Not helping someone grieve, but helping someone come to terms with their own emotions. All her training came into play in a session like this. While her training was used in some degree in every session, there was no bill from a psycho therapist.. The people that called her or walked through her door were far more likely to listen to a psychic than a psycho therapist. Celeste didn't mind. She was, after all, both.

The smell of Kielbasa had begun to permeate the house and it made Celeste feel hungry. Dinner tonight might be a little early. The phone rang again. The caller ID didn't identify the caller so it was decided to let it go to the answer machine. Dinner was ready. But, Celeste could hear the plea for help and couldn't ignore it.

"This is Judy Wells. My mother was wrong. There is still someone here and I need your help."

"Judy, tell me exactly what has happened," said Celeste picking up the phone before Judy could finish her message and hoping to handle this over the phone.

"There is a shadow man. At least there was. I saw him out of the corner of my eye, but when I turned he was gone. Mom must not have seen him, but he's here and I've heard a lot of terrible things about shadow people. They mean nothing but harm and they are evil and…"

"Calm down," Celeste jumped in. "Where exactly were you when you saw him?"

"I was standing in the dining room. I felt him and then I saw him to the side and slightly behind me. I think he's stalking me." Judy took a breath to continue, but Celeste took advantage of the pause again.

"You need to calm down, Judy. That is always the first thing to be done in a situation like this. I want you to go back into the dining room and stand as you were standing when it happened. Let me know when you are there."

After a minute or two Judy checked in, "I'm here."

"Now close your eyes for a minute and tell me what you feel," directed Celeste.

After a few seconds, Judy gasped.

"What is it, Judy?" asked Celeste.

"It's.... I don't know how to explain it, but... It feels like... It could be... No, no it couldn't be. But it feels like... my father."

Celeste closed her eyes and tried to connect with both Judy and her environment. It worked fairly quickly. She could see a large dining room with an elegant table, tall ceilings and a large bay window.

"Judy, are you facing the bay window?"

"Yes... yes, I am. How did you know? I didn't tell you there was a bay window," said Judy with a hint of concern.

"Psychic here, remember?" answered Celeste.

"Is the bay window important?"

"I don't know," said Celeste. "Was it important to your father? Did he build it or use it a lot?"

"I think he built it," said Judy. "You are amazing."

"He may be part of the room," said Celeste. "He may be attached because of the window. I don't think it is anything to worry about. That may be why your mom said it wouldn't hurt you. Can you live with the idea that he is part of the house?"

"I think so," said Judy.

"Good, then let's call this the end of the session and I will see you for your appointment next week. Does that work for you?"

"I may need to see you sooner. Do you have any opening tomorrow?"

"No, I don't. Do you want me to look at my Thursday schedule?"

"That would be great," said Judy.

"I can see you Thursday at ten a.m. Will that work?"

"Yes, ma'am, I will be there at ten sharp and thank you so much"

Celeste hung up the phone. "That was easy enough. Now I am truly starving. It's time for that sausage and veggies."

Chaos jumped up in her lap immediately. "No you don't. There will be leftovers for you when I have finished. But I will eat in peace."

Her clear crystal ball came rolling to a stop at her feet. She looked at it then looked at the cat then finished her meal. The ball would wait. The cat would wait. Celeste would have her meal and that, as they say, was THAT.

CHAPTER TWO

After finishing a delicious meal and tidying up, Celeste gathered up the crystal ball and carried it to the reading room. This ball was different from the ones used on a daily basis. This was more for show. It had the look of the traditional crystal ball. It was perfectly clear and pure crystal. It had a wonderful energy, but because it had no flaws, it was difficult to read. There was nothing to read, no flaws to interpret, no lines to decipher. She could only interpret the energy that emanated from it.

Anyone who was not a psychic would find this all but impossible. Only a true psychic could ever hope to use this ball. Celeste embraced the large ball, closed her eyes and let it "speak" to her.

To her surprise her mind called in an anchor. This was a ships anchor. There would be no such anchor in this area of the planet. Maybe a cruise was on the horizon. That was a nice thought. She had not seen the ocean in almost six months.

Immediately the anchor was replaced with a ring. It was a beautiful gold ring with a stunning blue sapphire as its center stone, surrounded by rubies. It made her sad. The sadness almost overwhelmed her. This was not about Celeste going on a cruise. *Darn the luck,* she thought.

The sadness lingered long enough for Celeste to shed some tears. Whatever was being foretold was very strong. More tears were felt while returning the Crystal ball to its pedestal near the window.

This day had been far from boring. There was a little anxiety about all these signs that were coming in. Apparently her days had been in a bit of a rut with her usual clients. Life had certainly shaken the bottle today.

The evening proved to be a tad tamer. Chaos convinced her (Don't ask how) to break up the routine and take a walk downtown. Maybe a small change in habit was a good thing. There was a tea room on the square. Celeste was craving one of their locally famous desserts. It was a wonderful chocolate creation which reminded her a little of Baklava, but not so messy and moist. The thought of it filled her taste buds with such wonderfulness.

The walk was pleasant. A few acquaintances were out this evening and stopped to talk two or three times. The last one was her massage therapist. "I do need to get back in to see you," she told Danielle.

"Call me tomorrow and we'll set up an appointment," said Danielle getting business out of the way, then switching to friend mode, "How have you been?"

"I've had a very interesting day," since you ask. "I've been receiving the most unusual signs. Two of my crystal balls rolled to me on their own today. Do you believe that? It wasn't at the same time either. They came over the course of the day… Rolled right up to my foot, they did. Even Chaos has been acting strangely." Celeste surprised herself with this outpouring of personal information. "Would you like to walk over to Tara's Tea Room with me for some dessert, my treat?"

"I'd love to," said Danielle. "It's been a long while since I've been in there. Have you talked to Tina lately? I know there was talk of cancer for a long time."

"I talked to her a few weeks ago. The cancer is in remission and doing much better. They're even keeping the tea room open late at night again," said Celeste.

"You know, it's just a short walk for me, but I don't make it over there often enough. I need to offer her a therapy session if we see her this evening."

"That will be great for her," said Celeste. "Tell me, have you heard of or do you know Judy Wells?"

"The mother or the daughter?" responded Danielle.

"So you've heard of them," giggled Celeste. "Do you know the daughter?"

"I was friends with her mother. Used to come to my yoga classes. Wonderful lady. I've met her daughter, but I don't know her that well. Brought a few of her mom's yoga tools to the studio after her death. I offered her some classes, but there was zero interest."

"From what I've learned of her, that girl could use some yoga classes. I'll see if I can guide her in that direction," said Celeste. "How did her mother die?"

"It was in a car accident. Killed instantly, they say. Had a head on collision

20

with a truck. The man driving the truck survived. Judy was not so lucky. The police arrested him for manslaughter at first, but the blood tests came back clean and it was determined that it was Judy who drifted out of her lane into his. So, it was ruled an accident. Is her ghost still around?"

"No… well…. Not after this morning."

They had arrived at Tara's and were seated at a table near the front window. "Anyway… I was basically left with her daughter's fear of the supernatural this morning."

"Who did?" said Tina as she joined them at the table.

"Tina," they squealed together as they saw her.

"Spill it. Who left their daughter in your capable hands?" insisted Tina.

"Now I really feel like I'm telling tales out of school," said Celeste as her face flushed with embarrassment. "I was really just looking for information from Danielle about the late Judy Wells."

"That was so sad to hear about her death. Such a nice woman. Would have gone out of her way to help anyone," said Tina. "I don't know much about her daughter, though. I don't think she's ever been in here."

"The girl is not exactly what you would call enlightened," chimed in Danielle.

The waitress came to take their order and Tina ordered right along with them. They all asked for something different to share a bite or two, so each would get to try three different desserts. Not that Tina needed to, being the owner, but it was fun.

"Well, she's on her own now," said Celeste. "Her mother's spirit moved on today."

"I don't know whether to be sad for the daughter or happy for Judy," said Tina grinning mischievously.

"A little of each, I think," said Celeste with a soft sadness to her voice.

There was a long pause in the conversation. "That looks like our desserts coming now," said Tina. "What have you been up to, Danielle?" changing the subject completely.

"I went to Dallas for a conference last week. Caught up with some old friends and learned a few new techniques for using hot stones in the massage therapy. You need to come over for a session, Tina. You are past due."

"My schedule just hasn't allowed for it lately," said Tina.

"First one is on me," said Danielle. "I'll call you tomorrow to set the appointment."

Conversation lapsed again while the ladies enjoyed their respective desserts and passed the plates around for tasting.

"I'd better get back to work," said Tina finishing hers off. "And don't worry about the check. This one is on me."

Celeste and Danielle thanked her and stayed a few more minutes talking before they left. They parted company on the sidewalk outside the entry to Danielle's loft apartment. Celeste reflected on the night's conversations while walking the remaining blocks home.

"Killed in a car accident," she mumbled aloud. "That one did not strike me as one who had left so abruptly. I wonder if there is more to this story."

Chaos greeted Celeste at the door. "Come with me, my sweet, I think it's time for sleep. Maybe some answers will come to me in my dreams. I'm so curious about this anchor. Maybe it's related to Mr. Scott's boat, but I hope it's about something more exciting than a toy boat."

CHAPTER THREE

Celeste awoke to Chaos's nose nudging her. Always awake by dawn there was never the need for an alarm, this morning. it seemed, was an exception. Chaos was, thankfully, her failsafe backup alarm. The cat was a tortoise shell which is like a Calico with the predominant color being black and little or no trace of white. It was, in many ways, like having a human around. And this morning Celeste was grateful for her little four legged alarm clock.

This was not a good morning to oversleep. There was an appointment at nine a.m. and a pretty full day. She wasn't late enough to feel rushed, but there was no time for a morning walk, either. Her nine o'clock would be a few minutes early, too, as always.

Her morning ritual went more quickly than usual, skipping tea and opting for coffee and an English muffin. It might have been unprofessional, but the thought was there: what did Mr. Scott want. And what was this nagging feeling about Judy Wells. Not the daughter so much as the mother. The daughter was going to be a handful, but her mother's death didn't set right with Celeste. There was more to it. That was sure. And the suspicion that Mama Wells had not really moved on lingered like the smell of fried fish.

Thinking of that... *When was Judy scheduled next? Was it written it in her appointment book? Was it today? Ah, here it is,* she thought. *I have her down for Thursday at ten a.m..*

Celeste perused the day's appointments. First was a nine o'clock and a ten thirty that would take up the morning. Then Mr. Scott was due at one and a regular at three-thirty that would take up the better part of the afternoon. All in all it would be a pretty full day. Prepping the reading room took less time than expected and done in plenty of time even though her nine o'clock was early, as expected. The reading went well and there were no surprises. Well, no surprises for Celeste. Clients were often surprised by what Celeste would reveal.

The morning went smoothly and if it weren't for her one o'clock there would be no thought that yesterday's signs had been fulfilled. Life was back to Celeste's version of normal. But her one o'clock had the potential to create some waves.

She half expected her crystal ball to pay her another visit, but it remained on its dragon bedecked pedestal all morning. At lunch there was time enough to read her runes. It was a simple three stone draw. The runes foretold mystery and danger. Celeste smiled at the thought of some excitement.

It was almost one o'clock when she moved to the reading room to do one last check that everything was in place. Mr. Scott did not arrive until five past the hour. Celeste made a mental note. There was no harm in people being late if they had a consistent modus operandi. It would take a few more times to establish a pattern.

Celeste showed him in and directed him to the reading table. "How are you today, Mr. Scott?"

"Please, call me John," he said. "I don't want us to have to stand on formalities."

"Very well, John. What can I help you with today?"

"I have something going on at work that I'm hoping you can help with," he said.

"John, have you ever been to a psychic before?"

"No, I've never believed in a psychic before," he responded bluntly.

"But you believe in me?"

"You knew what had happened to my son just from holding his boat," he said. "You're the real deal. And I think you're exactly who I need as a consultant at work."

"Consultant?" asked Celeste with more than a little surprise in her voice. She was not accustomed to being this surprised by a client. "So, you're not here for a reading today?"

"Not exactly, I have a situation at work that I need some help with. I don't want to hire you full time. I just need you for interviewing potential employees and maybe to look at this one particular, hmm, situation."

"Your company is interested in bringing in a paid psychic as a consultant?"

asked Celeste skeptically.

"We have had a lot of people leave without good reason. They don't work together in one department, or report to the same supervisors, but they all occasionally frequent one area of the building."

"I don't understand what you think I can do," said Celeste rather befuddled.

"For starters if you interview the new hires, you can help weed out anyone that's not going to stick with it. Also, you can poke around a little, literally, and see if you pick up anything like you did with my son's boat. I think I've narrowed it down to a loading bay near a clerk's office. Accounting has to come down there sometimes, so that would explain the clerk and the junior accountant and the loading dock hand. They would have all been in that vicinity for prolonged periods of time before they gave notice."

"What do you think I might find, John?"

"I think there is something supernatural going on."

"John, do you own the company?" asked Celeste.

"No," said John. "Why do you ask?"

"Do you really think the company is going to pay for a psychic to consult?"

"Oh... I see your concern. I don't own the company but, I'm the head of HR, um... human resources. I would be the one who would question it or approve it. And I already approve it."

"Still... Wouldn't it be better to hire me in my capacity as a licensed Psychotherapist?" said Celeste.

John's face belied his shock at this revelation. "You're a Psychotherapist? Why do you do all this mumbo jumbo if you have a license to counsel?"

Celeste smiled at John betraying his true belief. "Some people are embarrassed to say they go to a counselor, John. Since I actually am a psychic, it just makes sense to offer those services. If, occasionally someone needs a bit of therapy and I happen to lend an ear or some sound advice, who has been harmed?"

John's face lit up and he breathed a sigh of relief. "This changes everything. You're a bit steep for what we would usually pay for a staff social worker, but since you'll only be consulting part time..."

"VERY part time," interjected Celeste.

"Okay. VERY part time, I could justify a half day every week."

"Make it every other week. Make it on Friday mornings. I generally take Fridays off so I won't have to move any clients to accomplish that."

"Friday it is," said John.

"Do you start at eight o'clock or nine o'clock?" asked Celeste.

"I was hoping you could be there at six a.m. to interview a couple of people on the night shift."

"No, no, no. I do not rise before the sun and it is not yet summertime," she said with emphasis on the not.

"Okay, okay. I'll find a way for them to stay late one Friday. Who knows. Maybe you will have this solved before you get a chance to meet them."

"Do we want people to know I'm a Psychotherapist?" asked Celeste.

John belly laughed. "The question should be, do we want them to know you're a psychic," he said through the laughter.

"There are a lot of people in this town who know I'm a psychic. Very few people know I'm a psychotherapist and I wouldn't mind keeping it that way."

"I guess as long as you show up on payroll as a psychotherapist that should be all that's needed. You can maintain your psychic status and what the home office doesn't know shouldn't hurt me." He laughed again.

John was very satisfied with the meeting. "How much do I owe you for today? I haven't been here more than twenty minutes, but I know you set aside an hour for me."

"You have interviewed me and given me a job, I don't think it would be very ethical to charge for that."

"Still, I took up your time. Tell you what… You give me a, what do you call it? Reading? And I'll pay for a full session."

"We don't have time for an extensive reading, but we can do a three card draw or a rune casting."

"What about this crystal ball? Don't all psychics use this?"

"Not that often, but we can have a look if you like."

Celeste slid the ball on its pedestal closer to her, turned on a small light at the base of the pedestal, and then peered into the ball blocking out all other thoughts except those of John. As a picture formed of the model ship sitting in John's office she raised her head slowly, looking John in the eyes and asked,

"How is your son, John?"

CHAPTER FOUR

"He's doing fine. But… now that you mention it…"

"Yes," said Celeste with a stern face.

"There was a piece of the boat that was missing. It was an anchor. Actually it was a novelty key in the shape of an anchor. Did you see something like that around where you found the boat? He would really like to have it back. It's a piece of the boat, after all."

"I don't recall seeing it, but, I wouldn't mind going back after my last client this afternoon and looking around a bit."

"I wouldn't want you to go to that trouble," said John. "If you'll tell me where you found the boat, I'll go look for it myself."

Celeste didn't know why, but the thought wouldn't leave her that John was lying about something. *An anchor that looked like a key, who did he think he was trying to fool?* she thought.

"I couldn't come close to describing the exact spot," said Celeste. "I'll go over there around five o'clock to see what I can see."

"I'll pick you up, if you like. We can go together," offered John.

"John, is this for your son or is this for you?" asked Celeste. "That boat didn't look like a child's boat. It looked like a very nice model."

"Oh my, look at the time," moaned John. "I'm going to be late getting back to work. I'll see you around five o'clock. Thank you." He hurried out the door.

This is strange, thought Celeste. *There is so much more to this than I suspected. What is he hiding?*

Looking at the clock, there was just enough time to walk down to the creek now. John had left early and her next appointment was over an hour off. Grabbing two apples from the kitchen and hurrying on out the door allowed her a little more time maybe to visit with the horses.

The walk was pleasant and invigorating. There was no time to talk with the horses first. Her curiosity was high about this anchor/key that John was looking for. Could it be an anchor and would it satisfy part of her visions yesterday?

Celeste used the bridge to cross the creek this time and did a little slip slide down to the bottom of the side where the boat had been. The grade was much steeper on this side of the bridge. It took a minute to get her bearings and go straight to the spot where the boat had been. It didn't take long to find the anchor/key. It was cleverly made to appear to be an anchor. It had a hole ground in the key end for the anchor chain to loop through which only made it more realistic in appearance.

Picking up the anchor to put it in her pocket triggered a vision of a small office with large windows on one wall. They were covered with blinds. It was easy to see that they looked out on another room. There were tall metal file cabinets on the other walls.

In the center of the room was a very old banker's desk. The desk was so large the room seemed to have been built around it. There were papers stacked in neat piles all over the desk except for one small area closest to the equally old leather reclining office chair, leaving just enough room to work on active folders. Someone spent a lot of time in this office.

The calendar on the wall near the open door was current. Underneath it was a wall safe. The sounds coming from the outer room seemed to be those of a warehouse. Was this the area that John had been worried about? What was beyond the door was not visible from this vantage point and there was no way to change the vantage point.

There was no one in the room. Celeste wondered if the door was always left open. There was also a file drawer open as if someone had stopped mid search and left.

The image faded and Celeste raised her hand to cover her eyes from the bright sunlight. After almost falling down the steep side that she was on it seemed better to cross the stream and ascend on the other side.. The water was lower today than it had been yesterday so it was simple to walk from rock to rock without actually wading in the water.

As she started to walk up the slope there was someone moving towards her out of the corner of her eye. Imagine her surprise to find John Scott walking up the creek searching it high and low. He hadn't seen her yet, coming from the direction where he had found her the day before.

"Mr. Scott," she called. "How interesting to find you here."

John came to a stop. "I remembered that my next appointment wasn't for an hour, so I thought I'd have a look for myself," he said "I really hated the idea of wasting your time."

"I've found your anchor," said Celeste.

"Thank you," he said breathing a deep sigh of relief.

"Now, let's see… where did I put that?" Celeste searched her pockets and delayed delivering the key more to see what John's reaction would be than because of not being able to find it.

"You just had it, right?" asked John anxiously.

"I have it. Emphasis on the have," replied Celeste. It was almost as if the key wanted to stay with her. The key truly was being elusive with her. Her hand couldn't quite get hold of it in the pocket. Then, as if by magic, there it was. Celeste pulled the key from her pocket and John grabbed it immediately.

Celeste's curiosity was about to get the better of her. She wanted to ask John about the office and the safe and the key, but held her tongue. The universe would reveal what was needed at the perfect time.

"Would you like a ride to the office on Friday?" John blurted out obviously trying to salvage the situation.

"That would be most appreciated," said Celeste. Celeste owned a car, but rarely drove. When you are prone to go into trances it isn't really safe to be driving.

"I'll be there for you about ten till nine then. Would you like a lift now?" he asked.

"No, thank you. I have another errand before going home."

"I could drop you off," he offered.

"Thank you, but I'm already here. I'm looking for a stone. It's been calling to me since I arrived."

"Very well," said John politely. "I'll leave you here."

John walked south alongside of the creek. Celeste stood there watching until he was out of site. *What else is he not telling me?* She wondered.

Making her way up the west side of the creek the stone that had drawn her before beckoned her now. Glancing around and spotting it near the cleansing hole saved a few minutes. It was an amethyst. It had been left out in the sun which is not good for an amethyst. Retrieving it and holding it briefly before placing it in a special pocket made her feel better about having left it out. "I'm so sorry to have left you here unprotected," she said to the little stone. "I'll be more careful next time. I promise."

Celeste climbed up the gentle slope and walked over to the pasture fence. The horses had noticed her and were on their way over. They enjoyed her speaking to them and stroking their faces. The two apples were an extra special treat. They were delighted. Celeste reveled with them for a minute. Their joy was contagious and her reaction was to bask in it like warm sunlight on a cool winter day.

The walk had been a very good idea. She thanked her Spiritual team mates for their help with being in the exact right place at the exact right time. There was so much information to process. It was exciting to have all the new prospects that were popping up. It was a mystery how this would play out at John Scott's office, but her curiosity was as high as it had ever been about a new client.

Five minutes before her next session which was plenty of time to clean up and be ready saw her home. Chaos joined her in the dressing room/bathroom. The cat was being unusually clingy today.

The doorbell rang and Celeste moved to let Lori, her next appointment, in and escorted her to the reading table.

Lori was quite animated today. The excitement was about an opportunity for Celeste. "Have you ever been to the St. Mark's Church Craft show and Bazaar?" Lori blurted out.

"No, I don't believe I have," Celeste responded.

"I've convinced the board that it would be wonderful to have a psychic at the show. The table would only cost you twenty five dollars and you could do readings at your usual price. Wouldn't that be fabulous?" Lori said smiling from ear to ear.

"I would think the church might object," said Celeste calmly.

"I've told them that you will only use angel cards," said Lori. "like you do with me."

"I still don't know if that would be a good idea. There may be some people there who would object to a psychic. Not everyone is as open minded as you are." Celeste said thinking that Lori was one of her least open minded clients.

Lori would not let Celeste use any cards or stones or crystal balls when doing a reading for her. It was Angel cards only. In her opinion anything else was evil and must be aligned with Satan.

"I have talked with the board and they agreed that if you only do Angel card readings, it would be acceptable to them. And I've talked to a lot of members who would love to have their fortunes told in a Christian way. Please," plead Lori.

"Let me think about it, Lori," was all Celeste could think to say for the moment. It could be a disaster, but it could also be fun. It was worth considering.

Celeste proceeded to read the cards for Lori and, as always, Lori was thrilled with the reading.

"Please say yes," said Lori when leaving. "You are so good and I can't wait to share you with all my friends at church. We'll make sure you get a booth in the corner so that you can set up a little private area for the readings."

"As I said, I'll think about it. Do you want to come at the same day and time next week?"

"Oh, yes, please. I block this time out for the reading on my calendar for the month."

"I'll have an answer about the bazaar by then," said Celeste. "I'll see you next week."

Lori was a nice woman, but some days her sessions just wore Celeste out. It was difficult to incorporate her psychic abilities into the reading when all that was available was the Angel cards. They were a good guidance tool, yes, but they did not allow for as much as the Tarot cards or the runes.

Celeste was glad that Lori was her last appointment of the day. This was a good time to revisit what had happened at the creek and what Mr. Scott was hiding. He was definitely hiding something major.

Her mind took her back to the vision the anchor had revealed. Would there be an office like this at John's plant? And the anchor... it wasn't just a reference for the boat. It had shown her a scene from what could only be an office in a warehouse. It had to be at the heart of this little mystery.

The vision was neatly written down in a journal kept just for visions. Every detail that memory provided was recorded. "Maybe more will reveal itself in my dreams. I think I'll turn in early."

CHAPTER FIVE

Thursday came too early as Chaos pounced on Celeste repeatedly. Celeste looked at the clock expecting to find that it was late in the day when in fact it was an hour too early to be awake.

"Chaos! What is your problem this morning?" apparently expecting an answer.

"Mrow, Meow, Mreow," responded Chaos.

"I'm really not ready to get up, but here I am wide awake. No point laying here pretending. But, I'm warning you…" Celeste couldn't think of anything to threaten Chaos with so she just dropped it.

First stop was the bathroom and then to the kitchen to fix breakfast. There was a man standing in the door from the kitchen to the dining room. "Is this what you were trying to tell me about, Chaos?" Chaos did not reply turning to walk back into the bedroom.

"And who are you, sir?" Celeste asked the shadowy figure of a man.

He couldn't seem to talk, but she could see his face and his mouth was moving.

"I can't hear you. Maybe I could ask some questions and you can nod for yes. Shall we try that?"

He nodded for yes.

"Are you here because of one of my clients?"

He nodded yes.

"Do they have an appointment today?"

He nodded yes.

"Is Judy Wells your daughter?"

He nodded and then hung his head.

"Mr. Wells, I'll be seeing Judy this morning. Is there anything you want me to tell her?"

He nodded again.

"Mr. Wells, Are you the shadow man that Judy keeps seeing?"

He shook his head no.

"Do you visit her in the house often?"

He shook his head.

"Is there a shadow man?"

He nodded

"Does he mean Judy any harm?"

He shook his head no.

"Okay," said Celeste. "Let me go get my talking board and save us some time."

Mr. Wells nodded and disappeared.

Celeste went into the reading room and found her old talking board. It had all the letters and numbers of the alphabet as well as the words yes and no. It was handmade and most people thought it was like an Ouija board. It was not, but Celeste had found it best not to argue.

She set the board up at the reading table. Mr. Wells re-appeared. There was no time to explain. He was already pointing to a letter.

It was slow, but at least you could do more than yes and no questions.

"Why is the shadow man there," queried Celeste.

"HE IS STUCK IN A LOOP," spelled Mr. Wells.

"Is there anything we can do to release him?"

Mr. Wells pointed to the word no. then spelled out, "I WILL HELP HIM FROM THIS SIDE THERE IS MORE POWER HERE THAN YOU REALIZE."

"Judy is frightened of him. Is there anything I can tell her that would ease her mind?" she asked

He spelled out, "IT WILL BE TAKEN CARE OF BY HER FATHER"

"Your daughter will be here today. Would you like to be here to talk to her? I would surely appreciate it if you would. Her nerves are pretty raw," said Celeste.

He pointed to yes.

"I don't remember offhand what time her appointment is, but if you can give me a minute, I will check my book."

He pointed to yes.

Celeste pulled out her book. "She'll be here at ten a.m. It is seven o'clock now. You are welcome to wait here, but I would ask you to wait here in the reading room. I would like to shower and get ready for my day in peace and privacy," Celeste said as nicely as possible so early in the morning.

Mr. Wells nodded yes and took a ghostly seat on a chair that Celeste could not see. The whole scene would probably scare the wits out of most people, but Celeste was not most people. The psychic turned and left for her private quarters without another thought about Mr. Wells.

It was Mr. Scott that was on Celeste's mind. What was he up to and when would he admit that the boat belonged to him, not his young son. There was more. He was hiding something much larger than the ownership of a model ship.

Why in the world would he risk hiring a psychic to screen employees, both potential and existing ones? What could have happened in or related to the company that would push him to hire her? Where was the office she had seen? Who did that office belong to? There were so many questions.

Celeste went into the reading room at one point only to be startled by Mr. Wells sitting there. He had been pushed to the back of her mind by other things. He saw her and moved without standing to the talking board.

"JUDY NOT ACCIDENT" he spelled. "J SCOTT KNOWS MORE"

"Interesting," said Celeste. "How does he know more? Was he there?"

Mr. Wells shook his head then spelled "HAS REPORT."

"Do you know where it is?" she asked.

Mr. Wells nodded.

"Is it in an office inside a warehouse space?"

He nodded energetically.

"I think I've seen it in a vision," she said. "But I don't know where it is."

"AT HIS WORK" spelled Mr. Wells.

"That I believe. I know he's holding back on me. He has a lot more to tell than he is telling."

Mr. Wells nodded.

"I really must go get dressed and ready for your daughter. I want to ask you some more questions, but I have to get ready first. Will you stay?"

He nodded and moved his invisible chair back to where he had been sitting, then disappeared. Would he return before Judy arrived?

Celeste finished getting ready. There would obviously be no walk to see the horses this morning. There was much information to be gotten from Mr. Wells. He may not be able to share everything he knows, but it was possible he would share everything he could.

He would need to rebuild his energy before Judy arrived, but there was time for a short interview.

"Mr. Wells, what can you tell me about the accident that killed your wife?"

NO ACCIDENT

"Was it a successful attempt at suicide?"

He shook his head as if more than a little agitated then spelled NOT HER FAULT.

"But the truck driver was cleared, wasn't he?"

Mr. Wells' eyes became deep blue while the rest of him remained almost a shadow. He looked at her as if to plant the answer in her head. The driver had been cleared, but there was more to the story.

"Do YOU know exactly what happened?"

He nodded.

"Can you tell me?" the words came softly though she couldn't say why.

He shook his head. Celeste knew that there were some things the dead were not able to tell the living. Was it a rule or were the details not available to them in spirit form or what, she didn't know, but it happened. A spirit would know something and not be able to share it.

Celeste also knew that if that was what was happening here, there would be no point in arguing or begging or bargaining. He simply could not share the information. It was up to the living to find the facts in the physical universe.

"Thank you for your help. Maybe you will be able to help me more as I gather more details?"

He nodded.

"Your daughter will be here within the hour. Can you come back then or wait for her and help me with her fear of the shadow person she is seeing?"

He nodded again.

He sat down in his invisible chair again and disappeared.

Celeste shook her head thinking back (was it only three days ago) to the morning that everything in her routine was turned upside down with the help of a crystal ball and a few runes.

"Oh, my gosh! The runes!" gasped Celeste hurrying to find and hide them. Not her everyday runes, but her personal special runes. Who needed anyone else finding and requesting a session with them? They were more powerful than her everyday runes and there was no need to wear them out, so to speak.

"There! I think I will put this pure crystal ball away as well. The other two are much easier to read. I don't know why I keep this one. It's the most expensive one I own and the hardest to use. Still… I can't let it go."

The reading room had needed tidying anyway. This seemed an opportune time to just simplify it a bit. The talking board went under her chair. In case it was needed with Judy if her father had the strength. He was gathering energy for it now, no doubt.

Chaos wandered in and brushed up against her, weaving back and forth between her ankles. It was hard to move for fear of tripping over the silly animal.

"Chaos, what is it now? Honestly you are becoming a nuisance!"

Chaos purred so loud Celeste could hear it five feet away.

"Satisfied with yourself, are you? It was a good job getting me up to see Mr. Wells. Let's go see if we have any tuna on hand. You deserve it." They moved to the kitchen with Chaos right on her heals.

There was a small can of tuna. Chaos was rewarded in the only way that Chaos could understand.

Putting together a meal in the crockpot kept her busy while she waited for Judy. Judy seemed to be an early bird, so trying to be ready for her by nine-fifty seemed prudent. Everything was in the crock pot with a few minutes to spare.

Judy was early as anticipated and Celeste was ready for her.

"I hardly slept a wink last night. This shadow man won't leave me alone. He keeps showing up in the doorway. I know you said he meant me no harm, but he scares me. I don't know what else to do. I may have to sell the house. I've already called a…"

"STOP!" yelled Celeste. The words had been pouring out of Judy so fast that there was no keeping up. "Can I offer you some tea or coff… No, no. You don't need coffee. You need to calm yourself. You are here for a reading, so how about we let me do most of the talking today, okay? Besides, I have information for you. I have been contacted by your father."

Judy's father re-appeared in the same spot he had left from. Judy could not see him, but Celeste could.

"I have already asked him a few questions and he had a message for you about the shadow man."

"Really?" asked Judy excitedly. Celeste could see that Judy was about to launch into another verbal barrage.

"Let me get you that tea. Sit right here and calm yourself knowing that your father is right there," pointing to the spirit she had been entertaining this morning.

Judy's eyes grew wide. "He's right here?"

"Yes."

"And you can see him?"

Celeste nodded with a smile.

"I'll be just a minute with your tea. Do you like it with sugar?"

Judy nodded, having apparently run out of words.

Judy looked in the direction where Celeste had pointed to her father. Her face was pale and her eyes remained wide. Her lips quivered with fear. A tear had formed by the time Celeste returned with the tea.

"Oh sweetie, are you sad that you can't see him?"

Judy shook her head. "I'm frightened. Can you hear him?"

"No, we've been using the talking board to communicate. Can you hear him?"

Judy shook her head. "I'm afraid it would scare me too much."

"Your father is sitting here with us. He is very nice and has told me that the shadow man is stuck in the house. It's a little like he's in a recording that just keeps looping the same scene over and over and over. You can't stop it, but it can't hurt you. Your father says there is nothing for you to be afraid of."

"Is he saying that to you now?" asked Judy.

"No, he told me earlier, before you arrived. Do you have a question for him?"

"Let me think," said Judy.

"Take your time, Judy. I'll set up the talking board"

Celeste needed only to bring it out and put it on the table. There was really no setting up to be done. The board came in handy when a spirit could be seen but, not heard, which was most of the time for Celeste.

Some psychics could hear spirits, but rarely saw them. Some were like Celeste and could see them, but not hear them. And a very few could both see and hear them. Celeste was happy with her gift. There was always the talking board for in depth communication.

"I'm ready," said Judy.

"Okay, what's your first question?"

"Why are you still here?"

Celeste had a notebook and pen on the table. Her first job was to write down the letters as Mr. Wells pointed to them.

"He's pointing to letters. TO L O O K A F T E R M YFA M I L Y. To look after his family," said Celeste.

"Then why is Mom dead?" asked Judy.

S H E S W E R V E D I N T O A T R U C K.

"Why did she swerve into the truck?"

I T W A S I N T H E W R O N G L A N E.

"They said that Mom was in the wrong lane."

S H E W A S T H E T R U C K M O V E D B A C K I N T O T H E I R L A N E A T T H E L A S T M I N U T E.

"What does that even say?" Judy asked Celeste.

They looked at it together. "She was the truck moved back in tot heir lane at the last minute."

"There should be a period after She was. And that's not tot heir, that's to their," said Celeste.

"This is harder than it looks" said Judy.

"So, it was an accident like the report concluded?" asked Celeste.

N O

"That doesn't make any sense!" whispered Judy to Celeste.

Y E S I T D O E S T H E T R U C K W A S I N T H E W R O N G L A N E O N P U R P O S E

"Oh, my," said Celeste. "You mean someone wanted Judy to die in what looked like an accident?

Y E S

"Who would do that? Why? What could Mom possibly have done to deserve that?" Judy said through tears. Her face was red and the tears were flowing faster than Celeste could get the tissues. "We need to call the police! We need to get the investigation re-opened," cried Judy Jr.

"Let's think about this for a minute," said Celeste calmly. "All we have to offer for evidence is the word of a psychic who is seeing a dead man's spirit. What do you think the police will say to that?"

"You're right, of course," said Judy still crying violently. "We need more information. Is my dad still here?"

"Yes, he is," responded Celeste.

"Please ask him if he knows anything else that might help us prove this or lead us to more information."

Mr. Wells nodded. He seemed to want this to come to light.

STARTWITHTHETRUCKCOMPANY

"Which company is that?" asked Judy.

LOCALNAMEISHOLLYFARMS

Celeste circled each word to make it easier to read. "That sounds familiar. I may know the manager of HR there."

"Then she would know about everyone that works there!" said Judy. Her mood lifted immediately. They had a lead.

"As a matter of fact, I'll be visiting with **him** in the morning. I will see what I can discover then," said Celeste.

"Is there anything else we should know, Dad," said Judy.

DONOTFEARTHESHADOWMANIWILLPROTEC TYOU

Once again Celeste circled the words.

"Thank you for doing that," said Judy. "I was having a lot of trouble making it out."

"No problem," said Celeste. "It's difficult for me to read it, too."

"We've almost used up your time and I do have another client coming soon. Would you like to set up another appointment? I have an opening Monday at ten a.m."

"Are you kidding? I can't wait until Monday! I need to come see you after you talk to your HR guy. I want to know what you find out."

"I'll call you tomorrow afternoon then. I'll let you know if I find out anything when I call, but let's set you up for another session on Monday while you're here."

"Okay, okay, as long as you call me tomorrow."

"Good. I'm writing you in for ten a.m. Monday."

The doorbell chimed and Celeste put her arm around Judy's shoulder and steered her toward the door. "This will be my next appointment; I'll talk to you tomorrow afternoon."

Mr. Wells had already disappeared. Celeste asked the next client to have a seat on the porch to give her just a minute to put things back in order.

"I'm so sorry to keep you waiting like that. The last client had a lot going on. Please come in."

CHAPTER SIX

This seemed to be another day that was out of control. Celeste took care of her next client after which the only possible response was to collapse on the sofa to catch her breath. The appointment book showed that the next client was at two o'clock. This would give her a long break and some time to think about what was going on with the Judy Wells situation.

Judy's mother and father didn't seem to be aware of each other. The late Mrs. Wells left with barely a goodbye and never indicated that her late husband was also visiting their daughter, Judy. Celeste needed time to put all this information together and make some sense of it. "Oh, for a week ago when everything was calm and ordered and comfortable."

Chaos leapt on Celeste's chest and made herself at home. She seemed to think that the sofa was the best place for Celeste just now.

"I hope you're not trying to tell me there's another spirit in the house, Chaos. I don't need any more wrinkles in the fabric of my life at the moment. If you're here to nap then I will probably join you."

Chaos walked around in a circle on Celeste's stomach and then lay down and curled up. The purring began almost instantly and the feel and sound of it helped Celeste to doze off.

Her dream was of Mr. Wells. In the dream, he had a voice. He asked her how Celeste was doing. Celeste mentioned being a little tired.

"I'm sure you are," said Mr. Wells. "My daughter is wonderful, but that girl will wear you out."

He was smiling and obviously meant no harm. "This is a nice setup you have here. Do you think you're going to be able to help Judy Jr.?" he asked.

"Maybe," said Celeste. "I'm not sure how to deal with her determination to prove that her mom didn't die accidentally."

"Well that shouldn't be too difficult. It was no accident. The truck driver came into her lane. They would have had a head on collision if Judy hadn't swerved into his lane. Then at the last minute he moved back into his own lane and her car collided with his right front side."

"And you think he did that on purpose?"

"Seems like it to me. How else would you explain it?"

"Well…," said Celeste, "what if he was falling asleep at the wheel and didn't realize until the last minute that it was the wrong lane? Waking up caused him to correct too late for Mrs. Wells to move back to her lane."

"I think that's what the report said," sighed Mr. Wells.

"You know something you're not telling me," said Celeste.

"Look for the ring," said Mr. Wells as he faded into nothing.

Soon after, Mrs. Wells turned up in her dream. "Don't listen to him. Don't look for the ring. Don't look into anything. Leave it all alone."

"So… I was wrong about you two not being aware of each other," said Celeste shaking her head.

"I don't know what you're talking about but, listen. You tell Judy I came to you in a dream and told you to stop looking into this. It was an accident, nothing more."

"Didn't you indicate, when you pawned her off on me, need I remind you, that it wasn't an accident?" Celeste was getting a little irritated with the whole thing now. This family surely needed counseling before they died.

"One of us was probably confused," said Mrs. Wells. "There is nothing to investigate. You tell her that. You tell her I said so." And she vanished.

"What have I gotten myself into?" asked Celeste to no one.

But the dream continued; John Scott stood in front of her acting as if she wasn't there, then turned back to his labors. Was this the creek? He seemed to be looking for something with a flashlight. Celeste noticed it was full on dark.

"What are you looking for now, Mr. Scott?" Celeste called out, knowing it was falling on deaf ears.

"Who is there?" Mr. Scott turned and shone the flashlight directly into Celeste's eyes.

It took her by surprise. She held an arm over her eyes and labored to regain her vision. Mr. Scott shone the flashlight up and down the bank of the creek. There was no one to be seen. But he had heard someone speak.

Celeste recovered herself and resumed watching the man search. Then came the realization that a deep tiredness had overtaken her. Raising her arms in front of her, locking her fingers together and raising them on over her head an involuntary groan escaped her chest.

Mr. Scott twirled around again abruptly. "Who is there?" he demanded.

Celeste raised her hand but the man couldn't see her.

"Boo!" yelled Celeste and Mr. Scott jumped back.

Oh my, thought Celeste. *John Scott can hear me. This could be fun. I wonder if we are both dreaming. He can't be at the creek in real time. It's mid- day yet it is pitch black out here. I'm just dreaming. Oooh.... What if he has the gift of hearing and doesn't know it or doesn't know what to do with it? That would explain a lot.*

Celeste was deep in thought when Mr. Scott came up to her and started licking her face. The shock was so much she opened her eyes to find Chaos on her chest vigorously licking her and snuggling her face.

"That was an interesting nap!" she said to Chaos. "I wonder what it all meant."

It was time to make some lunch. "This clock can't be right. I can't have slept so long. Is it really quarter to two?" Celeste felt rushed now making a quick sandwich before the next appointment, but managed to eat and still have time to rearrange the reading room for the next client.

The door chimed and Celeste greeted an elderly woman with a huge smile. Dori was always on time. Celeste suspected the sessions were more for the company than the reading. Her standing appointment was every Thursday at two o'clock. Celeste regarded Dori as one of her sweetest clients. The woman walked straight to the reading table and sat down.

"I have a real question for you today," she said sitting down.

Why would that surprise me today? thought Celeste. "And what question is that?" was the response Dori heard.

"I want to visit my daughter on the East coast. It's a long flight with a stop in Atlanta. I'm not as young as I once was and my question is: Will it be safe for me to make the trip?"

"I know we always use Tarot cards for you, but today let's do both the tarot and the runes. It will give us a more accurate picture. Is that okay?"

"You are the psychic, dear. I will go with whatever you suggest."

"When did you want to travel?" asked Celeste.

"I'm thinking in May when the winter ice and snow are gone."

"Sounds wise to me," said Celeste while shuffling the Tarot cards. Dori was quite happy with the six card reading. Then Celeste brought out the runes.

"I don't think we've ever used these," said Dori. "This will be fun to do, something new. How does it work?"

"It's similar to Tarot in that I will pull one stone at a time and lay them out like we do Tarot cards. Each rune has a meaning and we will interpret the meaning together. Are you ready?"

"Oh! Heavens! Yes!"

Celeste drew the six stones and laid them out in a pattern. "This is interesting," said Celeste. "You may want to wait until June to travel. And see if you can find a straight flight. It will be easier on you."

"The stones don't say June," protested Dori.

"They don't say June, but they indicate that travel plans should be postponed and the journey made as easy as possible. You could make it in early June."

"That is worth thinking about," said Dori. "I'll check into flights this afternoon. Well, dear, it's been a pleasure as always. I'm going from here to a hair appointment. Don't want to be late for that. Here is your fee. I'll see myself out. Thank you for a wonderful reading."

Celeste smiled and walked her to the door anyway. After walking the frail old woman to her car Celeste wondered how Dori was still driving. Celeste waved her goodbye and went back inside. There was a phone consult at four o'clock. This was a good time to write down her three dreams, do a little meditation and then read her own runes.

This was certainly not the day Celeste had envisioned last night. Reading her runes didn't help. They didn't make a lot of sense which probably meant that the rest of her day wouldn't make much sense either. Celeste let out a long sigh then prepared herself for the four o'clock phone call.

To her surprise, it went smoothly with no upsets or complications or Spirits involved. It was a normal reading with predictable results and the client was both impressed and pleased. What a much needed reminder of how easy it could be.

The phone rang and Celeste hesitated to answer. Technically her work day was over. "Hello, this is Madame Celeste. How can I help you fulfill your destiny today?"

CHAPTER SEVEN

"Celeste, its Danielle. I have an opening in the morning for that massage. Can you be here at ten a.m.?"

"Oh, dear, I'm afraid I'm tied up until one-thirty tomorrow." Tomorrow was Celeste's first day working with John Scott.

"Hmm…." said Danielle. "I could take you at two-thirty. Would that give you time?"

"I do need a massage," said Celeste. "Yes. Yes, write me in. I'll be there."

"You'll be my last appointment of the day, so we can go afterwards to get some dinner."

"If you give me your usual massage, all I'll be good for is a long nap afterwards."

"Well, I didn't think about that," laughed Danielle. "Maybe we could get together Saturday for lunch?"

"That would be wonderful," said Celeste. "I'll walk over to your place around two fifteen."

"Perfect. I'll see you then," said Danielle hanging up.

A massage, thought Celeste. *What a wonderful reward for spending a half day in an office. Tomorrow will be a good day.*

Celeste felt refreshed just thinking about it. Picking a couple of carrots from the fridge and heading to the creek was the ticket. It was calling to her. Dinner would wait.

The horses were glad to see her and she gave a carrot to each of them. How it made her miss her own horses. It made her a little sad, but she was able to push the thought back. This wasn't the time to feel sad.

Her destination was the stream and to her crystal hiding place to check that they were all retrieved after the last cleanse. There was a small tiger's eye stone just under the edge of a rock used to mark her spot. It had occurred to her something was missing, but what took her back was the ring underneath it. It looked familiar. It was the ring from her vision. Why was it there with her tiger's eye? Where had it come from? This was a little alarming. What if the ring was stolen? It would need to be reported to the police. She would take a picture… no, a picture was no good. The person who lost it must be able to describe it in order to claim it. Maybe a classified ad would be the solution.. Yes. That would be the thing to do.

Maybe the ring had shown itself in her vision so that it could be found and returned. But why would it connect itself to a vision related to the key? It seemed the more answers were found the more questions were needed to be asked.

Picking up the ring it felt familiar followed by a vision of the key and the boat. In the boat was a secret compartment with no lock except that a mast needed to be turned in order for the drawer to open. Could the ring have been in the secret compartment with the key? Mr. Scott seemed far more interested in the key than the ring. In fact, he seemed to be satisfied once the key had been found.

The vision continued. The ring showed Celeste another room. This room was in a house. There were lace curtains on the windows and antique furniture. There was a small secretary desk and in the corner was a daybed. Was this a study or a bedroom? It was difficult to tell. The vision vanished

"I guess that's all I get for now. I think I will have to try this on." Sliding it on her right ring finger it was a perfect fit. Holding out her hand admiring the new addition took a few minutes.

"Hello," said John from a position a few yards behind her. "Did you find something else?"

"This is where I cleanse my stones. I was missing one, so I came here to look for it. I found it right where I thought it would be."

"May I see it?" asked John.

Celeste reached into her left pocket and withdrew the Tiger's Eye. "It's a humble rock, but necessary in certain…" she hesitated to reveal that her philosophy was pagan and practicing rituals and spellcasting then finished the sentence with "procedures."

There were very few people in town who knew that her use of Crystals and other stones was directly related to witchcraft and spells. Mr. Scott was not ready to be admitted to that circle.

"Well, I think it's a very pretty stone. What do you use it for?"

"It's a balancing stone. It helps restore balance in relationships, financial situations and more."

"That sounds very useful. Are you sure you didn't find anything else?" He seemed to be challenging her.

"I find lots of things here." What was this new urge to hide this ring from him? It was beginning to make her feel like a thief. "Mostly I find my own stones that I have brought to the creek to cleanse in the moonlight and the water."

"Well, you found my boat and my key, so I'm happy."

"Why are you here, Mr. Scott?"

"I was looking for you, as a matter of fact. I went by your house and when you weren't there, this was the next place I thought to look. Maybe I'm a little psychic, too," he laughed as he said it.

Thinking of her dream brought a smile to her face. It might be less of a joke than he thought. "Well, you have found me. What did you need? Has something changed about my working tomorrow?"

"I'm hoping I can get you to come in at eight a.m. tomorrow. I've arranged for the night crew to stay. It would only be for this one time. I promise."

Celeste decided that just this once, it wouldn't hurt to break her routine. "Will you pick me up, then?"

"Of course, of course," said John. I will pick you up around ten 'til eight. Don't worry about breakfast either. We will have donuts at the office."

"Deal," said Celeste offering her right hand.

"What a lovely ring," remarked John. "It looks familiar for some reason. I know I've never seen it, but it has a familiar feel to it."

That was my reaction, too, thought Celeste. *What is it about this ring?*

"Thank you, John," was all she was willing to say to him about it.

"I'll leave you to your cleansing," he said and walked back up the creek bank. His car was parked a few yards from the bridge.

Celeste had brought a few crystals to set out for cleansing. It bothered her just a little that someone now knew where her "spot" was. Looking around for a better one paid off. There was a place downstream a couple of yards. It was still under water and that pleased her. Cleansing by the moon in running water was her favorite method of cleansing. Depositing a large pink healing crystal and two smaller white crystals into the oval area of the crevice proved easy. There was a large flat rock nearby that would be perfect to place over it. The flat rock covered her stones almost completely. It left an opening that would allow the moonlight in tonight. And it would serve as a marker for her to retrieve them tomorrow.

It was nearing sunset when Celeste noticed the time. There was no place to be tonight, so watching the sunset from the bank of the stream was a treat. There was a great spot to sit down and meditate before the "show". It was hard to let go the thoughts of the day. The dreams were especially on her mind. It appeared that someone was flat out lying. It was up to her to determine whether it was a spirit or one of the living.

She opened her eyes to a beautiful sunset. The clouds in the western sky offered such a variety of colors. Her mind held no memory of a sunset so vibrant. It took her breath away. Basking in the glow for fifteen minutes wishing she had brought her camera, peace engulfed her. Then it was gone.

The walk home was in the fading light of dusk. There was a calmness that hadn't been felt in days. Even with the mystery of a potential murder haunting her dreams, at this moment there was calm. The universe was giving her a break this evening. It was palpable. Even after her encounter with John Scott.

There was a car in front of Celeste's house and Dori, of all people, was sitting on the front porch waiting.

"Dori, it's so nice to see you. Did we have an appointment that I've forgotten about?"

"No, I took a chance," said Dori. "I changed my travel plans and now I have a splitting headache. I was hoping you could help the way you did with my friend, Deb."

"She told you about that? Deb was not supposed to share that."

"Well, she did and I need help. Will you please help me?"

There was a limited number of people that knew about Celeste's other talent. Dori was now one of them.

"Let's go inside," said Celeste.

"Where should I sit?" asked Dori.

"At the reading table as always," said Celeste walking over to the Crystal case. "Let me find my... Here it is! Where is your headache?" asked Celeste.

"It's in my head, of course."

"Can you be more specific? It isn't your whole head down to your neck, is it?"

"It goes through my temples and then down to the back of my neck," said Dori.

"I want you to hold this crystal cluster to the temple that hurts the most and imagine you are pouring your headache into the crystal."

"That's it?" said Dori.

"No, if any thoughts come to mind I want you to say them out loud. Even if it's something trivial, like thinking about breakfast two years ago, okay?"

"Okay... I'm thinking about a cat I had as a child. Now there's a rabbit. Now I'm in a barn. The cat is eating the rabbit. It's horrifying," said Dori with tears streaming down her cheeks.

"You're doing excellent, Dori," said Celeste. "Keep going."

"There's a mirror. It's in a hospital room. I'm looking into it and have no makeup on. I'm embarrassed for people to see me without my makeup. I'm so ashamed. I look so old even though it was years ago."

"Now there's a scorpion in the kitchen. I'm frightened. I don't know what to do. It's so big. I put a bowl over it and call Jack, the handyman."

"Well, would you look at that? When I reached for the bowl another bowl landed smack on my head. What a headache I had that day!"

"This crystal is like magic. My headache is gone. How did that work so fast?" asked Dori.

"Well, this is one of my more powerful crystals. Dori, I really don't want people to know I can do this. Can you keep it to yourself?"

"But you're so talented, dear."

Dori tried to hand the crystal directly to Celeste, but Celeste held out a towel. She didn't want to touch the crystal directly until it was cleansed.

Dori paid in cash and was on her way. Celeste worried a little that this was going to send a flood of seniors looking for pain dissolution. That was not the clientele on her goal list. Celeste didn't mind helping current clients, but new ones? No, thanks. Her plate was as full as need be right now.

The phone rang and Celeste threw up her hands. *So much for a quiet evening.*

"Hello, this is Madame Celeste. How can I help you fulfill your destiny today?" the spiel came out with zero enthusiasm. Looking at the clock it was after six p.m. It was her policy not to answer the phone after six p.m. unless there was a phone appointment. *Why am I answering this?*

CHAPTER EIGHT

"Celeste, Its Danielle. Have you had dinner yet?"

"No, I haven't. In fact, I've barely eaten at all today," said Celeste.

"Good. I'm taking you to dinner. I'll be there in five minutes," said Danielle hanging up.

Celeste changed into a long flowing skirt. Her gypsy look would not do tonight. This was more formal and normal. Danielle was at the door before Celeste was fully dressed. She ran and opened the door then ran back to the bedroom to put on the finishing touches.

"Where are we going?" asked Celeste entering the parlor.

"There's a new place. I've heard lots of good things about it. I can't think of the name right now, but that's where we're going."

"Well, what type of cuisine should I prepare my palate for?" asked Celeste.

"It's Greek and Mediterranean food," said Danielle. "Hera's. That's what it's called!"

"Really? Do you think they know who Hera is?" asked Celeste.

"Some Greek goddess, right?"

"Zeus's wife and one of his three sisters," said Celeste. "This should be a very interesting meal."

As they walked in Celeste gasped, "There she is."

"Who? Is it a client of yours? Do we need to go?"

"No," said Celeste. "The statue that's in the middle of the restaurant is Hera. Why would the owners risk that in a small minded town like this?"

"I don't know, but I hear the food is off the charts."

Danielle was right. The food was excellent.Celeste knew just from the smell as they walked in. "I could imagine myself in Greece this is so authentic," said

Celeste. "Thank you so much for inviting me."

"You're welcome. I'm enjoying it too, so maybe I should be thanking you for joining me. Tell me more about Hera."

"Well… First and foremost the wife of Zeus… So, pretty powerful herself… And the goddess of women and…"

"Fancy meeting you here!" John Scott interrupted her mid-sentence. "This is my wife, Haley. And this is my son, Nick. This is Madame Celeste."

"Celeste will do, so nice to meet you."

"Celeste is the one who found your boat."

"Dad keeps calling it my boat, but really it's his. He built it years ago. I wasn't supposed to put it in the water. So I would have been in big trouble if you hadn't found it. Thank you," said Nick.

"You are a very articulate eight year old. I was glad to be able to help," said Celeste. "Oh, forgive my rude behavior. This is my friend, Danielle, the best masseuse in town."

"We were just leaving, so we'll let you get back to your menus. I would highly recommend the Greek Moussaka," said John Scott. He did an abbreviated bow by nodding his head, turned and escorted his family out.

"What a nice family," said Danielle. "Is that the one you told me about?

"Yes, and I start working for him one morning a week starting tomorrow."

"May I take your order ladies?" asked the waiter with a recognizably Greek accent.

"Should we try the Moussaka?" said Danielle.

"Might as well," replied Celeste giggling.

The Moussaka was a delight to the senses and Celeste was tempted to ask for the recipe, but had a feeling they were not about to share that. They each ordered a small glass of ouzo to finish the meal.

An extremely loud and annoying man arrived as they were finishing their ouzo. "Must be time to leave," said Danielle.

"Ready when you are," replied Celeste.

Just then Celeste heard a frail little voice call out, "Oh, look who's here. That is Celeste. The one I was telling you about." It was Dori, talking to the especially loud gentleman. "I'll introduce you. Come on."

"Celeste, this is my grandson's cousin's nephew. Did I get that right dear? Anyway, his name is Dean and he is in town visiting for a while."

Celeste nodded and said, "It's a pleasure to meet you."

"So you're the local snake oil healer?" the words boomed out of Dean's mouth. He apparently had no inside voice. A tall man and between his stature and his voice drew attention to himself without trying. The whole restaurant was listening now.

"I'm not sure what you are talking about," said Celeste while giving Dori a stern look. "I am the local psychic, please take my card."

"Gramms said you took away her headache today with a bunch of mumbo jumbo," countered Dean as he tossed her card back onto the table. "I don't like people taking advantage of my Gramms."

"I assure you, I did nothing of the kind" objected Celeste.

"Dean, you be nice to her. This is the best psychic I have ever met and we're so lucky to have her right here in town. I don't have to drive in to Dallas anymore and I love that."

"Gramms, you said she cured your headache."

"I arrived with a headache. I left without one. What would you call that? I am neither senile nor delusional and I know what happened. It was real and it was fast and it was such a relief. Do you know what it's like to have a relentless headache?" Dori was almost in tears.

"Gramms, it was a coincidence, nothing more," said Dean. "I don't think you should be seeing someone who claims to be a healer."

"I do NOT claim to be a healer. Look at my card. It says psychic. It says Tarot cards and Angel cards and Nordic runes. There's even a crystal ball for special cases, Do you see anything on that card that says healer? NO! you do not!" said Celeste in a huff. "Danielle, are you ready to leave?"

"You betcha'," replied Danielle. "Let's go."

The two women left Dean standing at an empty table fuming. Dori was in tears and the previously silent restaurant broke out into conversation about Celeste.

As they seated themselves in Danielle's car, Celeste started, "What was I thinking? It was just a headache. I should have told her to go take some ibuprofen. Why did I do it? I knew better. It was obvious she wouldn't be able to keep it a secret. But Dori's so sweet and the pain was real. Who could refuse?" Calm was starting to replace the wrath. Though still visibly shaken her face was no longer bright red.

"Honey, I know you don't like the spotlight, but that little scene in there is probably going to bring you a lot of business," said Danielle.

"I have enough business," argued Celeste. "I don't need a lot of business!"

"Maybe you could offer a gallery reading once a month. That would take care of a lot of people in a short amount of time."

"I really don't like doing Galleries. They're so.... public," she winced as she said the word.

"But you have to admit they are good money makers and take care of the maximum number of people in the least amount of time."

"I still don't like them."

"Just think about it. In case the phone starts ringing off the hook tomorrow."

"Banish the thought," said Celeste. "Let's change the subject. What did you think of the food?"

"Best Greek food I've ever had," said Danielle. "What about you?"

"Very enjoyable.... And the atmosphere of the restaurant, too. It was almost like actually being in Greece. That is, of course, until Mr. Loudmouth walked in."

"Yeah, right?" said Danielle. "Have you ever heard anyone that loud before. And to have a grandmother as quiet as Dori, it's just hard to believe."

"I meant to get some Baklava to bring home for dessert, but forgot about it when he started making a scene," said Celeste.

"Ooh, that would have been good."

"Do you want to come in for a bit? We didn't get to spend nearly enough time talking thanks to that big oaf."

"Of course," said Danielle who didn't want to leave her friend alone just yet.

"Oh no!" said Celeste as she walked in the parlor.

"What? What is it, Celeste?"

"My phone has six messages," said Celeste. "This can't be good."

She turned on the machine for message playback.

"Hello, this is Melody Graves. A friend said that you are also a psychic healer and I'd like to set up an appointment right away."

The next five messages were similar. Two wanted psychic readings, but the rest wanted psychic healings. Some had found her name on the card that she had handed to Dean.

"This is a disaster," moaned Celeste.

"It's only six people," said Danielle. "You can handle this. It's not a big deal"

The phone rang. Celeste didn't even pretend she might answer it.

"Hello, you don't know me, but I was in the restaurant this evening when that horrible man was verbally attacking you. I am interested in your work as a psychic. Are you taking on new clients at this time? If so, my number is 940 555 5555. I look forward to your call." Beep

"See? It's not all bad. That one seemed very nice," said Danielle as the phone rang again.

"Hello? I know what you're up to you evil child of Satan. You don't cure people in the name of Jesus, do ya'? You're just a devil worshipping whore, that's what. God is watching you and you will go straight to…"

Click. Danielle disconnected the phone.

"Sorry. You don't need to hear that nonsense."

"I've always flown under the radar. What I do is legal, but there are people who will hound me now because of this. It was a mistake to have helped get rid of that headache."

Danielle stayed for another hour. They talked about her business and her kids and Celeste's new job the next day and a couple of books they were reading and TV shows they were both watching and a movie they both wanted to see.

"Why don't you leave that phone unplugged until tomorrow?" said Danielle. It was more of an order than a question.

"I will, Thanks," said Celeste showing Danielle out. "And thanks again for getting me out of the house. We couldn't have known how it would turn out, though if I'm such a good psychic, I should have."

It was time for bed. Tomorrow promised to be another strange day.

CHAPTER NINE

Celeste rarely used her alarm clock, but six-forty five was going to come too early for her to rely on anything else to wake her. Setting the alarm was never an easy task, but falling asleep came easily.

It was another dream filled night. This night's dreams were more surrealistic. More like Celeste was accustomed to. It felt good to float through such normalcy drifting on the clouds and rowing a canoe through a rainbow. Floating on a red ocean for a time gave her a thrill. There were glittered and bejeweled dragons ridden by wizards in flowing gowns while angels hovered overhead. These dreams were so much more to her liking.

Chaos woke her before the alarm went off, but only by a few minutes. It was fun cooking an omelet to balance the donuts that would be waiting at the office. That kind of temptation was impossible for her to resist. When John arrived he found her ready and waiting. It was a quiet ride in. Celeste had brought a few "tools" with her, like a pendulum and her Tarot cards and runes.

"What am I supposed to do in these interviews?" she asked John.

"You are going to be given a folder for each employee you'll be interviewing. You'll see the night shift workers first. Ask them if they're happy working at the company, if they're satisfied with the work environment. Things like that. Get them to open up about anything weird that might have happened and use your psychic stuff to see what you pick up."

"That's a lot to ask out of a simple interview. What if I don't pick anything up?"

"You'll have lots of opportunities to scope everything out. And I will take you around to the place where I suspect the problem is."

"At least I'll have files to take notes in."

John showed her to his office and then to a conference room for the interviews. Sure enough there were a couple dozen donuts on the conference table. The chocolate one called to her.

The first man walked in. He looked at Celeste as if he were studying a horse, sizing her up.

"Come in. Have a seat. Have a donut," Celeste beckoned him. Having already sized him up psychically his file said he was a good worker who was never late and turned in all his paperwork. What the file didn't say was that he lived with his mom and probably always would. He went to church regularly with her and sang in the choir. He didn't even know he was hopeless, so there was no need to worry about him getting suicidal or going "postal".

"Has anything out of the ordinary ever happened to you while you were working in the loading area?" Celeste asked.

"Not really. I keep my head down as much as possible. Don't want to cause no trouble nor have no trouble," he responded.

"Nothing you say to me is going to get you or anyone else into trouble. Put that right out of your mind. Is there any reason you can think of why people who work in that area might be more likely to quit?"

"People are always talking about seeing weird lights and hearing someone talking when there ain't nobody there but them. But it never has happened to me. I'm fine with my job just like it is," he said reaching for a donut.

"What kind of weird lights? Do you mean lights turning on and off or lights where there shouldn't be any."

"Both," he said with a mouth full of donut. "Some of them people that left? They would talk about a light that would just float around the first loading bay. It seemed to scare 'em. Never saw nothin' myself. Never heard nothin' neither."

"Thank you, you've been most helpful. Will you ask Carol to come in?" said Celeste dismissing him.

It took a minute for Carol to make it in. In her thirties, wearing a very sharp looking pair of glasses, her pantsuit made her look as professional as the men in the accounting offices. Celeste waved at the donuts suggesting that the girl help herself. She declined. Celeste helped herself to another one.

This one's file was similar to the last except for being a bookkeeper. Going to college days made the night shift a perfect fit for the girl. Her hours were erratic, but she was always on time and kept her paperwork up to date and tidy.

Celeste had a hard time reading this one. Being an introvert made her more difficult to read. Introverts kept everything locked inside.

"How do you like working here?" Celeste asked.

"They let me set my own hours and are helping me pay my way through school. What's not to like?"

"Well some people think there is something going on in the loading area. Have you ever noticed anything out of the ordinary?"

"You mean like papers not being where you left them?"

"Yes, that would qualify," said Celeste.

"No, nothing like that's ever happened to me."

Why would she lie to me? thought Celeste. She's been told I'm a psychic. Is she testing me?

"Are you sure? I just have this feeling that you have experienced a few things."

"I'm not going to blow a good thing by talking about woo woo stuff going on in my office, okay?"

"I get it," said Celeste. "I understand. But if the company is willing to hire a psychic to help, do you really think they are going to let you go because of some "woo woo stuff"?"

"Well, I don't know. You make a valid point."

"I also understand that you have a guardian angel keeping you safe from whatever this is we're trying to find. I can see her standing just behind you."

Carol's eyes widened. How did this woman know about her angel.

"What does my angel look like?" asked Carol. "I've never seen her. I just feel her there."

"Hmmm…. She's shaking her head. I can't tell you more. But I still need you to tell me as much as you can."

"Okay. I'm convinced. Yes, papers do get moved around when I'm not there, but that could be anybody. And sometimes late at night it looks like someone is walking across the loading dock with a flashlight, but then there is no one there and the light goes out. It's a little creepy, but I trust my guardian angel to keep me safe."

"A little creepy?" asked Celeste.

'Okay. Sometimes it's a lot creepy. Sometimes I get really scared."

"That's what I needed to find out," said Celeste. "Thank you for talking to me. May I call on you again if I need more info?"

"Of course," said Carol.

"Would you ask Joe to come in?"

Celeste eyed another donut while waiting for the next interviewee. After a minute, Carol popped her head in the door and said "He's asleep. Should I wake him?"

"Are you sure he's asleep?" said Celeste.

"Oh yes, he's snoring. Reception is getting a giggle or two out of it," said Carol.

"I need a little break myself. I'll fetch him when I'm ready. Thank you. And by the way, where is the ladies room?"

"Down this hall and turn right," said Carol.

Celeste took her time. It wasn't in her heart to wake the man up. They had already disrupted his routine by having him stay late. Looking over the two interviews already done there was obviously something unusual going on. She could probably accomplish much more by just going to the loading dock and feeling around a bit. But it was her first day. Mr. Scott could call the shots for now.

Celeste was deep in thought when her next interviewee tapped on the glass door to the conference room. It startled her enough to make her jump a little in her chair. Looking forward to becoming more familiar with this place she longed for her abilities to kick in a bit more.

"They said you were ready for me. My name is Joe McFarren, but everyone calls me Mac," he said extending his hand for a friendly handshake which delivered a rush of information. Her interview questions had all been answered in that one gesture.

"Yes, Mr. McFarren, will you have a seat?" Going through the motions would give her an excuse to be writing down what the handshake had revealed.

"How long have you worked here?"

"Don't you have that in that file," he said playfully.

"I may, but I'd like to hear some things from you. Let's modify the question, though. How long have you worked in the loading area?"

"Couple years, I guess," he said.

"Do you enjoy working there?"

"As much as a man can enjoy working at all," he said with a wink.

"Did they tell you that you would be meeting with a psychic today?"

"Yeah, Mr. Scott mentioned it. He told us about you and his boy and that boat, too."

"How do you feel about psychics?"

"Well, I'm liking this one, so far," he said with a wink.

"Thank you, but I was looking more for how you view what a psychic does," she smiled at what seemed like flirtation. Was he flirting with her? He had to be ten years her junior and as fit a man as could be found.

"It's my understanding that they are all different and that there are a lot of phonies. But I don't expect that you would be here if you hadn't proven yourself to Mr. Scott."

"Good. Joe, when I shook your hand I saw a lot of things. It seemed like you knew exactly why we're here. You have seen and even heard some of the phenomenon that are scaring people away, haven't you?"

"That's a loaded question. You saw what you saw and I've seen what I've seen. Does that make me a psychic?" he said smiling.

"I'm afraid not. You see Mr. Scott believes that other people have also seen what you've seen. He thinks that may be the reason there is such a high turnover rate in that area. What do you think? Are the things you see and hear scary enough to make some people quit?"

"Well, Miss...." There was a pause as he tilted his head and put his ear forward.

"Oh my goodness. It's Celeste. My name is Celeste. I apologize for not introducing myself."

"Pretty name for a pretty woman," said Joe. "Some folks get scared off by things they can't explain, but I'm sure there's some logical explanation. It's just that nobody has gone looking for it yet."

"So, you don't believe there's anything paranormal going on down there?"

"I didn't say that. But I'd be more than happy to help you investigate it. You want to come by during the night shift and check it out for yourself?" he offered.

"I don't think you're taking this seriously."

"I swear I'm taking you seriously. I just believe in logical explanations. Has anybody looked for the logical explanations?" asked Joe.

"That's what we're trying to do now," said Celeste.

"How is a psychic going to help find physical explanations?"

Celeste couldn't tell if he was serious or making fun of her.

"Joe, have you ever witnessed anything down there that you couldn't explain?"

"Like those lights that everybody talks about? Yeah, I've seen them, but that doesn't make them magic or woo woo. It was probably just someone with a flashlight."

"That's what we're here to find out."

"You're not going to do it up here talking to people. You're going to have to go down there."

"I couldn't agree more, Mr. McFarren."

Joe looked surprised.

"I believe I have all I need from you for the moment. May I call on you again as we continue the case?

"I wish you would," said Joe with a twinkle in his eyes.

He grabbed a couple of donuts and left a puzzled Celeste wondering about everything to do with him. He was extremely pleasant both to look at and to talk to.

John walked in eager to hear what she had learned.

"Well? Is there something going on at night?"

"Yes, there is, but I don't know enough yet to say whether it is paranormal or physical. I need to see the area in question." Celeste had seen a lot of the area when she held that key and just now shaking Joe's hand, but there was nothing like seeing for herself.

"There may be a spirit down there, but it could just be regular people with a flashlight and a reason to hide what they are doing," she said.

"If its people, then we'll have to call the police in, but if it's paranormal, I'm hoping we can take care of it without bothering the police," said John Scott.

"Let's go to the area in question and see what I can see. That's the real reason you brought me in, isn't it?" said Celeste.

"Yes, I suppose it is. You need a break from interviewing anyway. Let me check in with my secretary and we'll head down there."

CHAPTER TEN

The building was larger than Celeste had imagined. It took five minutes to get to the loading dock. There was less office space than expected. Nothing here looked at all like her vision. They walked through a long warehouse. There was no disputing it was a tad on the creepy side. Two apparitions had already shown themselves by the time they arrived at the loading dock.

"Is that the office that's involved?"

"Yes, it is. That's where the bookkeepers have to come do some of their work," said John.

She hadn't seen the inside but knew it would match her vision. Its windows were covered with blinds on two sides. The office overlooked the warehouse/loading dock. That was it.

"Is there anyone working in there right now?"

"I don't know. Let's go see."

They walked the twenty yards between where they stood and the office. John knocked on the door. There was no answer. He turned the knob, but it was locked.

"Good thing I have a key," he said. "You met one of the people who work in here during your interviews. Carol is her name."

"Yes. Lovely girl... very pragmatic... So that was the last one in here?"

"Probably," said Mr. Scott.

"Is it customary to keep the door locked?"

"It insures that no one will be seeing things they don't have a reason to see. Management likes to keep most of the numbers to themselves."

The office was exactly like her vision, except for one thing. There was no safe below the calendar. Instead there was a two drawer filing cabinet.

"Is there a safe in this room?" Celeste asked abruptly.

"Yes," the answer came out before John had time to think. "I mean, there's a drawer safe in the desk. It's never locked, though. See?" He opened the "drawer safe".

Celeste knew immediately that he was hiding something. This was not the safe he thought of when he said "Yes". His thoughts went to a real safe. She saw his thoughts for a split second and he was thinking of the safe she saw in her vision.

"Do you trust me to be alone in the office for a few minutes?"

"I don't see why not. In fact, I'll leave you here for about half an hour while I go to my office. My assistant is going to have some papers for me to sign."

"That would be great!"

This was the room to be alone with. It was hard to interpret visions when you had someone standing over you. Celeste intended to touch everything possible to get some clues as to what was going on here. Carol and Joe both seemed to believe there was something paranormal. Celeste wanted some first-hand experience.

First there was the desk. Her fingers on the decade's old calculator revealed the dozens of people who had sat here using it. This was the original office. There was a time it was the only office. Back before computers and barcoding, there were clerks and stock boys and bookkeepers.

Feeling the desk was a rush. Although it bothered her that John was still watching her through the blinds.

The desk was older than the calculator. It was heavy oak. It bore the marks of age with grace and dignity. It had stories to tell. Celeste was flooded with a hundred years' worth of stories all at once. It was dizzying and almost nauseating. There was too much too fast. She pulled her hand away.

Leaning back and unwittingly resting her arms on the arms of the big leather chair the flood of stories started again. Jumping up afraid to touch anything her senses were wide open and there was too much to receive. Standing there not knowing whether it would feel better to go ahead and throw up or hold it in, there was no sense of anything evil here. There was just so much. It was overwhelming. *How does anyone get any work done here?* she thought.

Standing in the middle of the room as far away from touching anything as possible three separate apparitions appeared to be sitting in the chair at once. None of them seemed to notice the other and each of them was doing different sets of books. Her head was spinning just watching them. Not one of them noticed her.

Closing her eyes for a grounding ritual helped her take back control of her visions. When she opened her eyes they were gone. The office was back to whatever version of normal applied in this place.

Celeste remembered the safe. She put on her gloves and opened the two drawer file cabinet. It was a real file cabinet not a fake one covering up a safe.

Hmmm... Maybe the safe is behind the cabinet. Trying to move it caused a slight give. It was enough to see behind the thing. There was nothing. In the vision, the safe had been under the calendar. *What if it was actually behind the calendar?* The calendar was current. No risk of visions from it, but the gloves stayed on just in case. Raising the calendar there it was.... a wall safe. And it had a key lock!

"In for a penny, in for a pound," she said removing a glove and touching the keyhole.

No vision came of what was inside the safe, but there was a clear vision of John Scott using the funny shaped key to open it. This was the safe he didn't want anyone to know about. It was not an old safe either. It was fairly new.

Celeste wondered who had installed it. Had John done it by himself one night when no one was around? It had been a good decision not to tell him everything. She covered the safe again and went back to the desk. Even with gloves on it was hard to handle. But, the gloves helped. There was even a vision of Carol working at this desk then jerking her head to the door as if startled by a sound outside the office and in the end ignoring it and going back to work.

"How have you gotten on?" asked John as he popped his head in the door.

"You startled me, John. There are so many visions in this room it is truly hard to sort them out. I cannot imagine working in here. There are just too many people hanging about."

"Did you pick up on anything useful?" he asked.

"I have a lot of sorting to do. Some things are related and some things are not. It will take time for me to determine which is which."

"Have you walked around outside in the loading area?"

"No, I've been in here since you left and haven't touched more than three objects. There are so many stories, John. I can't get over it. If only I could hear what they are saying. Next time we'll have a talking board."

"What is a talking board again?" asked John.

"It's a board with letters and a few words and number on it."

"Oh! An OUIJA board!" he said excited to know what she was talking about.

"Not exactly, but similar," said Celeste.

"Well, by all means, bring it next time if you think it will help."

"Let's walk out to the dock. I want to show you where the people who have left worked most of the time."

"What about the office? Has anyone left who worked in that office?"

"We've had a few leave from there, but we mostly employ college students for that, so they're expected to leave. College students can be pretty flighty."

"More flighty than truck drivers and loaders? Really?" joked Celeste.

"Actually truck drivers are very serious and also very career minded. And most of the loaders are here to start at the bottom and prove themselves. It's like a rite of passage," said John trying to "unruffle" his feathers. "I, myself, started on the loading dock."

"No offence intended," said Celeste. "We learn something new every day."

"Just don't treat them like they're beneath you."

"I try not to ever treat anyone like they are beneath me," said Celeste. "Being a psychic, you can imagine how people treat me."

"I guess I can. But you have a lot of people in this community that take you very seriously, don't you?"

"It doesn't always feel like it, but you're right. I stay booked and busy."

"Do you feel anything out here?" asked John as they stopped at the edge of a bay.

"It's certainly a different feeling from the office. I feel something, but it's more spread out. The office is so small to hold all the memories it holds. May I walk around for a while?"

"Of course, should I leave you alone like I did in the office?"

"That would be perfect. Give me half an hour and then we can wrap up the day?"

"Absolutely!" said John as he turned and left.

Celeste was drawn to a spot between the loading and the warehouse itself.

She stood there and turned herself three hundred sixty degrees. It was a good vantage point to keep up with most of the facility. There was a vision of a great deal of hustle when a truck arrived. This must be where the supervisor stood to oversee the loading and unloading.

An apparition manifested beside her and walked over to the office. He went through the motions of unlocking and opening the door. Celeste followed him.

The door was still unlocked from her time in the room. She walked in and found the apparition sitting in the only chair other than the leather desk chair. He seemed to be waiting for someone. Soon "someone" walked in and seated himself at the big desk. There was a confrontation. Hearing them, or rather not hearing them, was not a problem. They were arguing like equals. They both pounded on the desk to punctuate their points. After a few minutes of this, the first to arrive offered his hand to the man behind the desk. They shook hands and he left.

Celeste could not tell what time period this was, but it seemed to be more recent than the desk. Guessing would place the scene within the last ten years. But there was nothing that would relate to the current situation except for the fact that the place was overrun with spirits.

It would probably take a spirit rescue team months to clear them all out, even with her help in finding them. There were just too many layers of time trapped in this place. What drew them here and what kept them here?

Back in the warehouse there was a real person standing in the spot she had stood a few minutes ago.

"Who are you? And what are you doing in my warehouse?" he asked sternly.

"I am Celeste. John Scott brought me here this morning to observe."

"He brought you here and left you unsupervised to wander through my warehouse?"

"You keep saying my warehouse like you own the company. Do you?" challenged Celeste. It was not in her nature to be made to feel small.

"It's my responsibility when I'm on duty. And right now, I'm on duty. That makes it **my** warehouse."

"I see," said Celeste. "Well, John should be back any minute. He will be able to explain my presence."

"Let me ask you; do you always work days?" asked Celeste.

"Yes."

"Do you ever notice anything amiss in the shipments or the warehouse?"

"What do you mean by amiss?" he said

"Things moved from where they should be. Papers out of order or missing?" said Celeste.

"This is a warehouse. Things get mislabeled or put in the wrong bins sometimes."

"Do you think it happens more here than in most places?" asked Celeste.

"Maybe a little more, but it's a big warehouse. And it's a very busy one. We have seven trucks due to be unloaded this afternoon. I have a good crew, but they aren't perfect."

"It seems very organized to me." Just then the first truck started to back in.

"Excuse me; I have to help with this. You stand right there. I don't know who you are at this point. I want to keep an eye on you." He shouted as he walked toward the bay the truck was backing into.

Out of what seemed like nowhere came a big piece of equipment for unloading pallets. Celeste felt very vulnerable. John saved the day.

"Are you ready to go?" he asked.

"I am, but the supervisor told me to wait here."

"Oh, that's Kevin. He's one of the ones I wanted you to interview. Did you get a chance to talk with him?"

"Yes, I did. He's very…" the right word wouldn't come to her.

"Efficient?" offered John.

"I guess that's as good a word as any," laughed Celeste. It had gotten quite loud in the dock area. They all had to shout now.

"Let's go back to my office," suggested John.

"I'll follow you," said Celeste.

As if on cue, Kevin came running toward them. "John, so this one is with you," shouted Kevin.

"Yes, we're on a mission to find out why we have such a high turnover rate down here," John replied.

"Good luck with that!" he said and walked back to his work.

The warehouse felt smaller on the way back to John's office. Celeste wondered how many spirits were here in the warehouse space. At least three peeked out at her as they walked back to the main offices.

John's office was larger than the office back in the warehouse. It was quite modern. The furniture all looked new and the computer seemed futuristic after experiencing the old office. John motioned her to have a seat.

"It's almost noon. But tell me what you think so far. What have you learned?"

"There is a lot of spirit activity here. And by here, I mean in the loading area. The office has more spirits than I could relate. Are they what is causing people to quit? I don't know. It does all seem to tie together."

"What does?"

"Oh, it's nothing. There's another case I'm working on that seems to point to that warehouse, too. Not everything that is here stays here, John. Some of them come and go. Others are stuck in a routine loop."

"What do I need to do?" John asked.

"First you need to take me home. It is noon and I need to think this all through. I will have more questions and maybe a recommendation when we meet again next Friday at nine o'clock," emphasizing the time she would start working next week.

"Then I'd like to set up a session at your..." John hesitated looking for the word.

"Just call it my home, John."

"Okay. When can I come in Monday?"

"I didn't bring my appointment calendar with me. I'll have to call you from the house," knowing perfectly well that one p.m. was probably available, but not wanting to say so without looking first. "I really need to get going. I have an appointment this afternoon."

"I thought you didn't work on Friday afternoons," he said, escorting her to his car.

"This is a personal appointment."

"I didn't mean to pry."

"Don't give it another thought. No harm, no foul."

They were silent the rest of the drive. John dropped her off in front of the house and waited until the door closed behind her before driving off. The neighborhood was questionable. He didn't realize how powerful Celeste was. Nothing living was going to hurt her. Not so long as she was surrounded by spirits.

CHAPTER ELEVEN

Celeste made herself a sandwich for lunch and bounced back and forth between thinking about the massage on the agenda this afternoon and the situation at Harper's. That was the name of the company of her part time employment as a consultant.

Settling after lunch and reviewing her collected information:

- John had a secret.
- There was a safe in the old office that he didn't want anyone to know about.
- There were spirits haunting the old office and the loading area as well as the warehouse.
- There was high turnover, but the employees that were currently working nights were a little spooked, but not enough to leave a good job because of it.
- Joe was a doll. Scratch that. (even though he was)

There was more to add to this list, but there was a massage waiting. There was no way Celeste would be walking after the full hour that Danielle would spend working out every ounce of stress in her body. It was close enough to take the car.

The room was uncluttered. There was a small waterfall running and massage friendly music. Just walking in was the most relaxing experience of the last few weeks. This was probably her favorite treat. After disrobing and sliding herself on the massage table Danielle poked her head in.

There was no idle chit chat when Danielle entered. The scent of the massage oils added another dimension to the already relaxing ambiance. Danielle began by massaging Celeste's feet. Danielle would find from the pressure points where Celeste needed the most attention. Today seemed to be a shoulder and neck day. Danielle was also a Reiki master. Working the pressure points of the feet and then moving up to the hands being sure to save time to do a little extra on the neck and shoulders.

By the time Danielle was finished, Celeste was snoring.

"I hate to wake you up, sweetie, but we're finished." Danielle said proud to have put her to sleep.

"Oooooh" moaned Celeste, "Please don't ask me to get up."

"Sweetie, you know I'd let you stay, but I have a three o'clock waiting. Take your time, but you do have to wake up." Danielle always allowed fifteen minutes for the client to wake up and get dressed, but there was more time spent on Celeste, so there was not time to wake up slowly.

"My limbs feel like jelly," said Celeste thinking that was pretty high praise to a massage therapist. "And I may have worked out a puzzle I've been pulled into. So, thank you for a perfect massage."

Danielle left the room for Celeste to get dressed. Celeste dressed quickly and walked slowly out of the room. Paying Danielle and setting up an appointment for next month, she realized this was needed at least that often, maybe more. Sitting for a few minutes allowed her to wake up more while Danielle prepared the room for her next client.

"You said something in your sleep," said Danielle.

"Really? What did I say?

"You said, "The ring is the key." Does that mean anything to you?"

"It means a lot, Danielle. Thank you for telling me."

The next client walked in, so Celeste gave Danielle a big hug and left. Her car was just out the door in a rear parking lot. Only living two blocks away from the best massage therapist in town had its advantages.

"The ring is the key. That could have several meanings. But I think it definitely ties Judy Wells' case to John Scott's case. This adds some interesting things to look for."

Celeste was known to talk to herself a lot. Many people suspected that it was spirits. Others thought her crazy and chalked it up to that.

Celeste tried to take a nap, but it seemed the very massage that had put her to sleep was now energizing her.

Looking at the ring which was still on her hand she took it off to study it closer. The inscription read, "Wherever I roam, you are my anchorage." The question was; who had it belonged to and who had given it to them with such a poetic inscription. But the anchorage certainly tied it to the boat and by association with John Scott. Yet, he had not acted like he had ever seen it before.

"Every answer I find gives me three more questions."

The phone rang and pulled her from her thoughts. "Go to voicemail. I am not in the mood for a phone conversation."

"Hi, Celeste, this is Judy. I know we're not set up again until Monday at ten a.m., but could you call me as soon as you can? You have my cell phone number. It's really important. I know: I always say…" click. The phone cut her off.

It immediately rang again. "Hi! Judy again. I have some new information about my father. Please call."

CHAPTER 12

"Judy, this is how it's going to work. You are going to put me on retainer. We'll start with one thousand dollars. Every time you call me, it's an automatic minimum fifteen minute charge. Do you accept that?"

"Yes, do you want me to bring you a check right now?"

"No," said Celeste. "I'm in for the night. Why don't you come by about eleven o'clock tomorrow morning?"

"I'll be there with bells on," said Judy.

"Okay. See you then."

In less than a minute the phone rang again. Celeste looked at the caller ID and didn't recognize the name or the number thus let it go to voicemail.

"I spoke with Dori this morning and my friend, Dori, said you could help me. I think the ghost of my late husband is stalking me. This is Mary and my number is 940 668 5555. I hope you will call me back."

Celeste hit replay and wrote down the name and number. The phone rang again.

"I've been trying to reach you all day. Your line has been busy. I was in the restaurant last night. I need a psychic. I have an important decision to make and I need help." The woman left her name and number and once again Celeste hit replay and wrote it down

This went on until Celeste couldn't take it anymore. Turning call screening off she started a warm bath. The lingering effects of Danielle's massage were wonderful, but she wanted to get the oils off before changing into her night clothes. A hot bath would be just the ticket.

It wasn't necessary to unplug the phone. Muting it now would allow her to listen to all the messages in the morning. This was bound to die down in a day or two. Maybe some higher rates for the new clients would thin the herd a bit. Judy would definitely be paying a new higher rate. That latest notebook would be devoted entirely to Judy.

Fortunately they sold the notebooks by the dozen. Maybe it was time to take Danielle's advice: Hire a part time assistant to drive her around, answer the phone, and take care of appointment setting.

All this could wait until tomorrow. For the moment, it was time to relax and read a few chapters of a new book ordered online. It came in earlier this week. She knew the author, C Derick Miller. The book was called A TASTE OF HOME. It was a thriller. Already hooked Celeste had found that changing her focus away from her own mysteries sometimes gave her a fresh viewpoint. Movies worked and sometimes TV, but the advertising on TV drove her batty.

Diving into her book for the rest of the evening her dreams that night were filled with vampires and werewolves and other horror story characters. This was certainly a change of pace for her. Not once was she visited by a spirit. It was exactly what the massage therapist had ordered.

Being Saturday she let herself sleep in. The day promised not to be as relaxing as hoped for. Getting ready for the day included a nice breakfast, then taking a notepad into the parlor to tackle the phone messages.

Apparently the phone had rung all night as the voicemail box was full. *Start at the beginning.* Surprisingly most of the calls were friendly, of those, only three wanted healing. The others were interested in her services as a psychic. The few calls that lectured her about being the devil's spawn were easy enough to ignore. These attitudes had been with her all her life. "You are charging for a gift given to you by God. You are corrupting the gift and now you are in league with Satan." There was always some version of that refrain. *Delete them and move on.*

With the mailbox now empty there was a list of twenty people who were seriously interested in her services and three of those wanted healing. Those would be her first call to let them know that she was not a healer, but sometimes there would be a recipe shared for a remedy with clients. That had happened with Dori. All three made appointments for next week.

Of the twenty, four thought her fee was too high. The rest made appointments for various times in the next few weeks.

Somewhere in all that, Judy showed up. Celeste had forgotten that she had scheduled Judy who arrived with a check for one thousand dollars. Celeste marked the start time in her book.

"Where did you get that ring?" gasped Judy.

"I found it in the creek. I meant to post a classified ad, but I haven't had a chance yet. Do you like it?" said Celeste.

"I guess I do! It belonged to my mother," said Judy.

"What did your father do for a living?"

"What does that have to do with it? You're wearing my mother's ring!"

"Have you ever seen the inscription in the ring?" asked Celeste.

"No, it was always on my mother's hand."

"Then maybe this is just one that looks just like hers. What did you say your father did for a living?"

"Accounting."

"Did he travel much?"

"Not really. I remember him usually being home every night."

"Did you have any uncles that were truck drivers or salesmen? You know people that are gone for a week or more at a time?" Celeste asked, beginning to wonder if Judy senior had a lover on the side.

"Uncle Hollis drove a truck. He would visit us whenever he was in town."

Bingo! Thought Celeste. *Uncle Hollis, where are you now?*

"Judy, have you seen Hollis since your mother died?"

"Once or twice, but not nearly as often as when Mom was alive."

"How long ago did your father die?"

"It's been a few years. That's when Uncle Hollis started coming around more often, sometimes staying for a few days."

"Was Hollis your father's brother or your mother's brother?"

"Beats me. I'm not real interested in all that genealogy stuff. Listen. Am I paying for this? Because, so far you haven't told me anything. All you've done is asked questions."

"This is how we're going to find the answers, Judy. If you don't want my help, we can stop now and part company."

"No! No, no," said Judy excitedly. "I do want your help and would just like to know what happened yesterday."

"That's reasonable. There were a few people in the loading area and some people in the offices interviewed. Then there was some snooping around the warehouse, but the name of this company is Harper's not Holly farms. So I really don't see a connection yet."

"What?!? Are you telling me that you were at the wrong warehouse?"

"Possibly, but nothing is certain yet. There is more digging to be done. Your mother, by the way, sent you a message that you should stop digging into this. It was an accident. Your father disagreed and said it was not an accident. I'm not sure anymore. Find out what you can about Holly Farms. Maybe they were delivering goods to Harper's." *That should be enough for now,* thought Celeste.

"What about my mother's ring? Do you intend to keep it?" said Judy.

"We haven't established if it was your mother's ring. Maybe next time we're in a room together it will be on my list of questions for her. If it was hers, I will give it to you immediately. But for now it needs to stay near me. It has given me a lot of clues on another mystery that remains unsolved. And it has an inscription that the owner should know," said Celeste.

"Did your mother start wearing the ring before or after your father died?" asked Celeste.

"For as long as I can remember" said Judy.

"Interesting…. I will keep it with me for now. If it was hers we will know soon," said Celeste.

"That is all I have for you right now. Look into Holly Farms and find out if their trucks ever go to Harper's and I will try to get in touch with your mom about the ring," said Celeste, trying to close the session.

"Why would my mother change her story now?"

"Let's take that up at our Monday morning appointment? Okay?" said Celeste.

Celeste felt like Judy needed her psycho-therapy help more than she needed a psychic. The girl was having a lot of difficulty accepting her parent's death. There was more to this than just a haunted house.

"Oh, if you talk to my dad, please tell him I can walk through the shadow man now. It doesn't bother me at all."

Celeste felt proud of Judy for overcoming the fear. There was a lot of work ahead of them and it would be done by a psycho-therapist working as a psychic. Judy would never have discussed the shadow man with a therapist. There would have been too much fear of being mocked or medicated or hospitalized. Celeste was proud of her own work, too.

Celeste took a break from phone messages (which were still coming in) to fix and eat a leisurely lunch.

The creek was patiently waiting for her and it was an attractive idea but then the thought came to her; What could be found out if a string was tied to the ring and it was used as a pendulum? Surely it was worth a try. The questions needed to be listed ahead of time.... right after lunch.

Celeste finished lunch and did a little meditation about the questions to ask:

- Did this ring, in fact, belong to Judy Sr?
- Was it a gift from her husband?
- Was it a gift from a lover?
- Was Judy wearing it when she died?
- Did Judy know how it ended up in the creek with Celeste's semi-precious stones?
- Did she want Judy Jr. to have it?
- Should it be returned to whoever had given it to her?
- Would someone get in trouble if Judy Jr kept investigating the accident?
- Would it be Judy Jr.?
- Was there anything paranormal about the accident

She looked over her questions and felt like they covered everything she needed to know except:

- Was John Scott involved in some way?
- Was the loading bay involved in some way?
- Was the company known as Harper's involved?
- Was the company Holly Farms connected to the company Harper's?

That seemed to Celeste to be a well-rounded list of questions. All that was needed was a pen to mark Y or N as the questions were answered. She found some string and tied it to the ring.

Relaxing, she emptied her mind and began to ask the questions. First one had to establish Yes and No. Top to bottom was Yes. Side to side was No.

"Let's get started."

- Did this ring, in fact, belong to Judy Sr.? Y
- Was it a gift from her husband? N
- Was it a gift from a lover? Y
- Was she wearing it when she died? N

- Did she know how it ended up in the creek with Celeste's semi-precious stones? N
- Did she want Judy Jr. to have it? N
- Did she want it to be returned to whoever had given it to her? N
- Would someone get in trouble or be hurt if Judy Jr. kept investigating the accident? Y
- Would it be Judy Jr.? Y
- Was there anything paranormal about the accident? Y
- Was John Scott involved in some way? no answer
- Was the loading bay involved in some way? no answer
- Was the company known as Harper's involved? no answer
- Was the company Holly Farms connected to the company Harper's? no answer

"Interesting," said Celeste. "Maybe a few more questions…"

- Do you not know the answers? Y and N
- Do you know some of the answers? Y
- Are there questions you just don't want to answer? Y
- Are you afraid Judy won't understand that you had a lover? Y
- Did he work for one of the companies I asked about? Y
- Holly farms? no answer
- Harper's? no answer
- Will you come visit me again? Y
- Was Uncle Hollis your lover? Y
- Was he really Judy's uncle? N

This was a lot of information and a lot of questions remained. But there was paranormal activity on the night she died. So, maybe it wasn't an accident, but maybe it wasn't anything caused by someone who was alive. More questions came to mind:

- Was your late husband involved in the accident? Y
- Was he helpful? N
- Did he cause the wreck? Y

"Now we're getting somewhere," said Celeste.

- Did Uncle Hollis work as a truck driver? Y
- At Holly Farms? Y
- Did anyone else call him Hollis? N

- Did anyone call him Holly? no answer
- Did your husband know about him? no answer
- Are you still here? no answer

"I sure appreciate you answering what you did," Celeste said. I will try to steer Judy Jr. away from this."

The lights in the room flickered for a few seconds. That seemed to be Judy's way of saying goodbye, thank you, and you're welcome.

Celeste put the questions on a table where they would remind her to share them with Judy. Maybe it would help her to accept the answers more easily if they were in black and white in front of her. She cut the string off the ring and placed it back on her finger.

"Time to get back to work. Let's go listen to some more phone messages, Chaos."

There had been ten more messages left since lunch. It was unbelievable there was this much reaction to one brief encounter at a restaurant. People were gossiping most likely. Surely, it was all over town by now. Danielle had been right. You couldn't buy this kind of advertising.

The first one up was different. "Hello. My name is Emma and I believe I have some psychic abilities, but need instruction. Would you be willing to take on an apprentice? That would give you free labor at least two hours a day. And I have lots of knowledge from books, but now I need a real teacher. Please call me at 940 667 5555."

"That one might be worth considering. It would answer my need for a part time assistant and be grooming a new psychic for the town. I'll put a star by it."

Next up: "Hello. My name is Kelly Ann. I heard about you from a friend. I lost my grandmother a few weeks ago and was hoping you could help me contact her. Grandma had the keys to my car and we can't find them."

An elderly woman appeared before Celeste nodding her head to say yes.

Celeste called Kelly Ann. "Kelly if you'd like to do a phone session I believe we can find your keys now. You can bring me payment later in the day." Fees were discussed and agreed to. Celeste continued with the elderly woman.

"Are they in your house?" asked Celeste. The woman nodded yes. "If I knew that, I wouldn't need you," said the snippy teenager.

"Actually I was talking to your grandmother, but if you're going to take that tone I'll stop," said Celeste a little miffed.

"You're talking to her now?"

"Yes."

"I'm sorry for interrupting."

"Are they in the kitchen?" No

"Are they in the bedroom?" Yes

"Are they on the dresser?" The lady gave her a funny look and kind of nodded and shook at the same time.

"Are they under the dresser?" The lady pointed at Celeste with her right hand and put her left hand finger on her nose.

"Did they fall there when you died?" The lady smiled and nodded and then faded from view.

"You're good," said Kelly Ann. "I'll be over in a few minutes with the money."

"That will be fine, dear," said Celeste.

"Do you have my address?"

"No," laughed the teenager. "I guess you'd better give it to me."

Celeste gave her the address and wondered if the girl would actually show up. Thinking about it for a minute, the answer was yes. The grandmother would see to that. It made her smile.

"That was an interesting break, Chaos. Now let's get back to work."

The next one on the list was looking for a healer, but hadn't mentioned what needed healing. Celeste moved her info to a different list. Her healer identity wanted time to decide whether to pursue that or not.

Offering healing was often a problem. People expected a guarantee most of the time and Celeste would not offer a guarantee especially since it was usually people who had exhausted all other possibilities. They had been to doctors and specialists and had not found relief. They were looking for a miracle and miracles were not in Celeste's bag of tools.

It would bear discussing with her own psychic next time they talked, but for now… She wasn't offering healing.

The phone rang. It was Dori's number.

"Hello, Dori. How are you doing today?"

"You may fool Gramms with that but I know you have caller ID," snapped Dean. "If Gramms calls again, tell her that you can't work with her anymore."

"I most certainly will not!" said Celeste in her most stern voice. "Dori is not just a client, but a friend. I will not abandon her just because her grandson's cousin's nephew or whatever you are to her isn't spiritually aware."

"Just because I don't go to church doesn't mean I don't believe in God," yelled Dean.

"Who said anything about God," asked Celeste.

"So, you do worship Satan!" Dean exclaimed.

"Hardly," said Celeste calmly. "I believe that every individual has the right to their own beliefs. We are all on a spiritual journey whether we know it or not. My job is to help people find the path that is right for them."

"Well, I didn't know that included bilking old ladies out of their money."

"Are you worried about Dori or your inheritance?" said Celeste remaining calm.

"Well, uh, well…"

"You should really come over and let me do a reading for you. I'll do the first one at no charge."

"So, that's how you sucker people in," said Dean.

"What do you have to lose?" asked Celeste.

CHAPTER 13

Dean was silent for a moment. Celeste just let the silence linger. Her best play in this situation was to make him comfortable with what Dori was doing. He had probably never been to a psychic nor even met one. This was an opportunity to help someone lose their fear and anxiety about psychics.

When he finally spoke, he said "When?"

"Dori has a standing appointment. Maybe you could come before and then stay to watch her session too. We'll have to ask her, but I'm sure she won't mind. Dori's a very open person."

"But mine would be private, right."

'Only if you don't want her there," said Celeste calmly.

"No, no I wouldn't."

Let me check her appointment time and day and I'll write you in an hour before."

"Okay. And it's free, right?"

"Yes, this first session will be free. I look forward to seeing you then, Dean," said Celeste hanging up.

Her appointment book was getting a little crowded. The phone calls had not stopped. The next number wasn't familiar so she let it go to voicemail. And it was a good thing.

"Hello? This is Martha. You don't know me but Lori said that you can do Christian readings using Angel cards instead of Tarot cards. I'm quite excited to get a Christian based reading. I have a couple of friends that would like to do it, as well. We were thinking we could have a psychic party one evening. How much do you think that would cost for a four or five hour party? Please call me at 940 321 5555."

Celeste had a psychic friend who specialized in Christian and Angel cards. This would be right up her alley. So began a new list that would be given to Michelle. Celeste had nothing against Christians. It just wasn't her way to deceive anyone into thinking that angel cards were her only tools. It was probably a poor business decision on her part, but there were ethical considerations that outweighed the business aspect of it.

By the time Celeste stopped for the day, there were lists of twenty three for herself, four for her friend Michelle and six that wanted healing. Returning calls would begin on Monday. No point in giving people the idea that their new psychic worked on weekends.

Calling Michelle was a must, though. *Might as well spread the good news around.*

"Hi! Celeste. I was just thinking about you. One of my clients was telling me all about a bit of a scandal involving you," said Michelle.

"Isn't it terrible? The man called me a snake oil salesman in front of a restaurant full of people. It was so embarrassing."

"So how do you feel about being the center of attention in a scene like that?" asked Michelle.

"It was not my favorite moment, but it had to feel worse for Dori. Such a sweet lady and she meant no harm. Of course, I had asked her not to mention it to anyone, so what does she do? The sweetheart makes a scene about it during the dinner hour at a new and popular restaurant. You can't help but love her."

"So, what can I do to help?" said Michelle.

"Well….. My phone has been ringing nonstop. I won't even pick up if it isn't a familiar number. There've been a few inquiries about a Christian psychic who will only use angel cards. I do that for one of my clients, but to present myself as a traditional Christian doesn't feel right. Would you be interested in any of these?"

"How many do you have?" asked Michelle

"As of this moment, there are only four. But that will probably change by tomorrow," said Celeste.

"My schedule could accommodate four more clients, but not too many more than that."

Changing the subject," said Celeste, "there is something I need to talk with you about." said Celeste.

"What's that?" asked Michelle.

"I um, well, um, I helped with getting rid of a headache and that is what this is really all about. Healings are not my thing for the simple reason that it's not me doing the healing, it's them."

"Does that part really matter if they are healed?" asked Michelle.

"It does to me. They shouldn't be thinking I can cure cancer or diabetes or any other incurable diseases," said Celeste.

"If you explain it to them and they are willing to take the risk, why should you not do the same?" asked Michelle.

"That's how I'm supposed to look at it, but it's not easy. They just look like potentially disappointed people; upset with me for not doing what was needed."

"That is you worrying. It's not a true vision. What are you really afraid of?" asked Michelle.

"That my practice would be taken over by people who want to be physically healed?" said Celeste hesitantly.

"Bingo."

"It isn't for me. My practice is fine the way it is."

"Then you know what to do," said Michelle.

"Thanks, Michelle. I really needed that."

"You would have figured it out on your own soon enough, but you're welcome," said Michelle.

"Call me for dinner next week," said Celeste. "We'll catch up on old times and create some new."

"Will do," said Michelle.

Celeste thought about who would be willing to help the ones who needed healers. Michelle wasn't interested or there would have been an indication of it.. There was a healer or two in Dallas and several in Ft. Worth, but these people had called Celeste because they wanted someone here in town.

"Aha. If they are desperate enough, they will travel to Ft. Worth," she said to Chaos.

After making a few phone calls and narrowing it down to one in Dallas and one in Ft. Worth who sees clients once a month in Denton which was less than half an hour from Gloryville there would be two names to give the people looking for healing. It was settled.

Celeste felt like a weight had been lifted from her heart. It was compelling to help with healing sometimes, but the energy it took was overwhelming. As her experience grew healing actually became easier, but it was still pretty rough to recuperate from. Dori's had been easy. Celeste let the stone and Dori do all the work. If it was possible to be picky about whom she healed...

"That's it, Chaos. I can see these people and if it's simple things that a stone will take care of, it will be handled here. But if it's a disease or anything major, just refer to the healers in Dallas and Ft. Worth. It's PERFECT!"

Chaos walked slowly across the room and jumped into Celeste's lap, obviously unimpressed.

The phone rang. Celeste checked the caller ID. Unfamiliar so it went to voice mail. One would think it would have calmed down by now.

The next call was from John Scott. Picking up was her first mistake. "Hello?"

"Where's your little speal about fulfilling destiny?" asked John.

"Caller ID," answered Celeste.

"Oh," said John. "Have you found out any more about my little problem at work?"

"To be honest, Its not on the top of my list today. There's been an emergency situation to deal with."

"Are you talking about the incident at the restaurant last night? You, Madame Celeste have been outed. Your business is going to boom and you call that an emergency?"

"I'm appreciative of the new business, John. It's the thought of people thinking they're going to be cured of physical illnesses."

"That is a dilemma," said John. "But you mustn't let that distract you from the problem at the warehouse."

"You have me on Fridays. Do you honestly expect me to investigate and spend time on that problem on the weekend? It's Saturday. Even psychics get the day off," said Celeste.

"Doesn't sound like you've been taking it off today," said John. "Sounds like you've been working on another client's case today."

"You know I have other clients, John. Did you expect me to work exclusively for you?"

"Well, a man can hope," he chuckled saying it. "Something might have come to you about my case. You can't blame me for that, after all."

"It's true," said Celeste. "But all I can think about since last night is the phone ringing on and on."

"Well then let me come and get you. I'll pay you for your time. We'll go over to the warehouse and spend half an hour away from these distractions and see if anything happens on the weekend that doesn't happen during the week."

"So you want me to get away from work by going to work... typical employer."

"That doesn't make it a bad idea. I could come over right now and promise not to keep you more than thirty minutes."

"Okay," said Celeste. "It would be nice to spend some more time in that office. There is an overwhelming amount of activity in that room."

"How about in five minutes," said John.

"You'd better give me twenty. It will take me that long to get ready."

"Fair enough, see you in twenty minutes. Bring your talking board and other tools?"

"Okay," said Celeste and hung up.

Celeste hadn't bothered to get dressed today. Jumping up and hurrying to her closet the choice was made for a long skirt with a matching blouse. It was a little bohemian, but most of Celeste's clothes were. It was her favorite look and as a psychic, it could be pulled off in almost any situation.

Her kit bag was ready to go when John arrived.

The phone was now ringing in unison with the doorbell. It went to voicemail.

"Can I listen?" asked John.

"It would be rude," said Celeste. "Not to mention a breach of privacy."

"Does your psychic profession have a code of ethics?"

"I have a code of ethics, John. That's what matters," said Celeste with emphasis on the "I" as she turned down the volume so that he couldn't eavesdrop. She suspected that Mr. Scott had no personal code of ethics.

"Alrighty then, shall we get going?" he asked

"Ready when you are," said Celeste.

John picked up her kit bag and carried it to the car. It was heavier than he expected. What was in there? A bowling ball?

Celeste was quiet in the car trying to switch gears. Focusing on all the phone calls had given her little time to think about the ring and the key situation all day. This would be a good way to clear her head and get those psychic juices flowing. It was time to go in that office with a talking board and get some answers that involved this situation. There had been too many answers to the "Judy" situation.

CHAPTER 14

Deep in thought when they pulled up to the warehouse, John didn't park at the office end. He drove straight to the unloading area.

"Here we are," he said.

"Where are we?"

"This is the warehouse entrance. The loading dock entrance," said John.

"Is it closed today?" asked Celeste having seen no sign of activity.

"There is a crew inside stacking inventory," said John. "Let's go inside and let you look around on a Saturday."

"What is your goal here, John? Do you just want to find something paranormal and get rid of it? Or are you hoping for something more than that?"

"I'm hoping to end the turnover rate. There are even some drivers who will not haul a load here, passing it off to anyone else who will take it. It's not about what the load is. They just don't want to come into this warehouse."

"My senses tell me there is more to it," said Celeste. "Is there something you hope isn't found?" she asked.

"Well, um, I, I'm sure there are plenty of secrets here. But none of them have anything to do with me."

Not the question, thought Celeste. *But it's something.*

The two walked into the building on the side furthest from the office. Celeste immediately saw three apparitions standing in the stocking area doing nothing; just standing with their hands at their sides and their eyes closed and their heads bowed low.

Then there was a lively apparition near the door to the office. He motioned for Celeste to join him at the door.

"We need to go to the office now," said Celeste.

"But you need to make sure you see this side of the warehouse," complained John.

"There is a spirit by the office door waving me to come over there," yelled Celeste. "Are you coming or not?" she said quickening her pace.

"You move fast for your weight," said John before realizing that that was probably not politically correct and might be taken as other than a compliment.

"That was a compliment, right?" replied Celeste.

Reaching the office, the apparition was still waving someone to join him.

"The door is locked," said Celeste.

"There you go," said John unlocking the door.

Celeste looked at the apparition and gestured to the open door. The spirit just stood there waving for someone to join him. It was just a memory stamped on the office. Like the shadow person at Judy Wells' house. It was called a residual haunting. He would be of no help to Celeste.

Walking into the office she remembered how confusing this place was with multiple spirits and apparitions layered one on top of the other. She shut down her abilities as much as possible to allow the most recent spirit to come through.

Her talking board was the first tool out of the kit bag. This was what John had perceived as heavy as "a bowling ball" when they were walking in. The piece of wood was overly heavy. All that was needed to run it was a spirit willing to cooperate. In lieu of that there was always a pendulum and dowsing rods. There was a perfect place for it on the desk, but not before noticing a card with her name on it sitting under an envelope. She looked at it without being obvious, and then slipped it into her pocket.

"Would you rather I be here or not while you do this?" asked John.

Truth be told, he hadn't believed in any of this mumbo jumbo stuff two weeks ago. But now… The more things that happened, the scarier it became. He would just as soon leave.

"Stay or go," she said waving him back. "You will have no effect on this. At least if I do it right, you won't"

Celeste looked around the room, paused and pointed to the corner sternly saying, "YOU! You in the corner! Come to this desk and help me."

This was not a request. It was an order and the spirit followed it like a soldier, immediately appearing at the desk.

"Do you speak English?"

His response was a nod for yes.

"Point to the letters to spell your name."

P A U L

"Thank you, Paul, for cooperating with someone who can see you, but cannot hear you. Can you answer my questions by spelling them out on the board? Can you do that for me?"

He nodded.

"Good," said Celeste. "How long have you been here?"

1 3 Y E A R S

"Can you leave this room?"

S O M E T I M E S B U T I D O N T L I K E T O

Celeste wrote down each question and each response.

"Are you afraid?"

Y E S

"What are you afraid of?"

T H E R E I S A M E A N S P I R I T H E R E

"In the warehouse?"

Y E S A N D I N T H E O F F I C E

"Is he here now?"

The Spirit looked around the warehouse peeping through the blinds like a child hiding from an angry parent. Finally he returned to the talking board and spelled out:

N O

"Then why were you hiding?" asked Celeste.

Y O U A R E H E R E S H E W I L L C O M E

"So, the spirit is a woman?" asked Celeste.

Paul nodded.

"What could another spirit do to possibly scare you? You are a spirit, too."

S H E T H R E A T E N S T O S E N D M E T O H E L L S H E S A Y S T H I I S I S P U R G A T O R Y

"Well, that's an interesting concept. Why would a spirit be able to send you to hell? Is this an angel, or a demon, or something else?

Paul ducked back into the corner. There was a loud crash in the warehouse. John ran to see what had happened.

"A pallet fell off an upper shelf. It must have been poorly placed and stacked too high. The boys will be busy with that for a few minutes," he was laughing as he walked into the office, but he stopped abruptly.

"What is that?" he exclaimed.

"I'm not sure," said Celeste. "But my theory is that it's responsible for the pallet falling. Paul has completely disappeared. Wait. You can see this, too?"

"I don't know what it is, but there is something unusual there."

It turned to look at John. "Evil comes for you." It said and slowly disappeared.

"Did you hear that?" said John.

"I heard something and that's unusual in itself. What did you hear?" asked Celeste.

"It looked right at me and said, "Evil is coming for you."

"At least we both heard the same thing. That is how it intimidates. It tells these poor souls that they are in purgatory and an evil is coming for them."

"Why would it say that to me, though," said John who was visibly upset. "This is not what we came here for. I may never come down here again."

"Nonsense," said Celeste. "That is exactly what it wants. It's a bully, nothing more."

"So, you don't find that thing scary? And besides, how'd you hear it? You said you can't hear spirits," said John.

"Not unless they want me to. And this one wanted to scare us, letting both of us see her and hear her. This will explain people leaving. How would you feel about being here alone now?"

"Won't be now," said John.

Paul reappeared. "Is it gone?" he asked.

"How is it I can hear you?" asked Celeste.

"By talking into your mind, just like the monster. It's a handy trick to pick up," said Paul.

"John, when was it noticeable that people were leaving?" asked Celeste.

"It's been in the last few months."

"And someone from the area died around the same time?"

"No one comes to mind," said John.

"The lady," said Paul. "The one that was so angry after having a fight with one of the drivers."

"Wait. One of the drivers had angry words with a spirit?" said Celeste.

"No, she wasn't a spirit yet by then. It was later, her spirit was still angry and yelling at him, but he couldn't hear her anymore."

"The rest of us heard her alright. Wailing and yelling and crying, saying a lot of mean things. In the end, she disappeared. It wasn't much later that this monster showed up threatening everyone."

"This is beginning to make sense," said Celeste.

"I'm glad it is for you, because I'm pretty much in the dark over here," said John.

They had been there for at least half an hour. Celeste was ready to get home. John agreed and helped her put her tools away then started for the door, still jumpy from the afternoon's experience, they couldn't leave fast enough for him.

"Paul, would you like to come home with me for a day or two. I think you'll find it comfortable there," said Celeste.

Paul nodded his head, wanting out of there as much as John did.

"What? You're offering a lift to a ghost in **my** car ?" asked John.

"Has Paul not shown you how helpful he can be? If he wants to stay at a more peaceful place, you can at least give him a ride," said Celeste with no room for argument.

"Fine, but no scaring me," said John.

Paul smiled and attached himself to the talking board for the trip. For anyone who could see spirits it looked like a balloon attached to Celeste's tool bag. Even Celeste would have trouble seeing him if Paul didn't want her to.

Celeste did most of the talking on the drive back to her house. "I think this answers your burning question, John. This spirit has probably done the same thing to other people and those are the ones who left. If it's bad enough to scare a spirit like Paul, then just imagine how much it must have scared the people working in the area. They must have felt the way you did and simply quit. There are a few who have ignored it and I will want to talk to them next Friday. Or there may be some "type" that she preys on. Paul, you have watched her. Are there certain types of people that she shows herself to?"

Paul hadn't been paying attention, rather playing with all the gadgets of the car. "There are so many buttons and lights. It's like a car from the future in a SciFi movie."

"Paul!" said Celeste sternly. "Focus on the task at hand. Are there certain types of people that the mean spirit shows herself to?"

"Mostly the drivers," said Paul. "But sometimes to brunette women with short hair. And a man or two in the warehouse."

"And other spirits," chimed in John. "And **me**!"

"You were just caught in the crossfire," said Celeste. "It was showing itself to me and you just happened to be there."

"That's an interesting point, though. How many spirits could see or hear her?"

"Never noticed many other spirits," said Paul. "Sometimes you would see her having a fit and yelling when you didn't see anyone there. Is it possible that not all spirits can see each other?"

"I've always thought that was possible," said Celeste. "No one has ever proven it one way or the other to my satisfaction."

"Well, no one has ever **proved** that there are ghosts," said John.

"Hey, what am I? Chopped liver?" said Paul.

Celeste was beginning to suspect that Paul had been a spirit for a lot longer than thirteen years. Time must be irrelevant in the spirit universe. Was it a mistake bringing him home with her? But it seemed awful to leave him stuck there in that terrifying office. They could go see the creek and the horses and he could travel about. Surely there was nothing wrong with that.

When they arrived at her house, John wanted to come in to discuss the afternoon, but Celeste pointed to her wrist as if to say, "off the clock." It was a Saturday and there were things to do.

"See you next Friday, John. There is some research to do and Paul is going to help."

"Have a nice weekend, Celeste, but do not labor under the misconception that you won't see me again before Friday," laughing as he said it, but Celeste knew he meant it.

Celeste walked up to the house with Paul bobbing off her bag like a circus balloon. It would have been a funny sight for passersby if they could see it.

When they were inside, Paul remained attached to the board.

"Why are you staying with the board?" asked Celeste. There's a whole house here for you to explore."

"What if letting go sends me back to the other place? Purgatory is no picnic," said Paul.

"Hmmm. I hadn't thought of that. If that happens I will call John and get him to take me back to get you and we will find something better for you to be attached to."

Paul detached slowly. He was smiling by the time he completely detached. His smile was the last thing to go. Celeste called John and explained the situation.

"I'm not that far. I'll turn around and come back."

When they walked into the warehouse there was a long haul truck being unloaded. Everyone was busy. No one paid any attention to Celeste and John going into the office. But, the part time clerk, Carol was at the desk doing some paperwork. Celeste looked at John. John nodded.

"I wonder if we could have the room for a few minutes," said John.

"I'm due for a break," she said. "How long do you need?"

John looked at Celeste and she said, "No more than five minutes, dear. We'll be gone by the time you get back."

Carol left and Celeste looked in the corner for Paul.

"Paul if you're here, please show yourself. I've come back for you. This time we will make sure you are tethered to something light. Ooh. I have a feather that could work."

As Celeste was talking Paul was slowly becoming visible to both Celeste and John. Celeste burst into tears of joy. She really wanted to help Paul and felt guilty for letting him detach at her house.

"Paul, thank goodness. You're alright."

"I may be alright," he said. "But it was scary. It was like being in a fog and not knowing where you're going only that you're getting there too fast."

"I'm so sorry, Paul. I brought a feather. Can you attach to it?" said Celeste.

"I can attach to it, but is it heavy enough to keep me from coming back here?" he said anxiously.

"Let's find out," said Celeste. "Go ahead and attach to it."

"Now let's go to the car," she said to John.

They walked to the car. Celeste let go of the feather. Paul was able to move around the car freely.

"This is awesome!" he yelled. "And a feather won't attract attention floating around."

"Some people believe that a feather means an angel has left a message."

"They got it part right," laughed Paul bouncing around the car.

Celeste left the car holding tight to the feather so that Paul wouldn't be carried off by the wind. She gathered her things and thanked John for coming back.

"My pleasure," said John holding the door for her while thinking of the nightmares coming his way tonight from todays' adventure.

Celeste let go the feather when they were inside.

"I can feel it pulling at me," Paul said, "But it is not as strong as my attachment to the feather. I'm very tired from manifesting. Do you mind if I go invisible for a while?"

"Not at all," said Celeste. "Make yourself at home. The only place that is off limits is my bedroom when I'm sleeping and the bathroom when I'm using it. Clear?"

"As a bell," said Paul.

"Who was president when you were alive?" asked Celeste.

"Eisenhower," replied Paul. "Why?"

"Paul, that is a lot more than thirteen years," said Celeste. That is several decades. This is the year two thousand seventeen."

"No, it isn't. It can't be. That would mean that my wife could also be a spirit. And if a spirit I need to find her," said Paul with an anguished look on his face.

"We need to do some more testing with the feather before you just take off. You don't want to end up back at the warehouse again, do you?"

"What am I attached to there that keeps pulling me back?" he asked.

"That's a very good question," said Celeste.

"What are you attached to?"

"I don't have a clue," said Paul.

"Do you spend most of your time in the office?" said Celeste? "Or do you wander around the warehouse?"

"I'm usually in the office."

"Then that must be where you are attached!" said Celeste.

"Do you remember being any place else besides the building that the office is in?"

"There was a place a few years ago. It was an office, but it was much bigger and brighter. Then one day I was in the office I'm in now."

"So it's likely that you were attached to some piece of office furniture or files or a file cabinet. The file cabinet is right there in the corner where you hide. Think about it. Do you feel any attachment to it?"

"Maybe," said Paul. "It's hard to tell."

"Try detaching from everything in the office, one thing at a time." said Celeste.

Paul imagined himself detaching from the file cabinets first. Each thing he detached from disappeared in his mind. This was going quickly and smoothly. Then some of the files that had been in the first cabinet returned. Not many, but at least three or four.

Paul looked at the files. They were about him. This had been his workplace when he was alive. The files contained the first application and all the payroll records and his death certificate. Everything had disappeared now except the death certificate. He held on to it not wanting to let go telling Celeste he couldn't detach from it.

"It's only a piece of paper and it will still be there when you let go of it. You will still exist. You just won't be stuck in that place," said Celeste.

"I'm trying," said Paul. "It's not that easy."

"I didn't say it was easy. I just said you could do it."

"Let me hold it for a while," he said. "I will try again later, okay?

"That is fine, Paul. You have to do what you can do when you are ready to do it."

Celeste went into the kitchen to make some dinner. Lunch had been early and long ago and her stomach was letting her know. Chaos accompanied her. Passing the phone she noticed that there were sixteen new messages.

"They can wait."

"Who can wait?" asked Paul.

"My voice messages," answered Celeste.

"I'm probably going to have a lot of stupid questions at first," warned Paul.

"We'll get through it," said Celeste.

"I'm going to have to go silent and invisible for a while," said Paul.

"See you later. Be sure and stay connected to that feather," came her warning as he slowly faded from view.

CHAPTER FIFTEEN

Dinner was especially delicious because her hunger was that great. Never mind that it had been prepared in the microwave. Tonight that didn't matter. It was food and tasty.

Having eaten, the phone messages finally took priority. They were up to eighteen now. It should have slowed down. But, no, the messages just kept coming. She considered leaving them all until tomorrow, then thought about the people who could have called and left real messages. Sitting down with her pad and pen the screening process started again.

Most were from the incident at the restaurant, but there were messages from Danielle, Dori, Carol, and Joe. Celeste didn't remember giving her card to Carol or Joe, but they had her number. She had just seen Carol this afternoon and Carol didn't say anything about needing to talk to her, but the message seemed rather urgent.

"This is Carol. I hate to bother you on your weekend, but you were just here with John. Coming back you were already gone. Something changed about the room and then after about five or ten minutes, one of the file cabinets started shaking. Is it safe in here?"

Celeste stopped to call Carol back, not wanting the poor girl to be frightened of being at work.

"I'm glad you called, Celeste. It feels like something in here is angry. There's a file cabinet that has turned over by itself and the boys are getting loud and cursing at each other."

"We seem to have upset the resident bully," said Celeste. "Try not to worry, dear. You shouldn't be in any danger. Just steer clear of the men for the rest of the day."

"What about the file cabinet. There are a lot of file cabinets in here. That's a lot of potential flying cabinets," said Carol.

"That cabinet was probably the only one she was interested in, so you should be fine."

"Why do you keep calling this "she"? Did you know about her when you ran me out of the office?"

"Yes, dear, we did, but we thought we had the situation under control."

"Obviously, you did not," said Carol with a less than friendly tone. "Should I call Mr. Scott?"

"No, he would just call me and I already know about it, don't I?" There was a pause. "Has anything happened while we've been talking?"

"Not in the office, no, but the guys on the loading dock are still acting like something is wrong."

"Just stay in the office until your shift is over. You'll be fine," said Celeste hanging up.

Was Joe working tonight, as well? she thought. *Was he one of the angry men arguing on the loading dock? That would explain a phone call from him.*

Celeste called Danielle. It went to her voice mail again. "Danielle, it's me returning your call. All in for the evening and possibly the weekend. Call me when you get this, please."

It was time to unmute the phone in case anyone actually called back. Picking up one of the three books by the sofa, all in the process of being read, she snuggled cozily under a blanket. Chaos jumped up and joined her. The purring started immediately.

"If it was possible my purr would be on, too, right there with you. This is as comfortable as I've been all day. And it was such a strange day. There must be a connection between Judy and that warehouse. It's not coming to me, yet. But, it will." she said stroking Chaos and increasing the purr factor with every stroke.

Celeste fell asleep on the sofa reading a new book about crystals. The book was new, but the information was old. It would probably not be finished. Awakened about three o'clock in the morning with a stiff neck, Paul appeared and startled her enough to get a small scream out of her. He thought it was funny. Celeste felt otherwise.

Moving into the bed was an effort, but sleep returned again in minutes. In the wink of an eye the sun was up. It was a leisurely morning with no place to be and nothing important to do. Celeste would make lists of people to call, but business calls would be returned tomorrow during business hours. Today would be devoted to rest.

"Paul? Are you here?" she called out.

"I am," said Paul appearing by the stove. "This is a very cozy place you have here. Hope you don't mind I turned on the TV. There is so much to learn. It seems we are traveling to Mars now and have invented something to teleport us across the planet and..."

Celeste stopped him, "The TV must have been on the SciFi channel last. That is mostly Science Fiction, Paul. A lot has changed since Eisenhower. Let me find you a more accurate channel to watch."

"No hurry. I'll hang out here with you, if that's okay."

"It's okay with me. Just going to have brunch and relax today. Maybe later a walk down to the creek. Would you like to come along?"

"As long as you don't mind carrying my feather," he smiled.

"You know it's strange for me to be able to hear a spirit. I usually can see them, but rarely hear one."

"Do you want me to go back to not talking?"

"No, I'm getting used to it. Does it take more energy on your part?

"It does and it doesn't. It does take energy, but having always talked it would feel funny not to. No one ever heard me before. Well... that's not really true. Every once in a while someone will hear bits and pieces."

Celeste set the TV to the Discovery Channel and went back to cooking breakfast. That should keep Paul busy for a while. Breakfast was good and debate over getting dressed was in the end won with a resounding "No." Curling up in an overstuffed chair and listening to her messages was as active as anyone needed to be on a Sunday afternoon.

Paul was fascinated. He was spellbound as Celeste pushed a button and someone began talking to her, but they weren't really there. Celeste had two more "hate" messages, which was always discouraging. Dori and Carol had called again. Joe had returned her call. It felt like they were all playing phone tag.

John had left a message about the ruckus at the warehouse. Danielle invited her to go drinking last night so the return call was a little hard to make out.

Celeste picked up the phone and dialed up Dori first who had tried to reach her twice now.

"Hello?" answered Dori.

"Dori, this is Celeste. Just listened to your message. What's up?"

"Did you tell my grandson's cousin's nephew he could sit in on my reading this week?"

"Only if you agreed, he would get a free reading before yours. But I made no promises about that."

"He thinks he's just going to sit in on mine. He has no intention of letting you read him," said Dori.

"You leave that to me, Dori. Will you mind waiting in the parlor during his reading?"

"Not at all," said Dori. "Readings should be private even for Dean."

"Well, you bring him an hour earlier than your appointment and let me deal with him, okay?" said Celeste.

"Oh thank you, Celeste. And thank you for calling me back on your day off," said Dori.

"Don't worry about it. Take care of yourself and I'll see you this week."

Celeste was not surprised at what Dean was up to. He was still trying to catch her in some kind of fraud. He might be in for a surprise himself. She would work extra hard to show him just how real this was.

Her next call was to Carol. "It got really nasty at the warehouse last night. They were throwing boxes and cussing each other up and down. Two of them even started throwing punches. But you were right, it was safe and sound in that office," Carol said in one breath.

"I'm sorry you had to see all that. But, I'm glad you are alright," said Celeste sympathetically.

"Is it going to be like that from now on?" asked Carol.

"Hopefully not. With any luck we're going to get to the bottom of it and help move that particular spirit on."

"Cuz I don't want to work in that kind of environment. If you hadn't talked to me, it would have been really scary. It's hard to work when you're scared."

"You hang in there, Carol. It's going to get better. Don't be afraid to call me if it gets like that again."

"Thank you, Celeste," said Carol hanging up.

"Paul?" said Celeste.

"Yes," he said appearing next to her out of thin air.

"What do you know about the being that is so upset that you left?"

"Uh…. what makes you think I know anything?" Paul said, stalling for time to think.

"I know that that's the being in charge of the warehouse who told me it was purgatory and if we didn't act right, we would either be stuck there forever or wind up in hell," he continued.

"She lied," said Celeste.

"I can see that now," said Paul becoming anxious. "But how was I to know? Her eyes glow red, did you know that? And she's mean. And she yells. And her eyes glow red! Red! Like a demon!"

"Paul," yelled Celeste. "Calm down. What can you tell me about the woman who was arguing with the driver?"

"That woman was pretty with long blonde hair and deep blue eyes. But really mad at the driver."

"Does the driver still work there? Do you ever see him anymore?"

"I haven't seen him in years," said Paul.

"But you saw the blonde arguing with him a few months ago," said Celeste.

"A few years, a few months, a few minutes… it all runs together," Paul shrugged as he said it.

"Think about this next question, Paul. Did you think you were in purgatory before the red eyed woman showed up?" asked Celeste.

"It's hard to remember."

"You can do it, Paul."

"No. No one ever told me about purgatory before her," said Paul after considering it for some time.

"What was the woman's name that became a ghost that night?"

"I don't know," said Paul.

"You don't know or you don't remember?" said Celeste.

"I don't remember," said Paul.

"I need you to remember, Paul. I need your help. What did the driver call her?"

There was a long pause while Paul strained to remember.

"Judes. He called her Judes," yelled Paul joyfully.

"What an interesting name," said Celeste. "It must be short for Judy. I knew there was a connection between Judy and the warehouse!"

"Was Judy having an affair while married? Or was this after her husband died? And was it even our Judy?" asked Celeste to no one really.

"How would I know that?" said Paul.

"You wouldn't, dear. Just talking to myself. Not used to having a talking spirit in my house."

"There have to be some death records, maybe some police reports to create a timeline for all this activity," said Celeste. "Too many things don't add up and too many unknowns."

"You're not supposed to be working today," said Paul. This is a day to take it easy and at most, take a walk to the lake."

"It's just a creek. There's no lake," said Celeste.

"It's outside. That's all that matters to me."

"Oh, you wanted to be outside. Let me get dressed and we'll go for that walk. Look at me being so selfish."

"But you still have phone calls to make," said Paul.

"They can wait," said Celeste slipping into her bedroom to change into a long skirt with a peasant top.

Spending a few minutes on her hair and face then they were off. Celeste put the feather in her pocket so it would stay put during the walk. They didn't want Paul flying away with no control of his destination.

He enjoyed the walk. As did Celeste who had remembered to bring treats for the horses. They walked down to the bottom of what was now almost a dry creek bed. There were patches of water here and there connected by arms of water. This creek filled up quickly when it rained and then emptied in a week or two.

"This seems familiar. Maybe I came here as a child," said Paul. "It was a little different, but I think this was it."

"Well, then its good we 're here today."

It was a pleasant spring day. There was a chill in the breeze, but the sun compensated. Her only regret was that it hadn't rained recently to fill the creek and make for a more enjoyable first outing for Paul. No sooner did Celeste think it, than the clouds rolled in and it began to rain. Turning to head up the bank and find some shelter under a tree near the horses Paul said, "That was a powerful wish. Are you a weather witch?"

"This has never happened before. Are you sure it wasn't you?"

"Let's test it. Wish for the rain to stop for fifteen minutes," said Paul.

Celeste wished that the rain would stop for a few minutes. There was a loud clap of thunder and the rain stopped. The sky remained black, so Celeste took off for home walking the last few houses in the rain.

"It was a coincidence," said Celeste.

"Nope," said Paul.

"Did you enjoy your first outing?" Celeste changed the subject.

"It was nice. You know I can't taste or feel the wind or the water or smell the flowers or the food that you cook. But it was nice to see what there was to see. It's all rather black and white to me, black and white and shades of grey.

"Doesn't sound like a wonderful existence," said Celeste. "Have you thought about moving on?"

"I don't know how anymore. The knowledge has left me. But back then there was reason to stay, to keep an eye on my family."

"How could you keep an eye on them from that little office?"

"That wasn't my first location. It was in a big office with lots of windows and my wife worked in that office. Then they moved me to the dungeon. Even now I can feel it tugging at me."

"When we were trying to free you from the office there was that last piece of paper that you couldn't let go. That was your death certificate, right?" asked Celeste.

"Yes, it was. Are you thinking…? I'm attached to my death certificate. It's what was available in the morgue. My wife must have gotten a different copy and mine went to the HR office."

"That makes sense," said Celeste. I'm sure people get attached to the wrong things quite often."

Celeste went back to screening and returning phone calls putting off calling Joe until last. His flirtations had an effect on her. She was hoping this was a call about the goings on at the warehouse yesterday, but in the back of her mind there was a desire for a little flirtation and flattery.

"Hello?" he answered the phone.

"This is Celeste returning your call."

"Perfect timing!" said Joe. "I'm at the warehouse and there is some weird s*#t going on over here. Yesterday was worse than today, but it's pretty bad today."

"What kind of things are we talking about?" asked Celeste.

"Everybody's mad. We've had two fights break out. People are throwing packages around, which is a no, no. You asked if I'd noticed anything unusual. Yeah, here it is."

"Do you work tomorrow, Joe?"

"I'm on the schedule, yes. But I haven't decided if I'm coming in. One of the guys said this happens every once in a while. I don't want to work in these conditions. Someone's going to get hurt and for what?"

"You said it's not as bad today as it was yesterday. Maybe tomorrow will be better. Can you call me tomorrow and let me know?"

"Of course, I'd love to," said Joe. "I'll keep you updated."

"Right now, though, I'd like you to call John Scott and let him know what's going on. He may want to come over and see for himself."

"I'll do it right away,"

"Thank you, Joe," Celeste hung up the phone smiling like a school girl. Was this a crush on a younger man? There was something drawing her to him and he didn't seem to mind talking with her. What was she thinking? He was at least ten years her junior. He couldn't possibly be attracted to her, could he?

Paul came floating through and startled her again.

"We should have tethered you to a bell!" said Celeste only half joking. "How have you enjoyed your first twenty four hours away from the office?"

"This is nice and I appreciate it, but it would be better to be really free. This is way better than the office, but being anchored to anything at all isn't good."

"Anchored? That's an interesting way to look at it. And an interesting word to use for it. I've been dealing with that word a lot lately. Your part of this is almost solved. You are attached to a death certificate even while you are attached to the feather the certificate is pulling at you. What would happen if we burned the certificate? Is it your main anchor? Would you then be free to detach from the feather and go wherever you like?"

"Maybe, but remember? I'm not ready to let go of it."

"Maybe that's part of the work of the anchor is to make you think you can't survive without it. Think about it. What need do you have for a death certificate? You are obviously dead," said Celeste.

"You may be right. We need to get the certificate and destroy it. Well, you need to. I obviously won't be much help."

"I'm going to call John tomorrow and ask him to bring it here."

"NO!" yelled Paul. "I will try to stop you. You must leave me here and do it someplace else."

"Then that is what we will do. Tomorrow," said Celeste.

CHAPTER SIXTEEN

Celeste enjoyed being able to hear Paul, but having him in her home all the time, not so much. It was time for him to let go of both the death certificate and the feather.

Monday was back to the usual schedule. Celeste warned Paul that other spirits may show up during readings and she would appreciate it if he would wait in the bedroom while she was seeing clients. He promised but she had her doubts.

Judy was early this morning, as usual. Celeste was glad there wasn't an earlier appointment. Judy at least rang the bell before walking in, then cut straight to the point.

"What have you learned about my mother and for that matter, my father?"

"As you know, your father doesn't think it was an accident and your mother wants you to stop looking into it."

"I'm not going to stop looking into it," said Judy adamantly.

Paul popped in in front of Celeste. Celeste signaled him to go.

"That's the lady at the loading dock," whispered Paul.

"What?" said Celeste.

"I said, I'm not going to stop looking into it," said Judy.

"I'm sorry, dear. I wasn't talking to you. There's a spirit here that may have some information for us," said Celeste.

"The brown hair makes her look a lot younger but, I think it's the one," said Paul.

"Judy, did your mother ever have dyed hair?" asked Celeste.

"The mother? That explains a lot," said Paul.

"It was blonde hair. I didn't realize it was colored until I was in my twenties. The odds are the natural color was similar to mine," said Judy.

"Can you think of anyone who ever called your mom 'Judes'?" asked Celeste.

"No. Not in front of me anyway. Uncle Hollis would use Jude sometimes. He would sing that old Beatles song when she was sad."

"So "Judes" could have been a pet name that he used in private," said Celeste.

"Eww! I don't want to think about Mom and uncle Hollis in "private". Yuck," said Judy.

"Well, I have a spirit that puts her arguing with a truck driver at Harper's sometime after your father died. He called her "Judes".

"And uncle Hollis is a truck driver."

"That's right," said Celeste. "But we don't know what they were arguing about. She died shortly after that. Of course shortly to a spirit could mean months."

"But I think Uncle Hollis works for Holly Farms. Why would he be at the Harper's loading bay?"

"We think maybe it was to make a delivery," said Celeste.

"That doesn't make sense," said Judy. "Holly Farms deals in dairy products. Why would they make a delivery to Harper's? Wait! Maybe it was a pickup." Judy exclaimed.

"That's right. There was a pick up. But how did your mother end up there? I mean, how would your mom know when Hollis would be there?"

"And who let her in. They don't just let anyone go back there, do they?" asked Judy.

"Have you been to the facility before, Judy?" asked Celeste.

There was a long pause. Judy seemed to be weighing her answer carefully. She finally nodded.

"I knew it!" yelled Paul in Celeste's ear only. "It **was** her I saw."

Celeste made another mental note to have a firmer talk with Paul when Judy was gone.

"How did you get in?" asked Celeste.

"I went with my father when I was little. He worked there, often taking me with him on a Saturday when Mom was out of town. We needed badges."

"Well, there's a clue we could have used earlier. Why didn't you tell me your father was an accountant at Harper's?" asked Celeste.

"I didn't think it was relevant. It was a truck from Holly Farms that killed my mother."

"True, but… Wait! You're right. I have neglected to investigate Holly Farms. I have focused on Harper's because of another client's case. I need to go visit Holly Farms."

"They're not as strict over there," said Judy.

"How do you know?" asked Celeste.

"Everyone in town has been to Holly Farms. They're a field trip for school kids every year," said Judy.

"I'll make an appointment to pay them a visit," said Celeste. "Having never been on a working farm, this will be fun."

"Me too? That place is awesome!" said Judy excitedly.

"Maybe this first trip should be by myself. Do you want me to read your Runes this session?"

"Nah, Tell me about this other client at Harper's."

"That's really not feasible. Client confidentiality, you know. You don't want me discussing your information with anyone, do you?"

"I guess not," said Judy.

"So, let's do a reading. We have just enough time left to do a three stone draw," offered Celeste.

"Okay," said Judy with zero enthusiasm.

"Or we could try the crystal ball?" said Celeste.

Judy brightened, "Yes, please."

Celeste handed the small yellow crystal ball to Judy, saying "Now roll this around in your hands like this," Celeste demonstrated with the clear ball the spinning in all directions.

Judy tried it and didn't do too badly for a first timer.

"Now stop. Hand me the ball with the top staying in the same position it's in right now."

Judy passed the ball to Celeste. The ball had so many flaws you couldn't even see through it. Celeste took it gingerly.

"This shows that you will get your answers, but they may disappoint you. Others have been hurt for getting involved in seeking answers to this. Some may have even died. Something evil is watching." Celeste seemed to be in a trance.

"How accurate is this ball? That's some pretty heavy stuff you just put on me," said Judy.

"Take heed. We are all walking into something that might be better left alone," said Celeste.

Paul whispered in her ear, "Red eyes."

"Leave it alone? The truth is important, even if I don't like it. We already know she was having an affair with my uncle. How much worse can it get?"

"**NEVER** ask how much worse it can get! The universe will answer that question in the only way it knows how. It will **show** you," said Celeste in her most serious tone.

"Then what do you want me to do? Just walk away and do nothing?" asked Judy in tears.

"No one is suggesting you walk away. But you must learn how to ask the right questions. You must learn to think in more positive terms. For now, our session is over. Would you like to set up an appointment for next week?"

"You know this isn't going to wait a whole week," said Judy.

"Let me get my calendar."

Celeste opened her book. Tuesday was full, but she had an opening Wednesday at four thirty.

"We can meet Wednesday at four thirty by phone. Will that work for you?"

"Yes, who calls who?"

"You call me, dear," said Celeste walking Judy to the door. "Now there's a new client coming in a few minutes, but we'll talk by phone on Wednesday. In the meantime watch a film called "What the Bleep Do We Know". You can find it on Netflix."

"Thanks, Celeste. I'll call you Wednesday."

Celeste had a few minutes to clear the reading room and straighten the table before her new client arrived. This was one of the first callers after the restaurant fiasco. The woman sounded truly interested on the phone and Celeste was looking forward to meeting her.

Melody Turner arrived exactly on time, but had brought a gentleman.

"Welcome," said Celeste. "Do come in."

"I am Mel Turner and this is Pastor Green. He will be sitting in on the reading to make sure that there is no satanic ritual or witchcraft involved."

"So, I'm guessing you would probably feel most comfortable using the

Angel cards," said Celeste.

"You have angel cards? You believe in angels?" Mel asked with great surprise.

"Of course, don't you?" answered Celeste.

"Take it slow," said Pastor Green. "This may be blasphemy Mrs. Turner. We must be ever vigilant."

Celeste brought out the well-worn deck of angel cards in order to placate Pastor Green that this was not her first time to use them.

"We have forty five minutes, so there is time for one full reading which requires nine cards to be drawn. I will shuffle the deck then you will cut the deck into three stacks. You will draw one card from each deck three different times. You will hand the card to me and I will place it where it belongs."

Celeste had a cloth with the pattern embroidered into it. Each place was labeled starting with the past.

Mel drew the cards as instructed and Celeste took them to their proper places. When all the cards were drawn, Celeste turned each deck over to display the cards on the bottom.

This was a fairly complex reading. It took the full amount of time plus a few minutes. Mel was thoroughly impressed. Pastor Green was apparently spellbound.

"That was amazing," said Pastor Green. "You seemed to incorporate so much information without asking Mrs. Turner any questions. And it all felt so accurate. I came here to appease Mrs. Turner and then shut you down, but I see no harm in what you are doing here. You have complete respect for our faith and I can think of no reason not to endorse you."

"What do you mean "endorse" me?" asked Celeste?

"We are from Lori's church," said Mrs. Turner. "We are from the committee that will approve you for the Spring Arts and Crafts event."

"So, this was like an interview?" asked Celeste.

"Yes, I guess it was. Now you won't be going into such lengthy readings at the event. There is a shorter one that you can do?"

"There is one that takes about fifteen minutes, but there is not as much information delivered in that one."

"As would be expected," said Pastor Green. "One cannot expect Amazing Grace to be played in fifteen seconds, can one?

Celeste laughed. This could prove to be a good event. It would be an interesting challenge. There might be some new props needed, like a cross, feathers, and a New Testament, or maybe Lori would lend her those.

"I thank you for coming and how did you want to pay for the visit?"

Pastor Green paid with cash and they were on their way.

It was lunchtime and Celeste had worked up an appetite. There was some lunch meat in the fridge to build a sandwich, and even give Chaos a few bites of it in the process.

"Paul?"

"Right here," he said. "How is your favorite ghost doing so far?"

"You were perfect!"

"Yeah, that last one would have blown a gasket to see me pop up in her face," said Paul laughing.

"When lunch is finished there is a phone appointment with John Scott," said Celeste. "You might do well to wait on the front porch while we're talking."

"Will do," he said saluting like a private in the Army.

After lunch, Celeste ushered Paul to the front porch and then made her phone call to John.

"Can you do something for Paul?" asked Celeste in a hushed tone. "Will you find his death certificate? It's in the small office in the loading area. It's in the two drawer filing cabinet. You'll have to search the drawers."

"What is his last name?" asked John.

"Hmmm…. Good question. Let me ask him. Hold, please."

Celeste walked out to the front porch. "Paul, are you here?"

"Yes, just reserving my energy," said Paul

It was difficult to see him in the daylight anyway. He tried to make himself more visible.

"No need', said Celeste. "You only need to speak. We have not asked your last name before?"

"Cramer, Paul Cramer at your service," he said.

"Thank you, I'll be back out in a few minutes. Do you mind waiting here a little longer?"

"Not at all," he said.

Celeste moved back into the house to continue her conversation with John Scott.

"Did you get that?"

"Get what? You were talking, but no one was answering. Are you okay today?"

"Never mind," said Celeste. "His last name is Cramer. That should make it easy enough to find, shouldn't it?"

"Yeah, what do you want me to do with it once found?"

"Set a match to it and make sure the whole thing burns. Do it there in the office, but expect that it's going to upset your resident bully spirit."

"Wouldn't you rather come take care of it? Or let me bring it to you! That would only take five minutes. I don't want to be the one that does it. You need to take care of this."

"Okay...." sighed Celeste. "Bring it over here. You'll find me sitting on the porch so that Paul doesn't see you arrive."

"Do you want me to call from my car. That will give you a five minute notice.

"That will be helpful. There's a client at two o'clock so try to make it as quick as you can."

"See you in a few."

Celeste went back inside. Paul was not to be seen. He had probably been listening in on the conversation.

"Paul?"

"Right here; He's bringing it here, isn't he? You don't listen. That's not the best way to do it. My attachment will only increase the closer it gets. And how do we know for sure that the fog won't just absorb me? Remember last time? Detach isn't easy and the fog is horrible?"

"We don't know, Paul. My thought is you went through that fog because you were traveling between two attachment points. So, maybe if we get rid of the main one and then detach from the minor one, you will just be free."

"That's easy for you to guess what might happen, but this is real for me. What if it lands me in some kind of limbo?"

"It's your decision, Paul. It's not for me or John to decide. You have to choose for yourself. When John gets here or tonight or tomorrow, but eventually, you will have to choose."

John called to let them know he was on his way.

Paul could feel John getting closer. They had definitely found the attachment. "It's getting so much stronger now," he said to Celeste. "It's pulling like a magnet."

"Hang in there, Paul. Soon it will be close enough that you won't feel the pull at all."

"I hope you're right," he said.

John made it with time to spare. Celeste took the certificate and John left. All that remained was to destroy the paper. Celeste had matches and a metal waste bin.

"Do you want to wait and do this after my next client?" asked Celeste.

Paul nodded then disappeared.

Celeste's next client was a longstanding one with appointments on Mondays at two p.m. and had done so for a decade. This was the woman who had referred Judy Wells to her last week.

"Christy Baker, you've been a busy little bee, haven't you?" teased Celeste.

"Whatever do you mean?" said Christy smiling. "How did that work out with you and Judy?"

"What a handful," nodded Celeste with a smile. "There is so much going on I'm on a retainer. But much more interested in how things are going for you. How did last week's reading work out?"

"Last week was great. Anything that came up I was prepared for because of your reading."

"Then let's get started," said Celeste leading her to the reading table.

The reading was uneventful. Christy was easy to read for, being surrounded by spirits who always gave Celeste a heads up on what the next week would be like. Christy didn't know the extent of her blessings.

After Christy, Celeste had a break. She called out for Paul who showed up immediately.

"Well?"

"Well what?" he answered as if he had no idea what the question was about.

"Are you ready to let it go?"

"No," Paul hung his head. "I'm afraid. I feel more comfortable being attached to it. Can we wait a little longer?"

"Of course, Paul, we can wait as long as you need to. Shall I put it in my file drawer for safe keeping?"

Paul nodded.

The doorbell rang a little before four o'clock. It was Emma, the potential psychic and assistant.

"Please come in, Emma." They walked into the reading room. "This is my reading room. Even when it's a phone reading this is where it's done. Like a sacred space."

Emma smiled and said, "Do you know that there's a man standing next to you?"

Celeste looked at Paul and with clenched teeth said, "Yes, he's not supposed to be appearing to anyone in this house right now. He is a temporary guest."

"I'm not appearing. This one can see me just like you can."

"Now he's talking to you, can't make out what he's saying," said Emma.

"That's because he wasn't talking to you," Paul said directly into Emma's mind as he did with Celeste.

Emma jumped and clutched her chest. "Is it always like this here?"

"No, it's usually pretty quiet. At least it was before Paul arrived. He's attached to a file that is in my possession. We are trying to determine the best course of action to give him his freedom without destroying him in the process."

"Can't you just destroy the object?" asked Emma.

"He's a bit scared of that option, dear," said Celeste. "But we don't need to continue this interview, do we?"

"I, um, well, was really hoping to apprentice with you. What did I do wrong?"

"Nothing, dear it's a perfect fit. What hours do you want to work?"

"I, I, I can start right now and can work every weekday from four o'clock to six o'clock?"

"My workday ends at five o'clock. Can you come any earlier?"

"Three thirty?"

"Three thirty to five thirty it is!" said Celeste.

"What's first?" asked Emma.

"There are a lot of phone messages that haven't been listened to. We will listen together and you can see how the sorting goes. That should be a good start."

Celeste showed Emma the lists and notes with each one already called. Celeste didn't leave the room. The two listened together and Celeste would let Emma tell her which list each one should go on. Emma did very well, missing only one.

The phone rang and Emma motioned pointing to herself to answer it. Celeste shook her head and picked up the phone.

"Hello, this is Madam Celeste. How can I help you fulfill your destiny today?"

Emma nodded writing down the greeting in her notepad then started playing with it to adapt it for her to answer the phone. Her version was, "Hello, this is Madam Celeste's . How can she help you fulfill your destiny today?"

It was Judy on the phone. "Are you busy?" Judy asked.

"Working with my new apprentice on a few things, but we're on your clock now. What is going on?"

"We have a tour of Holly Farms tomorrow. We can be there at either eleven a.m. or one p.m.," said Judy.

"This was supposed to be a solo trip the first time," said Celeste.

"Yes, but I got us in on a private tour," said Judy. "Please let me go with you."

"Let's make it one o'clock," said Celeste. "There's a ten o'clock that will run the full hour."

"Do you want me to pick you up?" asked Judy.

"That would be wonderful," said Celeste.

"See you at one o'clock then, bye," said Judy.

"That was quick," said Celeste. "That one usually has a lot more questions."

The phone rang again. Emma quickly showed Celeste her phone answering script and said, "Let me get it? Please!?" Celeste nodded.

"Hello, Thank you for calling Madam Celeste. How can she help you fulfill your destiny today?"

"This is Judy again. You must be the apprentice. Let me talk to Celeste."

"She'll be with you in a second," said Emma.

Emma handed the phone to Celeste and mouthed the words, "Judy again."

"Hello Judy, You forgot to ask if there was anything new about your mother, didn't you?" Celeste smiled. "The only thing new to report is that there is most certainly a link between Harper's and Holly Farms where your mother is concerned. We think her spirit is at Harper's now, but there is something wrong with her. As soon as we get more information, we may be able to do a ritual that could set her free."

"But, you said she left."

"Apparently not completely. Gone from me? Yes. Moved on? Maybe not."

"Will tomorrow's trip to the farm help?" asked Judy.

"I believe it will. I am looking forward to seeing what spirits may present themselves while we are there."

"Okay, well, I'll see you tomorrow at one o'clock. Bye"

"Bye now," said Celeste and handed the phone to Emma.

"Do you always see ghosts?" asked Emma

"No, but I see them a lot more often than most people do."

"Do you think you'll be back by three-thirty tomorrow?"

"Yes, I will," said Celeste with great confidence.

CHAPTER SEVENTEEN

Celeste spent time with Emma going over some of her tools. What was used when and why. Emma had been practicing using Tarot cards with friends and some of her relatives, still having to look in the book to understand the meaning of each of the cards, but it was getting better. Celeste was impressed.

Emma pointed to the big flawless crystal ball and said, "I bet you use that the most of anything, don't you?"

"Actually? The least. It's a very difficult ball to read; very powerful, but difficult to see. The smaller ball with plenty of flaws can be read more easily because of the flaws. Go ahead. Pick one of them up."

Emma complied picking up the yellow one.

"Now roll it around in your hands. Twist it in every direction. When you feel compelled to stop, do so."

Emma followed her instructions to the letter.

"Now look into the top of the ball. What do you see?"

"A lot of lines and flakes and swirls," said Emma.

"It is your job as a psychic to interpret those lines and flakes and swirls. What do they look like to you? Do you see any animals or people or symbols?"

"One looks a little like a horse," said Emma.

"Ah and what does a horse mean to you? Do you own one? Do you ride? Or is it a symbol of strength or endurance or transportation? That is how you use a crystal ball. Does the horse seem to be well or in distress?"

"Wow," said Emma. What is the horse a symbol of? And all those other questions…"

"It may be a universal symbol, but I am more interested in what it means to the client. Always make the reading about the client. Never superimpose your own wants and meanings onto the client. That is the most important thing I will ever teach you."

"Now pick up the large pure crystal ball."

Emma picked it up and began twirling it the way she had done with the first one. Celeste was impressed.

When Emma stopped swirling the ball, Celeste said, "Look deeply into it. What do you see?"

"Nothing," said Emma. "It's clear there is nothing to even guess at."

"That is why this ball is so much harder to use. Only a true and powerful psychic can use a ball like this. Take your time. Stare into it and let your mind show you a picture."

"There is a little bird in a nest," said Emma.

"And what does that mean to you?"

"I'm the bird," said Emma thinking about it for a minute, "And this is my nest!"

"Very good, little bird. With training you will be very strong and powerful, like an eagle, but remember that for now, you are the little bird."

"It is after five-thirty and I am ready to be done for the day. I will see you back here at three-thirty tomorrow. I have a phone consult at four p.m. so you will work on phone messages and dusting the reading room."

"Thank you so much, Madam Celeste."

"Call me Celeste."

"Celeste, thank you. I know I'm going to learn so much from you. I can hardly wait for tomorrow." She let herself out.

Chaos came walking in for the first time since Emma arrived. "Chaos, are you jealous, my love?"

"Mreow," said Chaos jumping into Celeste's lap purring immediately then making a bed out of Celeste's lap.

"Hello?" said Paul. "Did you forget about me?"

"No," said Celeste. "Why would you think that? You could have stayed with us."

"You said not to hang around for clients to see."

"And you know quite well that was not a client. You even talked to her, which didn't scare her nearly as much as I would have expected. You're just being sensitive."

"So that one's going to be here every day?" said Paul.

"For a couple of hours, yes."

"I like her," said Paul.

"I do, too," said Celeste.

Chaos hissed. "It is getting a little crowded isn't it, Chaos?" asked Celeste.

"So, Paul, have you tested to see how far you can go?"

"No."

"Let's go for a walk. I'm leaving the feather here."

Celeste was curious to see what his range would be. Now that the certificate was at her house, if he was snapped back, he could be found easily enough at her house.

They walked in the direction of the creek. Well, Celeste walked. Paul more or less floated. Making it to the railroad tracks, Paul started to feel uncomfortable like he was being pulled. Celeste asked him to continue with her.

It was another block before he vanished for a second and floated backwards.

"What happened?" asked Celeste.

"It was the fog. Any farther than here, there is a fog so thick you can't see through it."

"Well, you have a very large range. Look how far it is back to my house. You can't even see it from here. But, if my house is the center of your range, you have a lot of places you can go. Does that make you feel better?"

"It feels like it does," he said.

"Why don't you go up as high as you can to get back to the house and see if you can see your whole territory from there?" suggested Celeste.

"Are you sure? You'll have to walk back by yourself," he said.

"Go ahead. Walking is my favorite sport."

Celeste did enjoy her walk in solitude not having been fully alone for about a day and a half now. Hopefully Paul would find places to visit after viewing his territory from above.

This was an opportunity to look at the last few days. Had she been trying too hard to shove a square peg into a round hole? Perhaps John was not the bad guy he originally appeared to be. What would they find at Holly Farms? Was one or both of the Wells' lying to her? How much was Judy Sr. lying about? Paul was just unreliable. He had no concept of time since he'd been trapped by that death certificate. He wouldn't knowingly lie, but... his times didn't add up.

Back at the house none too soon; Danielle was sitting in the rocker on the front porch.

"I didn't think you'd be gone very long."

"How long have you been waiting?" asked Celeste.

"A few minutes, but I love sitting on your porch. It's so peaceful," said Danielle. "I came by to see if you wanted to go have dinner?"

"I'd love to. Maybe Italian this week?" said Celeste.

"Sounds good to me we can go to Luigi's. Do you need to grab anything from inside?"

"Yes, let me get my purse."

"It's my turn to buy this time," said Danielle.

"I don't think so," said Celeste.

"You bought Greek last week. Or have you forgotten our Greek experience?" asked Danielle laughing out loud knowing how embarrassed Celeste had been about that.

"Oh yes. It is your turn. But let me get my purse anyway."

"No problem. I'll wait here."

Celeste only took a few minutes to grab her bag, brush her teeth and run a comb through her hair. They drove the two miles to Luigi's and had a pleasant evening with no intrusions, interruptions, or insinuations, even staying for dessert.

Celeste was ready to be home, curled up reading a book. Thanking Danielle for the meal and the company, but not inviting her in, Celeste was done with this day and knew that tomorrow would be just as delightful.

Once again Celeste fell asleep on the couch reading. It did not occur to her until three a.m. waking with another stiff neck, that Paul had not shown himself since their walk. How rude she must seem to him. Moving to the bed, stopping briefly to change into night clothes she thought, *He'll show up in the morning* and drifted back to sleep.

By morning Paul was still "missing". He must have found a spirit buddy, thought Celeste. Chaos had let her sleep in which was not like Chaos at all. Celeste ran to check her calendar only to realize that her monthly Tuesday at ten a.m. was LAST Tuesday. So there was nothing today until her one p.m. with Judy at Holly Farms.

A morning off. This was like a dream. And the afternoon was a visit to a farm and one phone session. This was needed. Walking to her favorite nail salon, they squeezed her in to get her nails done. What a wonderful feeling to be pampered on a Tuesday morning.

"You have time for pedicure, too?" asked the Vietnamese girl who checked her in.

"Why not?" said Celeste. "I'd love it."

Pedis included a deep tissue massage of the feet and calves. Celeste felt like this was heaven. It was so relaxing she could fall asleep. Then came the scream from one of the ladies getting a pedi.

"What's cookin' ladies?"

Celeste knew that voice. "Paul?"

Paul popped into the woman giving her the pedi. "This is so much more fun than the warehouse," said Paul.

Celeste could still see the girl, but could also see the face of Paul. "You need to go invisible," whispered Celeste.

"You're the only one who can see or hear me now. This lady thinks you're nuts telling her to be invisible."

"Can you hear my thoughts?"

"Of course," he said.

"I'll deal with you when I get home," was "said" with a thought.

"Not if I'm not there, you won't."

"I will burn that certificate and you can take your chances with the fog!" screamed Celeste in her head.

"Calm down," he said. "I'll go back to your place. I was just having some fun with the straights."

"That's not funny," slipping up and saying that one out loud. Everyone stopped and looked at her. They had all calmed down since Paul's arrival. Now they had been reminded of it again.

Celeste left as quickly as possible, walking straight home. Paul joined her.

"Can anyone else see you?"

"No," he said, "just you and probably your new assistant."

"What was that? Is this what you do? Terrorize people? Isn't that what scared you so bad at the warehouse?"

"The first one was an accident. But it was so funny I had to try it again. There was a meeting at that church at the end of the street. I think it was a choir thing. They were trying to sing. They weren't very good. So, I decided to help the director. They could sure reach the high notes once they saw me. Ha! Ha! Ha!"

Paul's laugh was as spooky as seeing him. It was like a belly laugh gone sideways and it seemed it was coming through her ears not her brain.

"I can't have you running around town scaring people for your personal pleasure, or for any reason, come to think of it."

"I'm over it," he said. "I won't do it anymore."

"But will you do it any less is the question," said Celeste sternly.

"That's a good one," he said laughing that creepy laugh.

Celeste shot him a look that would stop a lion. Enough was enough! Being stuck with him for the foreseeable future was too much. He could be controlled with that death certificate. But controlling him wasn't the goal. It was to set him free. Maybe she should just burn the certificate and be done with it?

"No, please don't do that!" Paul shouted out loud.

"Seriously, you can hear **all** my thoughts?"

"People don't like that, do they? I've forgotten a lot since I've been like this. I'm really sorry. I didn't mean any harm, I promise. I'll be good. I'll help you with your work. Please don't banish me to the fog."

"I still think you won't be banished to the fog. You'll be set free. Besides, you're still attached to the feather, right?"

"I am," he said. "I should detach from that."

"Or," said Celeste, "stay attached to the feather, but let go of the paper. You need to try that."

"Maybe tomorrow," he said and flew into the house. They were home.

CHAPTER EIGHTEEN

Where was her mind? Getting a pedicure prior to visiting a farm may have been a bad decision. But here they were in Judy's car headed to a farm and her wearing sandals.

"You look nice today, Celeste," said Judy.

"Thank you, you look very nice yourself."

"Not fishing for a compliment. You really look nice. You had your nails done and you're wearing a touch of makeup. It looks good on you."

"Thank you. Sometimes we just need a little pampering."

"I see you're still wearing my mother's ring," said Judy.

"This may not be your mother's ring, Judy. But having used it to scry for answers to some of our questions, it is quite accurate. It could be useful in determining what happened the night your mother died."

"It's not polite to say died," said Judy. You're supposed to say it more gently like "passed away" or "left the world". Died is just so abrupt."

"But it was abrupt, Judy. One minute a person is alive, the next they're dead. Why do we need to avoid the word?"

Celeste was not known for being a politically correct person. It was better in her mind to call things what they are, especially when it comes to spirits. Granted, nothing really dies. It just changes form. But, dead is dead. It shouldn't be that difficult to say.

"We're almost at the farm," said Judy, changing the subject.

"Seems it should have more of a "country" feel to it."

"It's a pretty big farm. They do a lot of mass production," said Judy. You won't see some of their equipment on a "Mom & Pop" operation."

"What do they produce mainly?" asked Celeste.

"Eggs, milk, butter, general dairy products," said Judy pulling into the long driveway.

"There is a very negative feeling here," said Celeste. "We mustn't stay long. It will make me ill."

"Well at least let's make it to their loading dock so you can look for spirits and such there," said Judy.

A man in a business suit walked out to greet them as they pulled into a paved parking lot. If you didn't know you were on a farm, you would never guess it.

"Welcome ladies, welcome to Holly Farms distribution center."

"Distribution center?" said Celeste. "I thought we were going to a farm."

"Technically you are on the farm," said the gentleman in the suit. "What you would expect a farm to look like is about a mile behind us. This facility processes the milk and turns it into the various dairy products that you buy at the grocery store then distributes by truck to regional locations."

"Wow! This is already an education, isn't it Celeste?"

Celeste was not looking good. "I need to leave," mouthed Celeste to Judy.

"Let me give you the full tour," said the man in the suit. "I'm Mark Hollis."

Judy and Celeste gave each other a surprised look. "Is that where the name Holly comes from? Is it short for Hollis?"

"Actually, it's named after my sister, Holly who was born here as all we Hollises were, but Holly also died here at an early age. Dad changed the name of the farm to remember her."

"So, is this your farm?" asked Judy motioning to Celeste to come along.

Celeste was having trouble moving at all. Unable to shake the negative emotions emanating from the place, it was giving her a raging headache. Her stomach wasn't feeling well either.

"It's been in my family for generations. My brothers work in different areas of the place. One is in shipping which is where you are now. One oversees processing which you can see from here and the youngest takes care of the farm itself. We have a lot of help obviously. Would you like to see the processing plant?" asked Mark.

"No," said Celeste firmly. "We want to see the shipping area."

"Maybe we can look at processing later" Judy said to Mark. "You look very familiar to me."

Judy slowed her pace to allow Celeste to catch up.

"Have you seen any ghosts yet?"

"All I see is that something here is wreaking havoc on my body. I am extremely uncomfortable. We need to leave as soon as possible. Please hurry this up."

They walked to the loading area. In many ways it was similar to the ones at Harper's, except that they were air conditioned. Celeste assumed that was to keep the merchandise from spoiling.

"May we go up there?" asked Celeste.

"Of course!" said Mark enthusiastically. "Not many people are interested in the distribution aspect of our work. Most want to go directly to the farm."

Mark walked them around to a side door that put them up on the dock without having climbed any steps for which Celeste was most grateful. He held the door as Judy and Celeste walked in. Celeste hesitated for a few seconds.

"What did your sister look like, Mr. Hollis?"

"Please, call me Mark. Mr. Hollis gets very confusing around here."

"I bet it does," flirted Judy.

"Very well then, Mark, what did your sister look like?"

"Well, only six when she passed she was small with blonde hair,"

Judy shot Celeste a look that said, see? Don't say died. It's not polite and people don't like it.

"Was her hair short, blonde, and straight with bangs?"

"Yes, yes it was," said Mark.

Judy looked at Celeste with her eyes wide open, a questioning look on her face. Celeste nodded and pointed to the middle bay. No one could see it, except Celeste, but Holly was using the guard rails like monkey bars, swinging on them when a ghost truck backed into her. The truck pulled forward leaving her to fall to the bay below. Then as if by magic the whole scene began again. This was a residual haunting. Like a recording stuck in a loop. Like the shadow man at Judy's house.

Celeste suspected that no one here saw or heard any of this. And there was nothing to be done with a residual. There was no one there. Just a memory. It made Celeste sad.

"Don't be sad," came a voice from below her arms. "It's just a movie. I watch it all the time. I yell at her to move, but it's just a picture show. She always dies."

Celeste was more surprised to hear the little girl than to see her. "Do you like it here?" Celeste asked Holly.

"Actually, it's my least favorite place on the farm," answered Mark assuming Celeste was talking to him.

"Because this is where your sister died? Over there by the middle bay. When a truck backed into her?" said Celeste.

"You don't know what you're talking about," said Mark. "That's not how she died."

"How did she die?" asked Celeste.

"I'd rather not talk about it. That part of the family story is private and not shared with outsiders."

"I'm sorry to have intruded," said Celeste. "It's just that I'm a psychic and your sister is standing next to me talking."

"You need to leave," said Mark.

"We'll show ourselves out," said Celeste. "Your sister wants someone to talk to, though. Maybe if you listen, you will hear her."

"Wait! Come back," called Mark, "What is she saying?"

"Do you feel her hugging your leg right now saying, "I love them all very much, but I'd like to move on now. It's been so many years that I've been stuck here. Can you help me to leave?"

"Yes, dear, I believe I can with the help of your family," said Celeste.

"What can we do to help?"

"We will need to call in a friend of mine that specializes in crossing spirits over."

"I'm sorry, Holly. I should have seen you there. I wasn't paying attention. Please forgive me," said Mark.

"It wasn't his fault," said Holly to Celeste. "I wasn't supposed to be there. They were always telling me that it wasn't a monkey bar and I was going to get hurt one day." As Holly spoke the residual girl started fading away. "I was mad at him at first, but I see now that it was my own fault."

Celeste conveyed Holly's words to Mark verbatim. Mark started to cry. Celeste held him, offering comfort. Holly reached up and grabbed his hand trying really hard to appear to him, she managed it long enough for him to see her, then disappeared again. Even Celeste couldn't see her now. She could still feel her though. Still there, just conserving energy, it had taken a lot to reveal herself to Mark. Now it would be necessary to draw more energy from the atmosphere or something electrical, like the light bulbs which started to flicker.

Mark composed himself and said, "Ladies whatever you need. Name it. That was the most awesome thing I have ever experienced. How can I repay you?"

"Do you have any pictures of your brothers and father?" asked Celeste.

I do," he said. "Do you want to walk with me to the office?"

"Would you mind if we just waited here? I'd like to check for more spirits," said Celeste.

"No problem," said Mark as he walked out the door to fetch the photos.

"WOW! How did you do that?" asked Judy. "I never saw anything so convincing."

"That's because it was real, Judy. Haven't you seen enough yet to convince you that this is all very real?"

"Yes, I guess I have," said Judy. "But those are my own ghosts. This one belongs to someone else. That's different."

"I want to touch a few things in here to see if I can pick up anything paranormal."

"You mean more paranormal than a little girl hanging out on a so called monkey bar and falling to her death?" asked Judy sarcastically.

"You know what I mean. There is something here that makes me uneasy. I want to see what and where it is. I can deal with the distress if I know where it's coming from."

"Okay, so what do you need to do?"

"Just walk around and slowly touch things. Let the warehouse tell me its story," said Celeste.

Celeste did just that. There were a lot of stories, too. Poor little Holly was the saddest story, but there were others.

There was an older man that was stuck tight to the garage type door of the end bay. There was no ability to move about like Paul. The door had crushed him as it closed on him trying to get in. His timing had been off.

There was a young man in an army uniform. This facility must have been taken over by the government during wartime. Guarding the door he waved to Celeste and said something inaudible to her. Holly came back when Celeste walked near the place that she died.

"It's very rare for me to be able to hear spirits," said Celeste to Holly. "There is only one other spirit I can do that with. His name is Paul."

"I have a friend named Paul. He stays in a place similar to this," said Holly.

"Really, do you visit him often?" asked Celeste wondering if it was the same Paul.

"No, but he taught me this trick of being able to talk in your mind. And yes, it's the same Paul."

"You can travel a lot farther than Paul can. Paul can only go a few blocks," said Celeste. "If you can go all the way to Harper's, you can go for miles."

"It is miles if you go the long way," said Holly.

"There's a short way?" asked Celeste.

"Oh yes," said Holly. "Would you like to see? We just have to go through those woods."

"That looks a little dangerous," said Celeste. "Maybe I'll just take your word for it."

"I go into town sometimes, too," said Holly.

"Hmmm…. Is there any place you can't go?" asked Celeste.

"Home," said Holly sadly. "I try, but I can't get in. They had someone like you come and put a spell on it. Now I can't get inside the house no matter what I do."

"When did they do that?" asked Celeste.

Holly shrugged her shoulders and shook her head.

Celeste wasn't sure how much to trust spirits. Their concept of time was lousy and their concept of good and bad seemed to change rapidly. They were just not very good witnesses.

One thing Celeste was sure of; these two spirits had met.

Holly disappeared again as Celeste felt her way around the bay. The only spirits found were Holly, the poor man stuck to the bay door, and the soldier. There were plenty of stories, but no spirits. If not for Holly, Celeste would have called this endeavor a complete bust, but Holly made it worth the trip.

Mark came back in with the pictures. He showed them each brother and then his father.

"That's Uncle Hollis!" screamed Judy.

The room went quiet.

"What did you say?" Mark broke the silence.

"That is Uncle Hollis, who we now suspect wasn't my uncle at all. He was my mother's lover as best as we can tell," said Judy.

"My father? That's a laugh. After mom died we tried to get him to date. He wanted nothing to do with it. Said he was just as happy to stay home or go hang out at the VFW."

"Is he still alive?" asked Celeste.

"Yes. He works the main office buying, setting prices, consulting, and that sort of things. He's here two or three days a week. But also travels checking on the stores we ship to."

"Is he around?" asked Judy. "I'd love to meet him in person."

"Yes, in the front office," said Mark. "Let's go find him. But I'm telling you... my dad never posed as your uncle."

"His office is right over there," Mark pointed to the most prominent office in the place."

Judy walked ahead and poked her head in the door. She stood there for a minute as if in shock. Finally speaking, "Uncle Hollis? Is that you? It really is. I cried so hard when Mom said you were going away. It was like Dad leaving all over again," she started to cry.

"Judy? Look how mature you've become."

"Dad, you actually know her?" said Mark.

His father nodded. He went to Judy and held onto her while she cried. He found some Kleenex and handed her one.

"I guess you've met my son, Mark," said Mr. Hollis. "Maybe try thinking of him as a cousin."

"What did we do? Were we so horrible?" sobbed Judy.

"It's difficult to explain," said Mr. Hollis aka Uncle Hollis. "Your mother felt that it was in your best interest not to have me around anymore. I missed you, but I agreed with her logic."

"How is it logical to just disappear out of a teenager's life? What kind of logic is that?" asked Judy.

"Judes, it was what your mother wanted," he said. "Arguing with your mother never worked out."

The hair on the back of Celeste's hair stood up and a chill shot down her spine. He called her Judes. Not Jude, but Judes. What did it mean? The blonde in Paul's memory had been called Judes and when they had asked Judy if anyone called her mother Judes, she never mentioned that someone had called her that. Here was another answer that produced several more questions.

"Where did you get that?" asked Mr. Hollis pointing to the ring on Celeste's finger.

"In a creek bed," said Celeste.

"Does it have an inscription?" he asked.

"Yes, it does. It has a beautiful one, in fact," answered Celeste.

"May we have a few minutes alone?" asked Mr. Hollis

"We'll wait out in the lobby, Dad," said Mark.

Celeste started to leave. "Don't leave Miss... I'm afraid I didn't catch your name. What is it again?" asked Mr. Hollis.

"Celeste and it was assumed you wanted to talk to Judy."

"That ring was a gift to Judy's mother years ago. You can tell from the inscription the nature of our relationship," he said.

"Don't worry. Judy doesn't know what it says. But it has been mentioned that we suspect Uncle Hollis wasn't a blood relative."

"That is where you are wrong. Charlie Wells was my cousin. Technically that made Judy my cousin, but with me being a grown man when she was born, we just used Uncle. It was easier."

"But you and Judy had an affair, didn't you? This inscription is not the message a cousin would have for his cousin's wife."

"We fell in love the moment our eyes met, but she was already married to my cousin, Charles Wells. Charlie was unaware of our falling in love. We hid it and pretended it didn't exist, but it was always there. That ring was a gift for her birthday the year that Judy was born. At that point we had still not acted on our feelings. But I knew there would never be anyone else for me. My sons were already a few years old and my wife had died in childbirth with my youngest."

"This is all so sad," said Celeste. "Judy didn't seem to remember your sons today. Why do you think that is?"

"We stopped visiting as a family after my wife died. I would steal away when I could to spend time around Judy and we did have an affair that lasted for many years. But one day Judy came to me and said that Charlie was getting suspicious. We needed to stop seeing each other. I couldn't deny her anything, so we stopped. It was less than a year later that Charlie died."

"We saw each other at the funeral and I stepped up as the dutiful cousin to comfort her. And comfort her I did almost to the point of spoiling her."

"One of the things that was important to her was for Judy to never know the truth about me. I kept up the pretense even after Charlie died, but I visited less and less."

"If I had it to do over again I would surely do it differently. I loved her too much."

"And Judy Jr. never found out about Uncle Hollis living in the same town and owning Holly Farms? That's a hard one to sell," said Celeste. It was all too convenient for her. The pieces fit too tight in some areas and too loose in other areas.

"If you will promise to never show Judy the inscription, I will let you keep the ring," said Mr. Hollis.

"The ring is not yours to give or take," said Celeste. "Regardless of who it **may** have belonged to, it is mine now. Judy Jr understands that and you might as well know it, too."

"It was her mother's ring. It should rightfully go to her. I don't want it to, but it should."

"I don't want it to either. The girl has enough problems to deal with and doesn't need to have to reconcile the fact that "Uncle" Hollis was shtooping her mother her whole life." Celeste had no love for cheaters seeing too much of the aftermath in her clients. "It will stay safely in my care."

"Fair enough," said Mr. Hollis. "What will we tell Judy?"

"About what?"

"About me!" said Mr. Hollis.

"I'm not going to tell her anything," said Celeste. "That is for you to decide."

"So be it. Shall we join them?"

Celeste nodded.

"Well, Judy, I hate to spoil a good time, but I have a client at four p.m. and need to get back to prepare for it," said Celeste walking into the lobby.

The whole truth may remain forever hidden, but there had certainly been a great deal of information gained. Did any of it have anything to do with the accident? Only time would tell.

CHAPTER NINETEEN

"You two certainly talked for a long time in there alone," said Judy as she drove Celeste home.

"He had a lot of questions about how we found him and how he should handle it," said Celeste.

"Handle it? How he should handle it? What about me? Finding out that my uncle wasn't my uncle and learning that he was my cousin and what else? Oh yes, my mother's lover," barked Judy with as much attitude as possible.

"Those are questions you need to take up with him. You should probably call him when you get home and see if the two of you can get together for dinner or something. He has lots of questions and maybe a few answers for you."

"It's not like we have each other's numbers," said Judy with a bit of a harrumph.

"Way ahead of you. Here is his card with his personal cell phone number. No excuses. Get to know the man who may have loved your mother as much as your father did."

"This does not do anything to prove what happened to my mother that night," said Judy angrily.

"True. It was a dead end, but we won't stop trying, dear. And you did learn a lot from it."

"Well, here we are. Do you mind my just letting you out without coming in?"

"Not at all," said Celeste. "There's a client who will be calling soon. I must get ready. Thank you for the ride."

Judy left and Celeste went in and collapsed on the sofa. Immediately the doorbell rang.

"Judy? What did you forget? I really can't ans.… Oh," stopping mid word. "Emma! You had completely slipped my mind. Come in. You were only seconds behind me. Let me put my feet up for a bit."

Emma said, "No worries or need for supervision. If you're going to be on the phone at four p.m. you will keep the line busy while your new apprentice will clear off the messages from the answering machine. It will work out fine."

Celeste collapsed on the sofa again. Chaos jumped up to rub Celeste's belly while Emma brought her a Dasani. This was worth getting used to.

Emma started working the voice recorder while Celeste rested up for her four o'clock. Answering the phone when it rang and taking care of callers in real time instead of a day later. Celeste was impressed. Then there was a hate call. Celeste took the phone from Emma, who was blushing and looked on the verge of tears.

"This is Madam Celeste. You are calling for me?"

"You're a heathen and a whore," said the caller.

"Are you certain?" asked Madam Celeste.

"Anyone who has special gifts and charges people to use that gift, is consorting with the devil. It is not Christian and it is not ethical," said the caller.

"Tell me, how do you make a living, sir."

"I'm a gardener. What does that have to do with anything? Just because I don't wear a suit and tie to work doesn't make me any less than those who do."

"You must have a real green thumb," said Celeste.

"I do. I grow the healthiest best blooming plants in the county."

"Do you do that for free?" asked Celeste.

"Of course not," said the caller. "Why would I do that? I have bills to pay."

"I understand, but don't you think your green thumb is a gift?"

"Well… Yes… It kind of is, but…that's different!" he exclaimed.

"How is it different? I cannot grow a flower to save my life. You have a gift as unique as you are, as do I. But there are still bills for me to pay and I like to eat."

"Then you should get married so that your husband can take care of the bills."

"Are you asking me to marry you?"

"Of course not, I don't even know you!" he exclaimed.

"Then how can you judge and condemn me if you don't know me?"

The caller had calmed down now and was beginning to realize that he would not win this argument. It was true. He really didn't know her.

"I don't have to know you to know that what you are doing is against God's wishes."

"How do you know what I'm doing?" asked Celeste sincerely.

"I've heard people talk. I know a man who was at that restaurant. My friend said that man accused you of selling snake oil."

"And yet his gramms continues to come to me for advice and counsel." said Celeste calmly.

"Click"

"Emma, if you get any more calls like that, please, tell them to hold for Madam Celeste and give them to me. If that's not possible, you tell them that Madame Celeste will call them back as soon as her client leaves. Repeat their number to them from caller ID. And call them by name."

"Is that how you really feel?" asked Emma. "Do all gifts count as gifts even the common ones like being able to cook or do math?"

"Absolutely, my dear, we all have some kind of gift. That is what the universe or god or whatever you want to call the divine gives us to survive. Never doubt that the thing that is easiest for you to excel at is a gift that can support you."

"What if you don't know what your gift is?" asked Emma.

"Then you will have a very sad life until you find out," said Celeste shaking her head.

"I don't know what my gift is," said Emma.

"Then your first mission in life is to find out. Once you find out, your mission changes to using it to help others who don't have that gift," explained Celeste.

The phone rang and it was New York. "Hello Becky! How are you doing this week?"

Celeste found Becky's notebook and a pen and moved into the reading room. Emma went back to listening to messages. This had given her a much better idea of who she was working for and it was impressive. Emma was careful to work as quietly as possible so as not to disturb Celeste.

Becky had had a rough week. Her dear friend died the week before and she was still grieving. They had not had a session last week. They had just spent the hour talking. This week Celeste did a simple reading for her and it was a hopeful, yet reserved reading. Becky was going to meet someone new. It was in the Tarot cards. Celeste confirmed it with a drawing of Runes.

That almost cheered her up, but there was still too much sadness about the past to look forward. It was a start. Celeste knew that it would get easier to look at with each passing week. They finished the session and confirmed for next week.

Celeste was walking into the parlor when it hit her:

"Have you seen Paul?"

"No Ma'am," said Emma.

Paul popped in and said, "How long does it take to notice your ghost has been gone for days,"

"Actually, you've been gone for hours, not days. We haven't even known you for days, Paul," said Celeste smiling.

"Well.... it feels like days."

"Where did you go?" asked Celeste.

"I didn't go anywhere. I just stayed invisible. It's harder to do with you, but it can be done. I wanted to see how long it would take you to notice." Paul sounded like a spoiled child defending their position when they've been caught with the keys to the car.

"I met someone today," said Celeste changing the subject. "She said you taught her how to talk into a person's mind."

"You met Holly? Where? Will you take me to see her? Can she come here? Her being able to travel so much further and all."

"Yes, at Holly Farms, maybe, probably and yes she can. Why do you suppose that is?" said Celeste answering every question in order.

"Maybe there's nothing tying her to one place?" said Paul.

"It certainly seems that way to me. Wouldn't you like to try breaking your attachment to the death certificate? Isn't it worth a try?"

"It's not you taking the risk. You don't know how petrifying it is to think about risking everything. There's nothing to compare it to."

"Paul, isn't Holly proof that attachment to something isn't required in order to stay around?"

"Well… maybe… but maybe isn't proof positive. There's a chance of just disappearing into the fog. I just can't."

"You are definitely attached to the feather, right?"

"Right," said Paul.

"So if you let go of the certificate, you will still have the feather, right?"

"Right… maybe."

"So, let go of the certificate," said Celeste. "Keep the feather."

"Now?" said Paul.

"I can't think of a better time," said Celeste.

"Okay," said Paul. "Let's do it."

Celeste found the matches and a bowl quickly setting the death certificate on fire.

"I'm afraid!" yelled Paul.

"Hold my hand," said Celeste.

The certificate burned quickly. Paul cowered before the flame. He watched it decompose into ashes.

"You're still here," said Celeste. "The paper is gone and you are still here. Why don't you go see how far you can travel now that you are free."

Paul disappeared. Then in a second he reappeared. "I went all the way to the creek!" he exclaimed. There was no fog to be seen.

"See if you can go back to the warehouse," said Celeste, "or to the farm. It's very close to the warehouse."

Paul was appearing and disappearing every few seconds. He was traveling all over the county, it seemed.

"I think I can go just about anywhere now. This is wonderful. I went to the Eifel Tower just to see it. Is it okay if I still come here?"

"You are always welcome in my home, Paul. In fact, if you don't visit, I will be disappointed."

Paul disappeared again and returned with Holly. "This will be my traveling companion," said Paul. "I'll be back in a few days," he said and disappeared for the last time, at least the last time that night.

Celeste knew that with his sense of time a few days could be minutes or months or even years, but he would be back.

Emma looked at the clock and saw that it was after five-thirty. "I'd better get going. I've stayed past five-thirty."

"After a day like today, will you even be here again tomorrow?" asked Celeste.

"Wouldn't miss it for the world," said Emma.

Celeste went into the kitchen to fix some dinner and finally relax for the day. The ring had not led them to a solution regarding Judy Sr.'s death. There was still the issue of the anchor key, though the anchor may have been about the ring. Maybe it was time to read her Runes again.

While dinner was cooking Celeste went to retrieve her silver Runes. Wanting to keep an eye on dinner the reading would be done at the kitchen table.

The first Rune represented the past. The draw was the eolh which signified both protection and new adventures.

"Well that was accurate," she said to Chaos who had come in to see what was cooking.

The second Rune represented the present. The Sigel came up which signified the Sun, the center of attention, and the spotlight.

"That's surely where I am right now. Let's see what the future holds,"

The third and last Rune was Lagu which signifies water. Her first thought was the creek, but knowing that Lagu's deeper meaning was to go with the flow. Be receptive. Rely on your own intuition.

"Well if anyone is equipped to deal with their own intuition, it's me. What an interesting turn of events the last week has been. And tomorrow I have a full day booked with mostly new clients. There will be no time for the creek or investigating the mysteries of Harper's."

"Chaos, Let's eat."

CHAPTER TWENTY

Wednesday started with Chaos trying to sharpen her claws on Celeste's arm. Celeste came out of bed like a maniac surrounded by hornets. The sheets went flying and so did the cat. Celeste applied Benadryl cream to the scratches just to ward off any allergic reaction.

Might as well stay up. Her first client was at nine a.m. and her second was at ten-thirty. That allowed for some extra time with the new client at nine a.m. if needed. New clients tended to take more time. They had questions about the process and concerns about whether or not it was satanic or evil in any way. Having heard it all there was no offence taken when none was intended.

Beth, her first client of the day was a few minutes late. Celeste made a note of her arrival time in the book then showed her to the reading room.

"Lori referred me and I don't want any of that Pagan stuff. I want the angel cards," said Beth firmly.

"That is not a problem," said Celeste. The Angel cards were always kept handy for just such a situation.

"Lori says you are truly gifted and I can't wait to hear what you have to tell me."

"Lori gives me too much credit," said Celeste. "I just read the cards and interpret them."

"She said you were modest. That's why I was so surprised when I heard what happened in that restaurant. No woman should be put in the position of having to defend her honor in a public dining room. That's what I say. So, I'm here to show my support," said Beth.

"Well, thank you, Beth. That's appreciated. Shall we start?

It was an easy reading and Beth was sincerely impressed with Celeste. It was her intention to send all her friends to see her.

"Do you want to set up an appointment for next month?" asked Celeste.

"Will my future have changed by then?" asked Beth.

"Maybe," said Celeste, "Maybe not. But your present and past will have changed, won't they?"

"How often does Lori come?"

"Oh, Lori comes in every week, liking to fine tune based on what the angels have in mind. We never read more than a week ahead, as a rule."

"Well, if Lori gets a reading once a week then I should probably do that, too. Lord knows I need all the help I can get," said Beth smiling widely.

"Same day, same time?" asked Celeste.

"That will be fine, dear. God bless you and have a wonderful day."

Beth had arranged an auto draft to take advantage of a discount for prepay. Celeste was starting to be in high cotton, as they say. Maybe paying Emma was possible after all. Emma had been working for her for two days as an apprentice and was already making life easier for her. Who says you can't pay an apprentice anyway?

Celeste had a few minutes before Deb Riley showed up. Deb was a regular and had been for years. But her life was not an exciting one so her readings held very few surprises.

Looking at her calendar Celeste found that where there had been holes in the schedule a week ago, there were new client appointments now. Perhaps the debacle at the restaurant was a good thing after all.

Celeste never wanted to be this busy. But, with her new preparations it was becoming something to be extremely thankful for. Hopefully not all of these people would want weekly readings. They would be steered to monthly.

There was a short reading at eleven-thirty then a two hour break for lunch at noon. It was still her preferred policy to keep one p.m. open for emergencies. After making a sandwich it was time for a walk to the creek. It was a pleasant day for an outing. There were flowers starting to bloom. Some were weeds. But even the weed flowers were beautiful. Gathering some dandelions from a vacant field was a nice diversion. They would be used for a medicinal tea after sufficient drying.

The creek was still basically dry. There would be no crystal cleansing this month. Hopefully the rain would return by the next Full Moon. There were a lot of Crystals that needed to be recharged. Fortunately she had a small artificial waterfall set up in the back yard. It wasn't as good as a natural creek, but it would always do in a pinch.

The horses were glad to see her with a carrot for each of them. "Finally," said a man approaching from the direction of the house. "I knew someone was feeding the horses treats. Just never could catch anyone in the act."

"Have I done something wrong?" asked Celeste. "My horses used to love carrots and apples."

"I was just worried it might be someone trying to friend them so they could steal them, or worse, kids giving them things that were bad for them. Apples and carrots are fine." The man extended his hand, "The name's Norman West. Pleased to meet you, Ma'am."

"My name is Celeste and I always stop to greet these fine animals when my walks bring me this direction."

"You had horses but don't anymore?" asked Norman.

"I had to give them up on moving to the city," said Celeste briefly displaying her sadness at the thought. "They are missed, but I've grown too heavy to ride anyway."

"Nonsense!" bellowed Norman. "You're a healthy woman, yes, but too heavy to ride? That's pure nonsense. Let's make a date right now to go riding. How does Saturday at one sound to you?"

"I, uh, well."

"The word you're looking for is yes," said Norman.

"Yes," said Celeste. "I can't thank you enough."

"I'll look for you right here at one on Saturday," said Norman.

"I will be here with boots on," said Celeste feeling like a small child that had just been promised a pony.

They shook hands again and parted company. Celeste was glad to have chosen to walk at that exact time. Imagine all the times spent feeding those horses and had never met the owner.

With twenty minutes to spare before her new client at two p.m., she gave Chaos some attention and brewed some tea. Her excitement about riding kept her thinking about Saturday. It was only three days away. Finding her old riding gear proved a challenge, but it still fit. Her excitement geared up a notch.

Her two o'clock was a few minutes early. This one was new, had been at the restaurant that night, and wanted Celeste to cure her anxiety and depression. This was something that Celeste was actually licensed to do, but it was usually done with medication from an overseeing Dr. as well as Celeste's counseling.

"Have you seen a Dr. about this?" Celeste asked. It was a question of ethics. Treating something that could or should be treated by a doctor would not do. Unless the doctor had pronounced it hopeless or medication alone wasn't working.

"Yes, they have me on medication, but it doesn't work. I've told them it doesn't work, but they want to be the judge of that."

Celeste would have to use her therapist talents in a psychic disguise to help this woman, but felt it was worth a shot.

"Let's read your Runes first and see what the universe wants you to do," said Celeste drawing a short Rune reading. There needed to be plenty of time for talk therapy.

"I think it would be good for you to come in once a week until we see some positive results," said Celeste after this first session.

"I have to tell you, I feel lighter and happier than I have in ages," said Margie.

"Think of it as a weekly booster for a few weeks and then we'll talk about dropping it to every other week. Does that sound acceptable?"

"Yes. I'll be here next Wednesday at two o'clock."

The session had taken a little over an hour and Celeste was sure that Margie could be helped back to a normal life.

Next up was Lori Phane at three thirty. Lori was her original "Angel lady".

Celeste had told her last week that there would be a decision about the craft fair by today. It would be nice to surprise Lori with the news that Celeste had passed muster with the Minister and was going to do the fair.

When Celeste told Lori of her decision, Lori let out a little scream. That's how excited she was to show off her psychic.

The rest of the session went smooth with nothing out of the ordinary. Lori promised to get the necessary forms to Celeste by the end of the day. Walking Lori to the door, Celeste was surprised to see Emma hard at work. Once again Celeste had forgotten about Emma.

"Emma, I want you to take this key to the hardware store and get a copy made. If I'm going to keep forgetting you're coming, you're eventually going to need a key. Here's ten dollars. And keep the change for gas. In fact, here's another ten. Drive through and get us both a milkshake. I'll have a small chocolate."

"I'll get right on it," said Emma.

Celeste looked at her appointment book to find that Emma had resorted to even filling the one o'clock time slots. That would be addressed when Emma returned.

"Boo," said Paul as he appeared in front of Celeste. He had Holly with him.

"We've been exploring the state. There are places you can go into and they act like an elevator and take you someplace else. Some of them are mirrors and some of them are like wells and things with water. It's awesome!" said Paul.

"But, we have kind of run into a problem," he said.

"What's that?" said Celeste with true curiosity.

"Holly can't go as far as I can. Can you help her like you helped me?" asked Paul.

"I don't know," said Celeste. "It seemed to have something to do with what you were attached to and how long you had been attached to it. Are you attached to anything, Holly?" asked Celeste.

Holly seemed to be thinking about it when the phone rang. Without thinking about it Celeste answered the phone with her usual spiel.

"You can't fool me with all this angel reading stuff. You're a witch and I know it," said the caller.

"Yes, I am a witch," said Celeste. "I am also a Buddhist and a Christian and many other things."

"You can't be all those things at the same time," said the caller. "Christians worship one God. And they don't worship Satan."

"I can assure you, I do not worship Satan. I believe in God the father and I believe in the mother goddess."

"Well, you won't catch me around a pagan witch looking for a reading or healing."

"I understand," said Celeste. "Would you like the name of a good doctor or counselor? I have a list of several that I recommend.

"Click..."

The phone rang again and Celeste hesitated, but looked at caller ID. It was John.

"Hello, John. What can I do for you today?"

"I was hoping you would have some more info for me today. I have people talking about quitting. It's getting really scary down there."

"Hmmm…. I'm going to see if Paul will go over and have a look," she said eyeing Paul. He nodded reluctantly.

"Is that it, John?"

"For the moment, do you really think he can help?"

"Think about it, John. He has access to a dimension and knowledge bank we can only dream of. He can help if he wants to."

"I have to go, John," said Celeste hanging up the phone.

"Paul, Can you pop over to the old warehouse and see who is disturbing the peace and if there is anything we can do to help?"

"Sure. Holly, do you want to come with me?"

She shook her head, no. "I'll wait here for you."

As soon as he was gone, Holly asked Celeste, "Do I have to go everywhere with him?"

"Not to my knowledge, but I have to tell you that you have better access to the rules than I do. Paul may have needed my help to find out what exactly he was attached to that kept him from leaving the warehouse, but he had to do the rest."

"I like hanging out with Paul. He's a very nice old man. But there must be kids my age to play with, too."

"That's understandable. Where have you looked?"

"That's just it. I haven't looked. Paul says I have to stay with him for protection," said Holly.

"I don't believe Paul is lying to you, but don't think he really knows that officially. You might want to ask him," said Celeste.

"Thanks, I'll give it a try."

Paul popped back in. "That crazy lady is back; The one with the red eyes? Remember? I'm not sure what to do about her. That one's stronger than me and **PISSED!**"

"Is it all the time now?" asked Celeste.

"Pretty much" said Paul. "All the spirits are hiding or leaving and the humans are feeling her anger and hate and jumping on each other over stupid things."

"Maybe I should go over there and try to talk to her as a therapist."

"Good luck with that," said Paul.

"Paul, I'd like your help if you would. In case she doesn't show herself to me."

"Oh, I think someone like you will see her just fine," he said. "But I'll come with you. You may need some spiritual muscle."

Celeste called John back, "John, can you take me to the warehouse? It's best for me to see her while active."

"I'll be right there."

Emma walked in with Celeste's key and two milkshakes and could see that Celeste was concerned."

"I'm sorry it took so long. There was a long wait for the shakes," said Emma thinking that was what Celeste was upset about.

"I'll be going out and it may be after five-thirty when I get back. If so, let yourself out and I'll see you tomorrow"

"Will there be ghosts?" asked Emma. "Can I come, too?"

"You may join us to observe but, only if you promise to stay in the background. No jumping in, no trying to help unless I specifically ask you for help. Do you understand and agree?"

"Yes Ma'am," said Emma. This was the point of her apprenticeship. Handling Spirits and being able to see them and do battle if needed. Emma was in apprentice heaven.

CHAPTER TWENTY-ONE

They arrived at the warehouse at five-fifteen. Emma drove her own car in order to leave when Celeste told her to. Holly decided to come along. Her fear of the situation was outweighed by her curiosity.

Paul went in first to do a bit of recon. He poked his head through the wall to let them know the spirit was there and in a rage.

"Emma, there's an office when we first enter. You are to go into that office, close the door and watch from there. Do not come out for any reason. Nod if you understand," said Celeste.

Emma was dumbstruck by the whole scene. All she could do was nod. There were several ghosts at the loading bay. They were standing in front of two men. On the other side of them was a monster. It was twice the size of any man and had whips for hair which it seemed to be able to control. And the red eyes! They looked like the portals to hell. Emma was happy to hide in the office. Holly joined her.

"Do you see what I see?" said Holly.

Emma nodded appearing to be in shock. This was not a scene she had envisioned, but right now there was no telling what scene had been in her mind.

Celeste could see the "monster". The other spirits had formed a wall between her and two of the male workers. Celeste gasped. One of them was Joe.

Hurrying over to the men she asked, "What is going on?"

"Something we can't see has been turning over boxes," said Joe. "It feels angry. But then, so do I. You knew about this, didn't you? You knew there was something going on and you didn't warn us."

Celeste looked at the monster. It looked human, if you ignored the size and the whips and the red eyes. The monster recognized that Celeste could see her and sent a whip to coil around Celeste's arm. It didn't work. Physical control eluded her. That's why the boxes were flying. They weren't being randomly thrown on purpose.

The monster was aiming at the workers to punish them and all that happened was that a box would shift just enough to fall over.

The longer Celeste stared the more human the beast looked. Apparently the spirits had caught on to this trick, too. They just stood there staring at her. The whips became smaller. The beast became smaller. The eyes were not as red. Soon the whips were gone, replaced with blonde hair.

"Judy Wells?" asked Celeste "What happened to you?"

"My husband found out about Hollis," said Judy, but Celeste couldn't hear her.

Paul stepped in and relayed the message.

"How did that turn you into a monster?" asked Celeste.

"I resent the word monster," said Judy.

"He found a way to anchor me here. I can't escape. I can only manifest in this stupid warehouse. I used to be able to be anywhere I wanted. I would go and visit Hollis even though he couldn't see me. It didn't matter. I could give him a hug and I honestly think he could feel it."

"What makes you think Charlie did this to you?" asked Celeste. "Did he tell you?"

"He told me there was a curse that would keep me out of trouble and said it would keep me right here where I belonged."

"Well then," said Celeste. "All we have to do is find Charlie and either convince him to let you go or find out what he did to bind you."

"You're talking to ghosts, aren't you?" asked Joe.

"It's hard to explain" said Celeste, "but this is why Mr. Scott hired me. He wanted me to see if there was anything paranormal going on here and surprise! There is. Does that make you want to quit?"

"Are you kidding? This is awesome! Can you actually see the spirit?"

"There are several here. And yes, I can see them. Some of them are standing between you and a beast that is having a hard time adjusting to being dead.

Now, if you two would like to go watch from the office over there, that would be perfect."

Celeste turned her attention back to Judy. "Judy, did you watch him? Do you have any clue what he did?"

"He put something in that office. He knows how to jump into people to use their bodies. Where did you find my ring?"

"That's not important now. Right now we need to figure out how to unstick you."

"Whose body did he use to put something in the office?"

"His," said Judy pointing to John Scott. "He is here a lot and has a lot of keys. Charlie jumped into his body one day and did something in that office."

"So, he's very powerful. He's been doing his homework since dying. I wonder what else the man knows how to do."

"Okay, Paul was attached because he attached himself. He wanted to stay close to his wife and it didn't go according to plan and he ended up here," said Celeste.

"Do you remember attaching yourself to anything?" Celeste asked Judy.

"Not on purpose," Judy replied. "I was attached to my daughter, but she's never been here."

"Maybe he tricked you into attaching to something. Maybe there was an incident and he told you to hold onto an object."

"I remember now. There is a safe in that office," said Judy.

"There is?" said John Scott trying his best to act surprised.

"We already knew about the safe, John. And you are a lousy actor," said Celeste.

"He told me there was something important in the safe and I should keep a close eye on it at all times. Do you think that would do it?"

"It sure might," said Celeste. "Can you feel an attachment to the safe?

"Maybe," said Judy.

"Try to let go of it."

"I don't know how, said Judy.

"Let's go in there and see if you can feel it more," said Celeste.

Everyone followed Celeste into the office where Emma and Joe and the other worker were hiding. No one could see Paul or Judy and it appeared that Celeste had been talking to herself this whole time.

Emma could see both Paul and Judy. And didn't know that she and Celeste were the only ones who could.

Judy went straight to the safe.

"Touch it," said Celeste. "Put your hands inside it. Feel what's there then completely withdraw from it. Let it go."

"I can't," said Judy. "I'm stuck. I can't let go. What happened? This is worse. What have I done?"

"Calm down, Judy. We're going to get you lose, but you have to calm down. The harder you fight it the stronger it gets. Calm yourself. Think about your favorite place. Go there in your mind."

"Do ghosts have a mind?" inquired Joe.

"I think so," answered Emma.

"You can see them, can't you?" he said.

"Oh, Yes." Emma said smiling.

"Well, what's going on?"

"The beast has turned back into Mrs. Wells, but now they've gotten her stuck to the safe. I just hope that woman doesn't turn back into a beast."

"Like with glue?"

"Not exactly, that's what they're trying to figure out. What is making her stick," said Emma.

"Maybe there is something in there that she loves or loved or whatever the right word is for ghosts," said Joe.

"He's right. John, can you open the safe?" Celeste asked.

"Yes, this is the key that you found in the creek a few weeks ago," said John.

"Well...?" said Celeste.

"Well, what?" said John. "I'm not going to open a company safe just because it might be involved in a haunting. Do you even hear how ridiculous that sounds? There are important..."

"Open the safe, John. There is something in there that involves Judy."

"I can't even see Judy. How do I know this isn't some elaborate...."

"Open the safe, John."

"I could get in real trouble over...."

"Open the safe, John."

John opened the safe. He withdrew several files and a small metal money box.

"See," he said. "There's nothing in here that isn't company related."

Judy's hand seemed to be following the stack of papers. Then it snapped back to the safe itself. Apparently it had nothing to do with the contents. It was the safe itself. John started to put the papers and the cash box back in the safe.

"Wait," yelled Celeste. There is still something in the safe."

Sliding her hand on the floor of the safe there was something not readily visible, but it could be felt. It seemed to be taped down. Finding the end of it she pulled at the tape. The tape let go and Celeste almost fell backwards when it did.

"Hello," said Celeste. "What have we here? It looks like another certificate inside a brown envelope."

Celeste withdrew the paper. "This is a birth certificate."

Judy began to cry. "I remember. Charlie said I would always be attached to Judy Jrs.' birth and as long as no harm came to this then no harm would come to Judy Jr. I have been guarding it."

"Guarding it from what?" asked Celeste

"Anything or anyone that comes near it," answered Judy.

"I sure wish I could hear both sides of this conversation," said John. Everyone agreed except Emma who was keeping up quite handily.

"We took care of me by burning the certificate. Can't we just do that here?" asked Paul.

"I don't know," said Celeste. "Would you be willing to try that, Mrs. Wells?"

"Burn my daughter's birth certificate? No, she's going to need that. It's an important document."

"We'll order a copy. It happens all the time. People lose their birth certificates for various reasons," said Celeste.

"Why don't we just give it to Judy?" said Emma. "It seems like having her mother attached to her would please her no end."

"Wait," said Celeste. "When I first saw you, you were with Judy and that's only been about a week ago. How long have you been stuck here at Harper's?"

"And, John, when did you say this all started escalating?"

"There is something here that doesn't add up."

"A few weeks ago," replied John. "I might have exaggerated a smidge. I wanted you to take it seriously."

"You didn't even take it seriously at first, John. Why would you care if I did? And Judy, How long do you think you've been here?"

"It feels like months, but in reality? I don't know. Time is very confusing when you're dead. It's like it doesn't even exist. I can't really tell night from day, you know. I don't have to sleep so it's not like I keep count."

"I wonder if you were here, but not stuck here," said Celeste. "Maybe you were free to travel and then something happened to get you stuck here."

"Charlie showed up," said Judy. It was after I met you with Judy Jr," said Judy. "He showed up and scared Judy and then brought me here. He told me Judy's birth certificate was in this safe and I needed to guard it. He tricked me into staying here and attaching to it!"

Suddenly Judy was able to feel her hand. She quickly disappeared and then came back. "I can go anywhere I like. It was an illusion created by Charlie. But, why would he do that?"

"I doubt we'll ever know that," said Celeste. But the fact that you're free now is hopeful for Paul. He worries about being stuck in the fog."

"Oh, the fog is a horrible place," said Judy with no further explanation.

"You've been there?" asked Paul.

"Last week when I left here, I ran into a fog. It was terrible. I couldn't find my way. As soon as I thought about the safe, I was back here."

"Good information," said Paul.

Celeste turned to the living and said, "I think it is clear that while Judy ramped up the activity this last week, it was not her causing it months or even weeks ago. Perhaps it was Paul."

"You got all this from the conversation you just had with spirits we can't see and that none of us could hear?" said John.

"We have partially solved the mystery of why Judy was here, but not the mystery of what was causing all your people to leave. There will be less activity now, but there may still be some activity," said Celeste.

"John, sit down for a minute, will you please," said Celeste.

John sat in the big chair.

"You may have been taken over by a spirit."

"What? The hell you say. Now? Is it in me now? Get it out! Get it out!" John was predictably upset by the news.

"I believe that Charlie Wells used you to place that birth certificate in the safe and may have prompted you to go looking for that key and possibly more," said Celeste.

"More? I don't remember that birth certificate. I certainly don't remember putting it in the safe. Are you saying I was possessed? This is terrible. Do I need to call in a priest?" said John. John was not taking this at all well.

"I don't think so, John. I think that once Charlie and Judy work out their issues. He will leave you alone. You were just a way to move physical pieces that he was not capable of moving. But that is only a guess," said Celeste.

Paul was glad to have someone older to hang out with. Holly was fun, but she was a child, after all.

Paul and Judy disappeared.

"I think that is all we can do for tonight," said Celeste. "Emma, would you mind giving me a ride home?"

"I'd be happy to," said Emma.

"So, it's completely safe to go back out there to work?" asked Joe.

"I think so," said Celeste. "There are a few spirits here, but they were afraid of Judy as much as you were and three of them jumped in between you to protect you from her."

"Okay. I trust you,' said Joe.

Celeste turned to John. "I have an appointment with Judy in the morning. I'll let her know her birth certificate is in your company safe. May I give her your number?"

"Of course," said John. "I'll be happy to release it to her."

"I'm ready to be home for the night," said Celeste. "Are you ready Emma?"

"Yes. Ready when you are."

Once in the car, Emma had a lot of questions about the night. Like why did Paul have to repeat everything that Judy said? And why were those spirits standing between the beast and Joe and his buddy?

"Emma, could you hear Judy?" asked Celeste.

"Yes, but I had trouble hearing Paul sometimes," said Emma.

"Could you see both of them?" asked Celeste.

"Oh, yes," said Judy.

"You have a powerful gift, dear. We will begin your training with the Tarot cards tomorrow," said Celeste.

"Hot Damn!" said Emma with a little too much enthusiasm. "Uh Oh, I apologize. I didn't mean to…"

Celeste was laughing. "Do you think that shocked me? I have been known to use far worse. I'm happy to see you are excited to hone your gifts."

Celeste really was happy to be home. Chaos greeted her at the door and led her straight to the kitchen. Apparently they both needed some food. Celeste didn't see anything that would be ready fast enough. It was good that Emma had brought her that shake earlier.

Putting her feet up and ordering a pizza, she was officially done for the night. Tomorrow Judy was coming at ten a.m. But for tonight there was no thinking about all of that. Nothing was adding up anyway.

It was exciting to think that her new apprentice had so much talent already with no formal training. Teaching her was going to be a delightful experience, no doubt about it. The only problem would be when Emma discovered that she was more talented than Celeste, and Celeste knew that to be true already.

It's sometimes difficult to take coaching from someone who has less talent than you.

The pizza arrived and Celeste sat back and actually watched some TV. One of the few shows that she watched was on. It was called The Mentalist. He did not believe in psychics, but he was one. It was always entertaining to see him explain how he knew what he knew. Of course, he couldn't see spirits the way Celeste and Emma could, but he could sure solve crimes using the same clues that were available to everyone. He just knew how to use them to his advantage.

Celeste fell asleep on the sofa with a pizza box on her chest and a cat on her legs and the TV going.

But her dreams were as unusual as they had ever been. Waking in the night she shifted to the bed. Her dreams continued and almost made sense of a few things.

There was a fog that had her trapped. Then there was a safe, but it felt like a cave, a cave with a creek running through it and a ring sitting on a rock glowing as bright as a light.

CHAPTER TWENTY-TWO

When Celeste woke again, the sun was up and her body, mind, and soul felt surprisingly rested after what seemed like a restless dream filled night that ordinarily would have left her exhausted. Instead the night had been refreshing.

There was also more clarity about the mysteries that had recently presented themselves. They were not solved, but the extraneous information was falling away.

Celeste was still in the dark on how the ring came to be with her crystals in the creek bed. It puzzled her and tugged at her. It must hold some importance. The dots just weren't connecting yet.

And how, if at all, John figured in with Judy and the ring and her mother's still mysterious death.

"Ah, well. It will all come to light in the end. I know we are close and probably have all the clues already. We just need to sort out which clue goes with which mystery, eh?"

Chaos purred and weaved her way through Celeste's legs creating an invisible infinity sign.

Celeste had breakfast and was ready for Judy Jr's appointment at ten a.m. Judy was always early, so Celeste was actually prepared by ten 'til ten. Judy did not disappoint arriving at five before ten a.m.

"I felt my mother this morning," announced Judy walking in. "It felt like I was getting a warm hug."

"That's wonderful!" said Celeste. "Isn't it?"

"What if it means she came back to protect me from something?"

"Or maybe it was just a visit and to give you a hug," said Celeste. "But either way, I have some news to share with you about her."

"News? Did you see her?" asked Judy.

"Yes, I did. Your mother has been trapped at the Harper's warehouse this last week."

"I don't understand. How do you trap a ghost and who would do that?"

Celeste gave Judy the abbreviated version of what had happened the night before.

"My father did that to her? My father?"

"We suspect that he may have been angry about the affair with Mr. Hollis, but we haven't been able to contact him yet, so, we don't know for sure," said Celeste.

"But my father was such a gentle man. He wouldn't hurt a spider. I mean that literally. He would catch them and let them go outside."

"It's a puzzle right now, but we will get to the truth," said Celeste.

"Daddy? Please come and visit with us. Madam Celeste has some questions to ask you. Won't you show yourself again and help us find out what has really happened? I need to know," said Judy.

Celeste pulled out her pendulum. Steadying it over a small circular alphabet she asked, "Mr. Wells, are you here?"

The pendulum moved side to side which meant "no".

"If you're not here, how did you move the pendulum to "no"?" asked Celeste.

Mr. Wells appeared slowly. Even Judy could see him.

"I am sorry," he mouthed to Judy then disappeared.

"Daddy? Don't leave yet. We have questions," begged Judy.

"He must have his reasons to stay hidden," said Celeste. "Maybe he is hiding from your mother. She was pretty distraught about being bound to your birth certificate."

"My birth certificate?" asked Judy. "You didn't mention my birth certificate."

"Oh, it must have slipped my mind," said Celeste. "Somehow your birth certificate ended up in a safe in the warehouse at Harper's. We suspect that your father put it there because that was what your mother was actually attached to.

The attachment was so strong it trapped her inside a safe yesterday."

"Where is my birth certificate now?" asked Judy.

"It's still in the safe. John said if you would drop by with your driver's license for proof of ID, he would give it to you."

"Is that what daddy was apologizing for? Messing with mom?" asked Judy.

"I don't know, Judy. It could be. Or it could be something more. I just don't know for certain, yet."

Celeste was forming a couple of theories, but wasn't ready to share at this point. There were too many factors that didn't line up. It still wasn't clear how or why the birth certificate ended up at Harper's. Why did Mr. Wells want his wife to be trapped at Harper's? Why not at his office or his home or even Holly Farms where her lover would have to be haunted by her. Was that what he was so unhappy about?

Celeste needed to speak with Mr. Hollis Sr. again. He knew more than he had been able to convey with Judy present.

"Let's do a Tarot card reading," said Celeste. "Maybe we will get some answers there."

"Whatever you think will help," said Judy.

Celeste gave Judy a Tarot reading. It was quite informative, but didn't really help with the problem of why her father would go to such great lengths to hurt her mother or what had happened to her mother the night of her death.

They finished the session at eleven-thirty which gave celeste time to walk to the creek and check for more clues, since there was a creek running through a cave in her dream. Maybe there was a miniature cave at the creek. It couldn't hurt to look around for a few minutes.

Watching Judy drive away Celeste locked up the house and took off on her walk.

Mr. West was not around today, but her excitement for this Saturday was palpable. The creek was so low there was no water flowing or even trickling. There were a few puddles, nothing more.

Her stash spot was completely dry. Searching around the place where she had found the ring. There was nothing there. Walking over to the far side where the boat had been revealed nothing. There were no clues to be found this day. Then came a faint apparition of a man walking up the creek. He was so faint he could hardly be seen. He stopped every few yards to gather something that

Celeste could not see.

Then her eye fell to a bouquet in his left hand. He was gathering flowers. He walked right through her as if he didn't see her. This was a rarity for Celeste; to not be seen by a spirit. Perhaps he was residual. He walked further up the creek until, out of nowhere, there came a rush tide of water.

It was so realistic that Celeste ran for higher ground. But it took the apparition by surprise and he went under. Most likely he had died here in the creek. It was unsettling to see a man gathering flowers one minute and drowning the next. Celeste's thoughts went to the woman he was gathering the flowers for. This would, no doubt, have been a devastating loss. Celeste felt the sorrow swell in her. It was time to leave.

Having brought carrots for the horses, this was a good day to stop and visit with them briefly. They wolfed the treats down and looked for more.

There was a train today. Celeste watched all the murals go by slowly enough to take in the talent of the miscreant artists. It was too bad they could not be recognized for their skill and talent. Some of the art surely belonged in galleries.

She wondered if Dean would show up at one as planned. He had agreed to it, but would he back out at the last minute? Knowing that if he showed up, it would be to try to discredit her in front of his "Gramms". He was hell bent on getting his "Gramms" to stay away from Celeste. It would take more than coming to a reading to accomplish that mission. Dori was a most loyal client.

Dean and Dori pulled up at precisely one minute before one. Dean held the door for his "Gramms" and Celeste was impressed with his overall treatment of her friend, Dori.

"Dean, would you like for your Gramms to go first while you observe? You know, so you can see how it works?"

"I'll go first," said Dean. "I think I have a pretty good idea how it works."

"Very well, come with me please," said Celeste leading him to the reading room and indicating where he was to sit. Then sat down opposite him.

"I have many tools that I use including Tarot cards, Angel Cards, Runes, a talking board and a few others. Do you know which one you'd like to use today?"

"Whatever you think, it's all bunk," said Dean.

"I see," said Celeste. "Then why did you agree to try it?"

"Gramms needs to be convinced that I have given it a fair shot," said Dean.

"That's it. You use whatever mumbo jumbo you like best. I'm not going to be sucked in by it."

"Very well," said Celeste. Picking up her pendulum and mini talking board. "Is there anyone here that would like to speak with Dean today?"

The pendulum moved top to bottom indicating yes.

"Are you related to Dean?"

Yes

"Are you his father?"

No

"Sister?"

No.

"Brother?"

Yes.

"Do you have a message for him?"

Yes.

"Please spell it out with these letters."

"LET HER DO WHAT SHE WANTS TO DO"

"Let her do what she wants to do," translated Celeste.

"I didn't know you had a brother who had passed."

"I don't," said Dean. "That more than proves that this is all bunk. I'm going to go get Gramms and we are leaving."

He walked out into the parlor where Dori was waiting.

"That was fast," said Dori.

"It didn't take long to spot the fakery," replied Dean.

"But it's' not fake. There are things no one else knows. This helps me every week. I don't know how I'd get by without her counsel and friendship. What makes you think it's fake?"

"She told me I had a dead brother," said Dean.

"Oh dear, you do have a dead brother. You were only a baby when Peter died. We never found the right time to tell you and really, there was no need for you to know."

"How old was I when he died?" asked Dean.

"You were only one, just a baby yourself. He was almost three. You would point to his pictures and think it was you. No one ever corrected you."

"I had a brother?"

"Yes, dear."

"How did he die?" asked Dean.

"It was pneumonia," said Dori. "He was in the hospital for a week and then he died."

"This crazy woman says he's here today," said Dean.

"If she says he's here, then he is here, son. GO back in there and talk with him."

"I can't. I don't believe it."

"Let's just try," said Celeste. "It takes a great deal of energy to communicate from the other side. Let's give him a chance to say what he came to say."

"What do you have to lose?" asked his Gramms.

"I don't believe in psychics and I don't believe in ghosts," he said.

"Humor Gramms," said Dori.

Dean gave in and went back into the reading room with Celeste.

"What should we call you?" asked Celeste.

MARTY

"Do you have anything else to say to Dean?"

YOU MADE YOUR MOM AND DAD HAPPY JUST BY BEING BORN

"You made your Mom and Dad happy just by being born. Well, that's sweet," said Celeste.

"Dean, do you want to say anything to Marty?"

"I'm not even convinced he's there," said Dean. "Why would I have anything to say to someone who has been gone my whole life? You should have picked my father for this."

"I don't pick who comes here. They choose to come or not," protested Celeste. "You choose to talk to him or not. Everyone is free to choose."

"Okay, I'll humor you. Marty, have you seen Dad on the other side?"

"Interesting question," said Celeste.

YES

"Can you ask him if there was a life insurance policy?" said Dean.

NO

"No, there wasn't or No, you can't ask."

CANT

"But you said you've seen him," said Dean.

NOT IN A LONG TIME

"Not in a long time," translated Celeste.

"I'm not an idiot. I know what it says," said Dean.

BE NICE

"Bernice? I don't know a Bernice," roared Dean.

"I think it says, "Be nice"," injected Celeste.

"That sounds more like you than a big brother of mine."

DAD ISNT HERE NOW Celeste went back to "translating".

"Well, where is he? Can't you just go get him?" Dean was still roaring. He was not convinced and he was getting testy.

NO

"So, why are you here?"

GUARDIAN

"My guardian?"

NO GRAMM

"So, If Gramms weren't sitting in the next room, you wouldn't be here talking to me?"

RIGHT

"Do you talk to her?"

NOT MUCH JUST GUARD

"Yet you let her waste her money on a psychic?"

NOT WASTE

"The psychic is putting words in your mouth," said Dean.

TRY TAROT

"That's an excellent idea!" said Celeste. "Let's do a Tarot card reading. It's one of your Gramms's favorites."

"Okay. What do I do?"

"I shuffle and you cut into three piles."

Dean cut the cards and set them in front of Celeste. Celeste spread the cards out in three fans.

"Now choose one card from each pile starting with the one on your right. Just line them face up in front of the fan."

"This card represents your past. The middle card is your present and the card on your left is the future. We will start with the past."

Celeste read his cards and he was impressed with the whole thing. Maybe this wasn't such a terrible thing for his Gramms to do. And Celeste seemed to genuinely like his gramms. He would watch her reading and make up his mind then.

"I think it is Gramms's turn now," he said in a much calmer tone.

"Let me go get her," said Celeste.

He took the time to look around the room. There was no artificial smoke, but there were plenty of candles. There were a lot of Angels, too. But, there was a Buddha and several statues that he didn't recognize. It seemed to have something for everyone.

He stayed around for his gramm's reading and found it to be pretty harmless. And it made his gramms happy. How could he object to something harmless that made her happy even if it involved talking to fake dead people.

"I'm satisfied you are not going to harm my gramms or bilk her out of my inheritance," joked Dean. "I won't object to you seeing Celeste."

"Not that you could have stopped me," said Dori sternly. "I'm glad you approve, but you need to understand that I don't need your approval to live my life."

"I understand, Gramms. But you need to understand that I will always be compelled to protect you."

"Now maybe on the ride home, you can tell me about my big brother," said Dean leading her out of the house.

Celeste walked them out and waved them off. It was an hour before her next appointment (a phone session) and half an hour before her apprentice arrived.

"I have a bag of chocolates in the fridge that needs my attention."

"That's one thing I miss," said Paul. "Chocolate. We can't taste, you know."

"Why do you have to do that?" said Celeste.

"Do what?"

"Scare the wits out of me."

"I didn't mean to, I've been here for a while. I thought you would have recognized my energy."

"I guess I had my mind on other things," said Celeste.

"Yeah, chocolate," said Paul teasing her.

"Well, yes, that, but I'm still trying to find the connection between the haunting at John's and the haunting at Judy's and the ring. Maybe this ring isn't even the ring they were talking about when they said the ring is the key."

"I'm thinking you have everything you need. You just need to piece it together," said Paul. "What do they all have in common?"

"I'd say Judy Sr. except that she was not at the creek where the key was found and John Scott showed up," said Celeste.

"What about the ring?" said Paul.

"What about it? It has no connection with the haunting at Harper's or the wreck."

"Maybe it does and you just haven't found it yet," whispered Paul as he disappeared.

"You know, don't you?" yelling at him after he disappeared. "You know all the answers, don't you? You make me furious sometimes," shaking her fist at the air.

"Who are you yelling at?" asked Emma having let herself in. "I rang the bell, but you must not have heard it."

"Paul was here. I think he knows what happened the night Judy died."

"Maybe he's not allowed to tell you," said Emma.

"Probably not, but at least he doesn't have to tease me about it. He's such a little stinker. And now that I think of it, Holly wasn't with him today. I wonder if the little thing has learned to let go."

"I'm going to get started on the phone messages. I noticed yesterday that they are slowing down. Is that a good thing or a bad thing?"

"It's a good thing as far as I'm concerned," said Celeste. "I don't like being this busy. But it's giving you some work to do, so that's good. In fact, I want to pay you for your time. We'll start with a dollar over minimum wage and see where it goes from there."

"I'm an apprentice. I can't take money for that. This is like taking a class at college, only way better," said Emma.

"I have a secret for you. Can you keep a secret?"

"Oh, yes," said Emma nodding her head so hard Celeste worried it would give her a headache (Which it did.)

"I have a master's degree."

"They have a program to be a psychic?" asked Emma.

"No, my degree is in social work and psychotherapy."

"I haven't been able to decide on a major. Do you think the social work degree has been helpful in what you do?" said Emma.

"It's very useful. Sometimes people need a reading and sometimes they just need someone to talk to. I can be whichever they need me to be. That's probably why I have so many regulars who come on a weekly schedule. They get their cards read and then they get some talk therapy to help them deal with what their cards said."

"That makes so much sense. I was about ready to just quit college, but you have given me a lot to think about here."

"Good."

"Don't forget you have a four o'clock phone session. Would you mind if I listen in? It would be as an apprentice of course."

"I think that would be a good idea. I will ask Pam if it's okay with her. If so then you will use the base phone."

"Thank you, Celeste."

"Be sure to be so quiet that I forget that you are there."

"I will put it on mute," said Emma.

The phone rang. Celeste answered. Pam agreed to have Emma listen in. It was the first of many sessions for which Emma would be a spectator. Silent and attentive, and learning so much from Celeste it was tempting more than once to quit pursuing a degree and to just start full time as an assistant to Celeste. Celeste would always talk her out of it.

But this was the first session and she would always remember it.

CHAPTER TWENTY-THREE

Pam's phone session was excellent. Celeste read her cards and was spot on with every card. Pam hung up the phone happy and Emma hung up ecstatic.

"That was awesome!" said Emma joining Celeste in the reading room. "Did you have help from a spirit?"

"No, that was just me," replied Celeste.

"I hope I have your confidence one day," said Emma.

"You will. You just have to give yourself time to learn. Have you been studying the meanings of the Tarot?"

"There are so many to memorize. It's difficult. But I'm working on it."

"One day you will just get it. It will all click and you will wonder why it was so challenging."

"I hope you're right. Well, I better get to work on the phone messages. Are you finished for the day?"

"I don't have any more appointments, but I have a feeling John Scott will be calling me soon."

Sure enough it was less than five minutes before John called.

"Things were much calmer today. Maybe the problem has been solved. What do your senses tell you, Celeste?"

"I think they will continue to calm down, but there is still something to be resolved. Do you want me to come in tomorrow?"

"Of course," he said eagerly. "Do you want me to swing by and pick you up?"

"That would be great," said Celeste. "I'll see you then."

The minute her hand left the receiver she called out for Paul. He didn't show up. Where was he when there were so many questions to ask?

Emma popped in to say, "Good night. I'll see you tomorrow at three-thirty. Is there anything I can pick up for you on the way in?"

"No, I should be fine. I don't often work on Fridays, you know. Maybe we should just hold off until Monday."

"Please let me come in," said Emma. "I can clean the reading room and catch up on all the phone messages and I just scheduled you a new client for tomorrow at three o'clock. I didn't think you'd want to turn it down. This is a Dean at my college."

"Then it's settled. I'll see you at three-thirty tomorrow," said Celeste. "And use one of my notebooks to keep your hours in."

Celeste made some dinner and grabbed a book from her side table. It was her intention to stay in and rest with a good book tonight. Still reading about the werewolves and in the mood for that tonight, she needed to let her own mysteries simmer in the background for a time. Maybe they would sort themselves out.

The phone rang in the middle of a horrific scene, having forgotten to mute it when leaving the "work area". It caused her to jump up and throw the book across the room, it startled her so. She picked up the wireless, but said nothing

"Hello? Hello?"

Celeste recognized the voice. It was a man. "Hello," she said breathing heavily from the recent fright.

"This is Joe from Harper's. You asked me to update you on the activity over here? I'm the one you intervie…"

"I know who you are Joe and after this phone call I am not likely to ever forget you," her breathing was returning to normal.

"What happened?"

"I'm reading a horror novel and your phone call came at a most inauspicious time."

"I'm sorry. Do you want me to call back later?"

"No, the damage is done and I will be fine. I've been turning the phone off and forgot to do it this evening."

"You should have a cell phone," said Joe nonchalantly.

"I'm usually home, so I rarely need a phone."

"Then you need to go out more and you need a cell phone," he said laughing.

"What does any of this have to do with what is going on at the warehouse?" said Celeste.

"Not a thing. Will you let me take you to a movie some time?"

"What? I mean…. Why would you want to do that?" stammered Celeste.

"Because you are a beautiful woman that I would like to get to know better?" responded Joe.

Celeste thought he was pulling her leg and called his bluff. "When would you want to go?"

"I have Sunday off. We could go Sunday evening for dinner and a movie."

"Okay. It's a date. What time?"

"How does seven o'clock sound to you?" he asked.

"Perfect," said Celeste. "Now tell me about the situation there at the warehouse. Have there been any more fights?"

"Not even one," said Joe. "It still feels like there are ghosts here, but nothing malevolent."

"So, you called to tell me there was no news?" laughed Celeste.

"And to ask you out," said Joe. "Well, okay. Mostly it was to ask you out."

"Mission accomplished," said Celeste.

"Why are you reading a scary book at night when you're home alone?" asked Joe trying to prolong the conversation.

"I'm not alone. I have my cat here with me and the occasional ghost."

"If I weren't working, I'd come over and be there for you while you read," said Joe blatantly flirting.

"I don't know you well enough for that yet."

"You're a psychic. I would think you would know everything there is to know about me."

"I can't read minds. I'm a psychic, but I'm not telepathic. Telepaths can read minds and project thought to others."

"So what can psychics do?" he wasn't flirting now. He was seriously interested.

"We're all a little different. I can see ghosts. I can also see the future and the past of certain things I touch."

"That is so cool! If you touched me, would you be able to see my future?" He was back to flirting.

"I didn't pick up anything when we shook hands."

"I think I'm glad of that. It means I don't have to worry about you poking around in my past." He smiled as he said it.

"You should probably get back to work," said Celeste.

"There you go being psychic. Can I call you tomorrow afternoon before work?"

"I may be busy being a psychic. My new assistant has scheduled me tomorrow afternoon by mistake."

"Maybe Saturday," he said.

"I'll be horseback riding."

"I give up. I'll see you Sunday."

"I'm looking forward to it, Joe."

Hanging up with Joe and retrieving her book there was a horror scene that begged for closure in order to stave off the nightmares. This was a lesson learned many years ago.

The remainder of the night was uneventful for which she was eternally grateful. The rest was needed though her wolf book was not yet finished.

John was right on time Friday morning.

"What will I be doing today, John?"

"I thought maybe you could go through the files of the ones who have quit. Maybe you can pick something up with your psychic senses the way you did with the desk and the safe."

"That sounds like a good plan. Will I be working in the conference room again?"

"Yes if it's available. Were you comfortable there?"

"Yes. It was fine, just curious."

John had not been joking about the number of people who had quit or asked for transfers. There was a pile of files to go through. The fresh notebook would be filled fairly quickly with visions if these people had seen or heard even part of what was going on in that warehouse.

The files were sorted by job area. There were more loading bay workers than anything else. Next were the warehouse workers and last were the bookkeepers.

They dated back to about three months ago. That could have been when Judy Sr. arrived. Though her death was months before that. But that could be attributed to the lack of sense of time in the spirit plane.

The first file was pretty bland. There were no visions until the last page. Picking it up there was a vision of the loading bay. There was a large crate rolling towards the man. He had no place to go to get out of its path. He was boxed in. He managed to climb up the containers left in the truck to avoid being smashed by the loose crate.

"That would do it for me if I were him," said Celeste to no one.

That file went into a newly created larger file marked "activity noted". The incident had not been reported on his exit file and his reason given for leaving was "found a better job".

The next file had a "feeling" to it before even opening it. This was a woman who worked in the loading area of the warehouse. Every page Celeste touched seemed to be screaming "Get out!" This woman had had several different encounters with the spirits here before quitting.

It had permeated the whole file. Celeste went to the exit interview and held the paper in both hands. The vision started instantly. It had started with boxes being misplaced in the bins. Then whole bins would be in the wrong place. Then a bin tipped over from the highest shelf. Its contents pelted her and then the bin itself landed on her. The vision was in fast forward. These incidents had taken place over the course of a few months.

That file went into the activity folder, as well. The next file was less active. In fact, even the exit interview did not spark a vision. Her reason for leaving was that she was finished with school and would be pursuing her career in English as a teacher.

Celeste created a new file, "no activity".

The morning passed quickly. Celeste estimated that one half to two thirds of the files ended up in the "activity" file. It was tiring. Visions required energy and hers was running low. Leaving the files on the desk she went in search of John.

"Mr. Scott is in the warehouse. Would you like me to page him?" said his secretary.

"I'll go find him if that's okay," said Celeste.

"It's a big warehouse, but it's up to you."

Celeste walked to the warehouse. It was much louder today than it had been before. John was in the office. There were three trucks unloading and lots of people working. The trucks were running and that ramped the sound up considerably. The whole scene helped clarify why the bookkeepers needed an office and not just a cubicle here.

John saw Celeste and jumped up to let her in. "You didn't need to come down here. My secretary should have paged me," he said apologetically.

"I asked her not to. I needed the walk. My mind needed a break from those files. You were right. Most of those people had had repeated incidents and they were escalating."

"How does it feel down here to you now?" John asked.

"Very loud," said Celeste.

John laughed. "I know that, but how does the ghost activity feel?"

"They are still here, but they are not as agitated. I think that Judy was probably stirring things up for a few months before getting a true feel for where and what she was."

"So maybe the mass exodus is over?" asked John.

"Maybe, but we need to keep an eye on it. Judy may yet have a role to play in finding her killer."

"Her killer?" asked John with surprise in his voice. "That was an accident. Judy fell asleep at the wheel or something."

"That is not what the spirits are telling me."

"Maybe the spirits are wrong this time," said John.

"They're timelines get mixed up, John. But they are usually right about the details," said Celeste.

"Boo!" shouted Paul in her ear.

"Did you just hear that?" said John.

"Hear what?" said Celeste with a fake grin that hid the anger harbored towards Paul at this moment.

"I distinctly heard someone yell, "Boo!" said John. "It was not my imagination, either."

"No, it wasn't your imagination, John. It was my friend, Paul. Who, thinking of it, I met right here in this office. He is the one with the death certificate issue."

"But I heard him, too" stammered John. "I don't want to be able to hear any of them."

"Hopefully, it won't happen often and you will get used to it."

"Paul, I warned you about that."

"I heard you talking about Judy. Have you seen her?" asked Paul.

"No. I assumed she was out exploring with you. Are you saying you haven't seen her?"

"Not since we were all together."

"What about Holly? Have you seen her?"

"Nope."

"It seems there was mention of wanting to find some people closer to her age. Having friends her own age is important to a young girl," said Celeste sympathetically. Or maybe Holly and Judy took off together. Judy was ready for some serious traveling. It would be nice to see her, though. I'd love to ask her a few more questions."

"Holly or Judy?" asked Paul.

"I was thinking about Judy, but I'd love to talk to Holly some more too. There's more information there."

John was sitting in the big office chair white as a sheet and shivering to boot. "How can I be hearing this? How did this happen? Make it stop! I don't want to hear ghosts!"

"John, calm down. We will work on it together and I will teach you how to block it."

"You can do that?" asked John, calming down a little.

"We can certainly try."

"Paul, will you please try to find one or both of them and bring them home?" asked Celeste changing her focus to Paul.

"I can certainly try," he said mocking her.

"Just go do it, please," said Celeste sternly.

"I'm ready to call it a day," she said to John. "Will you give me a lift home?"

"Oh, it is almost one, isn't it? Good call. Let's head out to the front exit. There's more air conditioning that way."

"That suits me just fine. I have a new client this afternoon and I'd like to eat and get a little rest before then."

CHAPTER TWENTY-FOUR

John drove through a fast food place to pick up lunch for Celeste. It was the least he could do for all the information found today.

"When can we start working on my hearing ghosts problem?" asked John. "I'd like to start as soon as possible."

"We'll have to ask Emma to check the schedule," said Celeste. "I'm so booked up after that incident at the restaurant. I can't keep up with my own schedule."

"Sounds like it's a good thing that Emma came along," said John sincerely.

"It is and her talent as a psychic is remarkable, too. I think she has more talent than I do. It's going to be amazing watching her hone her skills. I've never had an apprentice who was truly psychic before we even started. I'm afraid there'll be a bigger fish for her soon enough," Celeste smiled saying it but the fear was real.

"So you are working with her to teach her how to control her gift?"

"In a sense…yes. You can never fully control these kinds of gifts. At best you learn to adapt to them and that's what you'll be learning, too."

"You said Emma has a lot of talent and studies under you every day. I don't have time to come apprentice for two hours a day. How long do you think it will take me?

"You are not trying to learn as much as Emma is. You only want to be comfortable with one very small aspect of psychic abilities. We should be able to work one afternoon on a Saturday or Sunday and have it all sorted out for you.

Does that sound like something you can do?"

"Absolutely," he said, "How about this Saturday?"

"NO. I have a date this Saturday to go horseback riding."

"Sunday?"

"It would have to be early. I have a dinner date for Sunday."

"Celeste I didn't know you were such a socialite."

"I'm not. I'm usually sitting home alone, but this week I seem to have become quite popular."

John pulled up at Celeste's house and dropped her off. As always Celeste was happy to be home all the more so with food cooked by someone else. The meal was too big so Chaos was a happy beneficiary.

There was over an hour before her only appointment of the day. After finishing a perfect burger with fries it was time to rest her eyes in the bed for a half an hour. There was no need to worry about falling asleep when she only wanted to rest her eyes a bit.

Chaos woke her at about a quarter 'til three o'clock.

"Oh my, I must have needed some sleep after all."

Quickly making herself presentable, splashing cold water on her face to get properly woken up. Having fallen asleep in her dress it didn't appear to be too wrinkled.

Moving to the front of the house she checked the appointment book to see who this new client was. Her first name was Tia. Emma had failed to write in the last name.

There was a knock at the door and Celeste answered it instantly. The woman was in her forties like Celeste, with blonde hair, blue eyes and wearing a small fedora.

"You must be Tia. Please come in."

Tia walked in without saying a word. They went to the reading table where Celeste had just finished getting the table prepared.

"Let's start with your full name and address. I like to get the paperwork out of the way first," said Celeste.

"Tia is a nickname I go by," said the small woman. 'My real name is Cynthia Bell."

Celeste brought out a new notebook and marked it Tia Bell then wrote down the rest of her information and made payment arrangements.

They did a long Tarot reading which took most of the hour. Tia was impressed.

"Do you have any openings during the week besides Fridays?" Celeste was delighted with the question.

"I don't usually do Friday readings at all," said Celeste. "Let me look at the book and see what is available. How soon did you want to come back? A week, two weeks, a month?"

"A week, but not on a Friday, so maybe a Thursday or a Monday?"

"I seem to have two openings next Thursday at nine o'clock or three o'clock," offered Celeste.

"Oh, nine o'clock is too early for me. I'll take the three o'clock."

"Perfect. I'm writing you in as we speak."

Celeste walked Tia to the door and wished her a good week.

"Emma? Are you here?"

"Yes. I let myself in and have been taking phone calls and messages." said Emma.

"You are doing a great job," said Celeste. "But there are a few points we need to go over together."

"What did I do?" asked Emma sheepishly.

"You scheduled a reading on a Friday and you didn't even get her full name for me."

"I'm sorry. There was no place else to put her. she was desperate to get in before this weekend."

"We are getting so booked I'm not going to be able to keep up with it. We may need for you to learn to do readings with tools less complicated than the Tarot."

"Me? You want me to do real readings?" said Emma in disbelief.

"Not yet and not until you can read for me, but starting today, I think you need to either read my runes or read my palm, which would you prefer?"

"I don't know enough about them to choose. Which one do you like to have done?"

"Good! That was the exact right answer for a client. Today we will do a palm reading. But by Monday I expect you to have your own set of runes. You can find them at Barnes and Noble with a book about interpreting them."

They sat at the reading table and Celeste walked Emma through a typical palm reading.

"That can't change much from week to week, can it?" Emma asked.

"It's highly unlikely. That's why you need a set of Runes," she showed Emma her own sets of Runes. "You can even make a set yourself if you go to a craft store and find either stones or pieces of wood that are basically the same size and shape. But if you're going into town, the stones that come with the book are worth the investment."

"I will go to Denton this weekend. They have Barnes & Noble and two craft stores."

"Perfect. Now I think you promised to give this room a good cleaning today," said Celeste with a wink.

"I'll get right on it," said Emma.

Emma left at five-thirty and Celeste was left to choose between finishing her wolf book and going out to a movie. A movie meant driving. All a book required was getting comfortable. So, the book won. Celeste spent the evening at home curled up with a book and a very purry cat.

She was reaching to silence the phone when Joe called.

"What are you doing this evening?" he asked.

"I'm determined to finish my horror novel tonight."

"Will you promise to call me if you get scared?" said Joe.

"I don't think I'll get that scared," said Celeste. I would have been fine last night if you hadn't called and startled me."

"So it's my fault?" he asked laughing.

"Who else?"

"I can hardly wait for Sunday evening," he said. "You have my cell number if you need to call me, right?"

"Are you on your cell phone now?"

"Yes."

"Then I have your number."

They hung up and Celeste went back to her book.

Within minutes Paul showed up.

"I can't find Judy," he said.

"Okay," said Celeste. "What do you want me to do?"

"I can't find her. Don't you understand? What if Charlie has attached her to something? What if she needs our help? Don't just sit there. You have to help me find her."

"How do you think I'm going to do that?" asked Celeste.

"You're the psychic. How do you summon someone when you do a séance?"

"I don't do séances," said Celeste. "I am no good at summoning anyone. It is not my gift."

"Well, what about your new assistant? Maybe it's one of her gifts. Maybe that girl could summon her."

"I'm sorry, Paul. I'm not going to drag Emma into this at this time of night."

"It's only seven-thirty," said Paul.

"Oh, I see how it is. Now you can get the concept of time correctly. Where was this sense of time when we were trying to determine how long the beast had been around Harper's? You take the cake. I'm tired and I'm not getting involved with your search tonight."

"Just try calling for her. Do that for me and I'll leave you alone for the rest of the night."

"Make it the rest of the weekend," said Celeste.

"You drive a hard bargain, woman," said Paul.

"Judy, if you can hear me please come to my house or send a message if you can't come. We are worried about you. We are worried that you might have gotten stuck again."

"I'm not stuck. I just wanted a little time to myself," said Judy Sr.

"I can truly relate to that," said Celeste. "I just want to finish reading this book."

"You thought you couldn't summon a spirit," said Paul. "Look what you did just by calling her name."

"This is different, Paul. This is a spirit that I know."

"Still… You did it."

"Can I go now?" asked Judy. "I was in Paris with Holly and I've left her alone."

"I thought you wanted time alone," said Paul. "Now you admit you're with Holly? How do you think that makes me feel?"

"You want me to care how it makes you feel? I don't belong to you. There's fun to be had. My freedom is mine to enjoy. In a few days you and I can hang out again."

"Can you two do this someplace besides my bedroom?" asked Celeste. "I would really like to finish this book tonight. And I am not a spirit counselor. Go to the park and discuss it there."

Judy vanished with Paul right behind her.

"Phew," said Celeste. "It's become like Grand Central Station in here. I'm going to have to stop being so nice and friendly."

Eventually, Celeste finished her wolf book, but it wasn't that night. Once again she fell asleep reading. But this time at least it was in bed.

Saturday morning was beautiful. The weather was perfect for a ride. Where were they riding? It didn't matter. It had been far too long since Celeste had been riding. And the horse both knew and loved her. Celeste was excited for the day to begin.

Turning the phone on brought reality crashing in. It was ringing as soon as the volume came up. There were ten messages. Three were from Joe. There were some spooky things happening in the warehouse.

Two were from John for the same reason. Joe had called him and so had Carol. The remaining five were new clients trying to get a weekend appointment. she deleted the ones from Joe and John leaving the other five for Emma to deal with on Monday.

Breakfast was eggs, bacon, toast, and waffles. The ride would require plenty of energy. Sleeping in until eleven o'clock, made this brunch.

There was no hurry preparing and eating. By noon she started getting ready. It would only take her five or ten minutes to walk over there, but in order to be early, would require her to leave by a quarter 'til one o'clock. That was plenty of time to wash up and do her hair and makeup.

The walk was at a quickened pace and made her early. Where were they supposed to meet? Maybe at the fence. Mr. West was standing there waiting.

"I had a feeling you'd show up here. Let's walk around to the gate. I have the horses saddled already. I thought I'd let you ride Belle. That's the more laid back of the two."

CHAPTER TWENTY-FIVE

Belle was indeed a laid back horse, seeming to enjoy having Celeste on her back. They took off first down the dry creek bed. When they would get to a bridge they would get off and walk the horses under.

"You have a particular destination in mind, don't you?" asked Celeste who was enjoying this more than expected.

"I do, indeed," said Mr. West. "What gave it away?" He had a handsome smile and Celeste found his company as enjoyable as the ride.

They came to a small wooded area. At this point they left the river bed and headed for a part of the town that Celeste had never seen. There were no roads to get there and no walking paths. In fact if not for being on a horse she would be concerned about snakes.

"I'm glad I wore my riding boots. If we're going to dismount around here it could be a little scary to walk in the underbrush."

"No, we won't dismount in these woods, but there's a place about a mile upstream that I want you to see," said Mr. West.

"Are we heading for the Red River? Does this creek join with it?"

"No, this dumps into the Elm Fork. I'm taking you to see where it starts."

They rode another mile and the woods opened into a field or meadow. Celeste wasn't sure what the difference was. But this was a hidden treasure. They followed the east tree line and came to a small pool of water. The pool was very low, but it was obviously not man made.

"Where is the water coming from?" asked Celeste. "I don't see a source."

"There is a small spring in the pool. It doesn't produce enough water to feed Pecan Creek more than a trickle. But the water is cool. Would you like to feel it?" Norman asked as he dismounted.

Celeste was even more thankful for the boots now. This was a beautiful place that seemed to have been forgotten by man. Which meant snakes would be lurking around the rocks.

They walked over to the pool. It was so clear one could see the fish several feet down in the water. It was only about ten or fifteen feet across. And Norman was right. The water was so cool it was soothing in the heat of the day.

"How have I not heard about this?" asked Celeste. "This is so serene and beautiful."

"This is the beginning of Pecan Creek," said Norman. "Look over there and you will see a small creek bed."

"But the creek bed is dry," said Celeste. "This small pool can't possibly be what causes the flooding."

"You're exactly right. It's the heavy rains that cause the flooding downstream. It would be a very small creek if it weren't for the rains."

"How far are we from civilization?"

"That's the funny part. This tree line is only about fifty yards across. The other side is where everyone goes shopping."

"How far does this tree line run? Does it go to Holly Farms?"

"I think so. It stops at the expressway, but then picks back up on the other side and continues to the Red River. Though there's no creek running through it on that side of the expressway. You want to ride over that way? We can. And it's a pretty ride."

"I would love to, Norman. Is that what friends call you?"

"Yes Ma'am, for my whole life."

"Have you lived here your whole life?"

"I sure have."

"Do you like it?"

"I do."

"You don't talk a lot do you?" smiled Celeste.

"I live alone. I do most of my talking to the horses and the dogs."

Norman pointed to an outcropping of trees in the distance. "You see those trees sticking out up ahead?"

"Yes," said Celeste.

"I'll race you to them. Ready. Set. Go."

They both took off in a flash. She hadn't been on a horse in years, but still knew how to ride. Norman finished first, but Celeste ran him a good race and was only a length behind.

"You're good. And I'll tell you now. I gave you the slower horse in case you weren't as good as I thought. Turns out you're seasoned."

"You make me sound like a roast, Norman," chuckling.

They came to a stretch that was recognizable from the road. She had always wondered what it was like in the woods beyond that. It turned out to be more magical than imagined.

Soon they were at the expressway with no way to cross.

"We'll go up the access road about two blocks and there is an underpass we'll take to get over to the industrial area," said Norman.

"At least I know where I am now," laughed Celeste. "Are we safe on the access road?"

"Oh yes. In fact horses have the right of way on local streets and that includes access roads."

Celeste had never ridden in the city. Her horses had been left behind in the country, partly because there was no place for them, but also because she didn't believe there would be places to ride them in town. Norman had certainly proven her wrong on that.

They rode single file until they were back in the woods. Celeste was a little frightened by the cars racing past. Not wanting to offer them the target of two riders abreast, she breathed a huge sigh of relief when they were off the road.

"Was that scaring you?" Norman asked.

"It gave me pause," said Celeste.

"I wouldn't have done it if I'd been thinking. We would have headed back at the end of the woods."

"I'll be okay," said Celeste. "It was just a new experience for me. I'll get better at it, if you invite me again."

"Consider yourself to have an open invitation to ride either one of these horses anytime you can."

"Wow! That is especially generous. I have missed horseback riding so much."

"There it is," He stopped.

"Holly Farms?"

He nodded, "This is the view most folks don't see."

It did look very different from the farm she had visited. That one was like a mini farm compared to this. There were cattle as far as the eye could see and huge buildings that must house the chickens.

"Wow."

"Pretty impressive, isn't it? It used to belong to my Dad, but he sold it off years ago."

"Do tell."

"He was just tired of running a big farm and none of us boys wanted anything to do with it. We wanted to go to college and live in the big city. Yet I ended up here in the sleepy little town of Gloryville. Sometimes I miss the farm and sometimes I miss the big city. But I'm happy to have settled here and kept a few acres for my horses."

"Can we ride through the woods and see what lies beyond them?" asked Celeste.

"Sure," said Norman. "It isn't too far."

They rode through the woods and emerged on the back of the Harper's warehouse parking lot. So Holly had been right. Harper's and Holly Farms were practically back door neighbors.

"Let's ride along the tree line and look for a path between the two," said Celeste taking off to do just that.

Norman was puzzled but joined her anyway.

"Norman, does that look like a path to you?"

"Yes, yes it does. Looks like it hasn't been used since Spring started. I see some new growth that hasn't been trampled, but, I'd say it was a path up until very recently."

"Looks like it to me, too. Interesting."

"Why would anyone need a path between Harper's and Holly Farms?" he questioned.

"Doesn't seem like there'd be any need of it," said Celeste. "And if there was, why not make it a paved pathway."

"Makes you think someone's been up to something they didn't want anybody to know about, doesn't it?" Norman asked.

"Yes, it most certainly does," said Celeste. "We'll never know, though."

"It's getting late. Should we head back?" asked Norman.

"We probably should," replied Celeste.

"But let's go back through town. That'll give a lot of people a thrill."

"Then we should do it," laughed Celeste.

Norman was right. Kids came out of their houses to see the horses. So did some adults. They went right past Celeste's house, too.

"This is where I live," she told Norman.

"If you want to get off here, I can lead Belle back in."

"That wouldn't be fair to you. I had so much fun and you have to brush them both down? No, I wouldn't hear of it."

"It will be my pleasure," said Norman dismounting his horse at her front door.

He was making it pretty clear that was how it would be.. There weren't many gentlemen like him left in this world. She dismounted. He bent to give her a kiss and Celeste let him.

"Can I get your phone number to call on you some time?" said Norman.

"I happen to have a card here in my pocket. It has all my information. I look forward to hearing from you."

He waited for her to step inside before he returned to his horse and led Belle back to his place.

Celeste was exhausted after riding all afternoon. Putting some soup on to cook and slipping into the shower to get the dust and dirt off her, her mind drifted back fondly to the pond. Maybe next time they could take a picnic basket for the two of them. It felt like some magical dream. There were two men who seemed to want to be romantically involved with her despite her weight. This must be how skinny girls feel all the time. It was wonderful.

Celeste was about to eat dinner when Joe called. Letting it go to voicemail so as to eat it while it was hot, she would call him back after dinner. The runes had been right a scant week and a half ago. Her life was now filled with adventure and mystery and romance and it all felt weird but wonderful.

As soon as her meal was finished the phone rang again.

"Why aren't you on silent?" she yelled at the phone.

It was Danielle. "Hey girl, do you want to go out with Tina and me? We're going to the Casino."

"I'd love to, Danielle, but I'm exhausted. I've been out riding horses with a gentleman here in town."

"I want to hear about it. We'll stop by on the way to the Casino for a quick visit," said Danielle hanging up before Celeste could protest.

"Well, Chaos, it looks like I need to get dressed, after all."

Chaos was unsympathetic. Celeste had left her alone all afternoon and Chaos wasn't speaking to her.

It was time to return Joe's call.

"Celeste, where have you been? I've been trying to get in touch with you for two days," said Joe.

"Ooooh…. I forgot to call you back yesterday. I was so excited about going riding today. Ask me how it went," said Celeste, still feeling like a giddy school girl with two dates to the prom.

"First let's talk about what's going on at Harper's," snapped Joe.

"Okay, your messages said it wasn't as bad as it had been. Has the situation changed since yesterday," said Celeste feeling like a child who'd just been scolded.

"No, but you should have called me back. I thought you liked me."

"I do like you Joe, but I've had a lot going on this last week. I'm sorry if I made you feel unimportant. It's just hard to believe that you are really interested in me like that."

"That doesn't say much about your psychic abilities," joked Joe.

"They don't always work for me when it's about me," said Celeste.

Her doorbell rang. That would be Danielle and Tina.

"Joe, I have to go. A couple of my girlfriends just rang the bell. They won't be here more than an hour. Can you call me back in an hour and a half or two hours? Please," begged Celeste.

"Or you could call me," he said.

"I will. As soon as they leave, I will. I promise."

"Okay. I'll talk to you in an hour or two."

Celeste answered the door while saying goodbye to Joe.

"Was that the horse man?" asked Danielle.

"No, that was a worker at Harper's. I was supposed to call him back last night, but I forgot. He was a tad upset,"

"So… You're juggling two men?" asked Tina.

"I'm not really juggling. Today was my first outing with the horse man, as you called him? And tomorrow I have a date with Joe. Our first date, I might add."

"Is that what they're calling it these days? An "outing", said Tina making quote marks around the words "an outing".

"Oh my god, you have to tell us everything," Tina and Danielle said together.

"Well… The ride this afternoon was incredible. He took me to a place that you can't get to except on foot. It was a beautiful pool of cold water. And it was the perfect day for a ride."

"That's nice, but what happened between the two of you. Was there chemistry?" asked Danielle

"I guess you could say that," said Celeste. "He's a little on the old side for me, but I like him."

"How old is he?"

"I'd guess he's about late fifties or early sixties," said Celeste.

"Well how old is Joe?" asked Tina.

Celeste blushed, "He's probably only in his mid to late thirties."

"Wow. One too old and one too young, sounds like no contest to me," said Tina.

"You haven't met either one of them. The problem is I like them both and I want to spend time with both of them. I just have to keep them apart for a while."

The phone rang. It was Norman.

"Hello?" answered Celeste.

"I just wanted to let you know how much I enjoyed todays ride. I was wondering if you would have dinner with me one evening," said Norman.

"Dinner sounds lovely," said Celeste.

"We'll just let ourselves out," whispered the girls waving and winking.

"Do you have company? I didn't mean to interrupt," said Norman.

"It's just some girlfriends of mine wanting me to go to the Casino with them. I had already told them I'm too tired after today's ride."

"Well, I don't want to take you away from your friends. May I call you tomorrow afternoon?"

That would be wonderful," said Celeste. "I'll talk to you then."

The girls were already gone. She needed to call Joe, but her eyes were so heavy. They just needed a few minutes of rest and then she would call him.

Chaos woke her at ten-thirty.

"Oh no!" yelled Celeste "I haven't called Joe!"

"That was the longest two hours I've ever experienced," said Joe. "Did you end up at the Casino with them?"

"No, would you believe I fell asleep?"

"Really?" asked Joe, "I guess that's better than you went to dinner and a movie with someone," said Joe.

"Were you calling about activity at the warehouse?" asked Celeste trying to change the subject.

"Well, that was part of it. There is still a creepy feeling in certain places and we've had a couple of boxes fall, but nothing as bad as the night you came over. I'll never get over watching you talk with ghosts I couldn't even see. It was so cool. You're like one of those TV people that talk to ghosts and see them. It was awesome!"

"I'm glad you enjoyed it. I doubt that I will be able to do any better than I did that night. You'll probably be disappointed with how average I am tomorrow night."

"Never happen. You fascinate me. I want to hear all your stories. I can tell you have some good ones."

"I'm looking forward to it," said Celeste.

"Well, I need to get back to work. We're unloading a truck that the driver refuses to come into the warehouse because he's heard too many stories. What a chicken. Ha, Ha, Ha. I'll see you tomorrow at seven o'clock."

CHAPTER TWENTY-SIX

Celeste woke up Sunday morning without the help of Chaos.

"I guess you decided to sleep in, too," she said to Chaos who was sound asleep and apparently not ready to wake up just yet.

Waffles with strawberries was on the breakfast menu. Thinking about it made her realize that they were on the menu every Sunday.

Celeste was ready for a relaxing day There was still a wolf book to be finished. No answering the phone or the door today until Joe picked her up at seven p.m. Breakfast was delightful and the sofa beckoned as did a certain wolf. At five-thirty the book was closed and Celeste was smiling. She was going to miss it, but knew there would be a sequel.

"Five thirty," she said to Chaos. "I'm done with time to spare. I think I'll take a short nap after I lay out my clothes."

The phone rang waking her up at seven p.m..

"Oh my god, I can't believe I slept this long. What happened to my alarm clock?"

It was Joe on the phone, "Hello," said Celeste working wildly to get her clothes on.

"It's me, Joe," he said. "Where are you? I've been ringing your bell for a few minutes."

"I'm running a bit late. I might have had the hair dryer going. Would you mind waiting on the porch for a minute, I'm not dressed yet."

"I like the sound of that," he chuckled. "But I'll wait."

Celeste freshened up her makeup, checked her outfit and was good to go. Oh, wait, perfume. I need perfume. Finding her favorite and spritzing the air she walked into it letting the fragrance envelop her.

Joe was waiting patiently on the porch. "You're not going to invite me in?" asked Joe.

"Not now, we're already late."

"Late for what?" said Joe. "There's no reservation. We can get there when we want."

"I guess I think too much in terms of appointments.".

"Well, let's try footloose and fancy free tonight, okay."

"Okay," said Celeste grinning. "Am I dressed appropriately for footloose and fancy free?"

"Everything is appropriate, but you look great. Did I tell you that yet? If not, you look great!" said Joe. "Do you like Italian?"

"I love Italian. Can't you tell?" doing a model twirl on the porch to prove her point.

"Did I not just say you look great?"

"For someone so heavy..."

"I personally don't like women to be skin and bones," said Joe.

"So we're going for Italian? I love Italian, but when I go out, I usually just get spaghetti with meat sauce. Isn't that funny? I make it myself at home. You'd think I'd get lasagna or something Alfredo, but I rarely do."

"I'll be ordering for you tonight," said Joe. "Do you trust me?"

"No, but you can hardly go wrong with anything Italian," said Celeste hoping that he would at least order one of the things mentioned.

"No? You don't trust me? I'm hurt."

"Don't be. I don't really trust anyone. It's a psychic thing."

"I can't wait to hear about some of your psychic adventures. You must have some interesting and exciting stories."

"It's usually pretty boring, but the last two weeks have been abnormally active."

They arrived at the restaurant and Celeste was delighted with his choice. It was an older restaurant. It had dim lights and real tablecloths and Italian music soft enough that you could still have a private conversation.

"I hope you like it," said Joe

"I love it," said Celeste.

They were seated by the fireplace. It was warm, but cozy. He ordered Seafood Alfredo for both of them and a bottle of white wine.

He wanted to hear all about her experiences with ghosts.

Paul popped in. "You should tell him that you can see them, but you can't hear them unless I'm around."

"No one invited you. Go away," said Celeste.

"There's one here with us now?" said Joe.

"He's here. His name is Paul and he started following me when I unstuck him from Harper's. The truth is I can't hear ghosts, with the exception of Paul here. I see them. I see them talking. I just don't hear them."

"There's one sitting with us?" asked Joe.

"Well, he's standing really. There's no chair. Though, I do know someone who brings his own chair. And Paul is only unique because I can hear him. Right now there are at least five ghosts standing near people in this restaurant."

"I don't see them," said Paul.

"Paul just told me that he doesn't see any of them," said Celeste. "That's true of a lot of them. They cannot see each other most of the time. It's like they are on different frequencies."

"But you can see at least six?" asked Joe.

"Yes."

"Did you tell him what you did yesterday afternoon?" asked Paul.

"You need to stay out of my personal life," said Celeste.

"You're talking to the ghost, right?"

"I'm sorry. I'm trying to tell him he needs to leave and let you and me talk with each other," said Celeste.

"About me!" screamed Paul. "I know you're talking about me."

"I promise we won't talk about you, okay? Now please, go find Holly or Judy or someone to hang out with."

"What about the ones here? Any of them seem like my type?"

"How would I know what your type is? I've only known you for a week."

"True," said Joe, "but I keep trying to tell you that you are my type. You don't seem to want to hear it."

"I was talking to Paul. But I'm done. I simply won't respond to him for the rest of the evening."

"I kind of knew you were talking to him. It was sort of a joke on my part," said Joe.

"I'm glad you have a sense of humor about it."

They spent the rest of the evening talking about everything from the paranormal to sports and movies. The food was excellent. And they enjoyed a comedy movie after dinner.

Joe walked Celeste to the door, but was not invited in. There was an early appointment in the morning and it was already late. Joe seemed disappointed, but they both enjoyed the goodnight kiss. Celeste would have loved to have invited him in for more, but didn't pull all-nighters on a work night anymore.

Celeste fell asleep thinking about Joe. But her dreams were about Norman and the horses and the pond. Somewhere during the night there was a dream of someone crossing the woods between Holly Farms and Harper's. They were carrying a large box on a wagon behind them. They only went halfway in and there was a box sitting on an identical wagon. They left their wagon and returned to Holly Farms with the other wagon.

So it was an exchange point; But an exchange of what? What kind of goods were going between Holly Farms and Harper's. It wasn't eggs and office paper.

Waking up she immediately wrote these new clues down in a special notebook kept on the two cases that had become so entangled as to be one case. Her first client this morning was Judy. So the timing was good for the vision. It gave her new information to share with Judy.

There was no evidence of what year the dream had taken place. This vision could be ten years old or five days old. When Norman showed it to her, they could tell that no one had used the trail recently. So, the vision must be months ago up to years ago. Maybe the day would shed some light on it. Dream visions were unreliable at best. And sometimes they were just dreams. But this had all the markings of a vision.

Chaos jumped up in Celeste's lap pawing at Celeste's arm like a child tugging at mom's blouse.

"What is it Chaos. Do you have something to show me?"

Chaos jumped down and started for the reading room. She would stop and look back periodically to make sure that Celeste was following. Jumping up on the reading table Chaos pawed at the velvet pouch.

"Well, you can't be clearer than that, can you?" said Celeste. "Do I need to read my special runes?"

Chaos jumped down and curled up in the client chair. Her job was apparently finished.

Celeste had not gotten ready for the day yet, but stopped to read the runes.

The first draw was the Ur also known as The Auroch. The rune implies that a challenge awaits one of growing into new and larger shoes. This was talking about one or all of three things. The first was the healer that Celeste was being pushed toward becoming. The second was the corporate detective role that had been recently thrust upon her. The third was becoming a mentor to a student who was clearly more talented than she. The rune suggested dramatic change and that was certainly happening. This was the Rune of the wild bison. It spoke to Celeste of grabbing the bull by the horns.

"Thank you, Chaos. I did need to hear this on this very morning. You are such a good partner."

Chaos purred and basked in the sunlight of her partner's praise. It was nice to have one who listened to her. She completely ignored Celeste during this appreciation, as was customary for her people.

"I guess I'd better get ready for Judy at ten o'clock," said Celeste aloud out of habit. "Look at this reading room. Emma spent a lot of time in here and it shows. I'll have a few things to move, but not much."

Pouring one more cup of coffee to help get the cobwebs out she said, "This should do the trick."

Judy showed up five minute early. In Celeste's book that was right on time. It was her technique to de-stress about appointment times: establish the client's pattern and adjust accordingly. Judy's appointment was for ten o'clock. In Celeste's calendar was written "nine-fifty five".

"Do you have any news on my mom's death?" Judy didn't stand on tradition jumping straight to the point.

"I have a few more clues."

"Like what? What do you have? Have you found a ghost that was there?" said Judy.

"I have several ghosts telling me their versions, but none of them line up, which is not unusual. Ghosts are rarely reliable when it comes to time and place memories."

"Even your mother hasn't come up with a story that jives with the facts we have."

"So what do you have that's new?"

"Apparently there are or were two people involved in something questionable going on between Holly Farms and Harpers. There was an actual exchange going on in the woods behind Harper's.

"Well, how does that help us determine what happened to my mom?" asked Judy.

"It's just one more clue. We don't know who was doing the exchanging. Was it your uncle Hollis? Was it his son Mark? Was it your dad at Harpers'? Who else at Harper's is involved? Did your mom figure out what was going on and need to disappear? Or was it the truck driver who was meant to disappear?"

"That's a lot of questions," said Judy. "Do you have any answers?"

"I think your mom could answer some of them, but she took off for Paris and I haven't seen her. Maybe we can summon her together now."

"I'm up for it. What do you need me to do?" asked Judy.

"Hold my hand and think about your mom. Let me do the rest. I'll tell you when it works," said Celeste to Judy Jr.

Celeste began chanting something in Latin or Greek. Judy couldn't tell until hearing the name Judy. Then hearing it again.

"Judy Sr. is here. Judy was there something going on between Holly Farms and Harper's? Something illegal," asked Celeste.

Judy raised her hand as if to say, "How would I know?"

"Judy, do you know what happened to you that night?" Judy nodded as a yes.

"Did the truck swerve into your lane?"

Judy nodded.

"Did you swerve into the other lane as well?"

Judy nodded.

"Why did you swerve?" asked Celeste.

Judy tried to answer but Celeste couldn't hear her. It was time for the talking board.

"Point to the letters and I can right them down," said Celeste.

THERE WAS A GIRL IN THE ROAD A YOUNG GIRL

"There was a girl in the road, a young girl," read Judy.

"A small girl on the road at that time of night?" said Celeste.

"Did the truck driver see her, too?"

There it was. The question no one had asked because no one knew it needed to be asked. No one knew Judy's side of the story. How had Celeste missed this? Having been so focused on the dead, she had forgotten about the living.

"Did anyone interview this man?" said Celeste. "Who has talked with him?"

SHERIFF TALKED TO HIM THAT NIGHT I WAS IN THE WRONG LANE END OF STORY.

"I need to talk to this man. I need to know what, if anything, he saw. Why am I just now thinking of this? I feel like an idiot!" yelled Celeste.

"Don't," whispered Paul. "You didn't know and there were spirits who didn't want you to know. They gave you misleading information." He tilted his head towards Judy Sr. and raised his eyes.

Paul and Judy Sr. were now having a heated discussion that only they were privy to. Celeste couldn't even hear Paul's side of it. Judy Sr. left in a huff.

"That one is not going to get you any closer to what you are looking for," said Paul defending the fact that once again, he had run off one of only two people who could really help her.

"You don't know that. There could have been more. Like a description of the little girl. Or why Judy had been at Harper's that night. Now I'm going to have to summon her again after she has time to calm down. Are you trying to sabotage my investigation, Paul?"

"So Paul showed up and Mom left. Hasn't this happened before?" asked Judy Jr.

"I'm afraid it has," said Celeste boring holes in Paul's thin veneer with her eyes. "Paul, I appreciate your help, but this was not helpful."

Celeste turned her attention back to Judy. This was, after all, taking place on her nickel.

"Judy, were you ever told who was driving the truck that hit your mom?"

"Yes. I have it written down at home. But I remember it. He was Joe. I can't remember the last name. It was something weird and Irish."

"McFarren?" asked Celeste.

"Yes! Something like that," said Judy.

Celeste was silent for a few moments. This was a complete miss on her part. There had been nothing picked up from Joe that indicated he was involved with this. Maybe her psychic abilities were all imagined..

"I need to talk with Joe. Judy, let's call this the session. Let me spend the rest of the time remaining talking with Joe."

"Can I stay and listen?" asked Judy.

"I don't see any harm in that," said Celeste. Just sit right here. I'll be back in a minute."

When Celeste came back Joe's number was already dialed.

"Hello beautiful, Do you miss me?"

"Joe, this is a business call," said Celeste stopping the flirting in its tracks.

"Wow. That sounds very serious," said Joe.

"Joe, why didn't you tell me that you were the driver that was in that fatality accident a few months ago?"

"It never came up," said Joe quite seriously. "I had better things to talk to you about than an old accident that could not have been avoided."

"Joe, I'm working with the ghost of the woman that was killed. Or at least I'm working with her daughter."

"It wasn't my fault. There was something in the road," said Joe.

"Something?" queried Celeste suspiciously. "You mean something like a deer or a person or what?"

"Celeste, I wouldn't say this to anyone, but you; there was a man standing in the road. He was near the shoulder but he was in the road. And then he was gone. I screamed for help and no one came. Why would he have done that and then not answered my cries for help?

"Could he have been a ghost?" asked Celeste.

"I wouldn't admit that to anyone else," he said. "But I could almost see through him."

"This next question is going to sound crazy," said Celeste.

"After what I just told you?" said Joe.

"Did you notice if there was a little girl in the other side of the road; A little girl that Judy might have seen in front of her?"

"I was too busy trying to deal with my own delusion at the time."

"Joe, I don't think it was a delusion. I'm sure you saw what you say you saw. And I understand not mentioning it to the police. What good would that do for anyone?" said Celeste. "What I don't understand is you didn't mention it to me."

"I just did," said Joe

"After I specifically asked about it you did. There were several ghost stories told last night. You didn't even bother to tell me then or to tell me you were the truck driver in Judy's accident."

"Why did you ask about a little girl? I never heard anything about that," asked Joe changing the subject.

"Judy said there was a little girl on the road in front of her and Judy veered off to avoid hitting her. But according to her there was no one on your side. I was hoping that maybe you had seen the girl on her side. The fact that you both claim to have seen a similar version of something paranormal, makes a good case for revenge on someone's part. I wonder if they were after you or Judy or both of you."

"Me? Who would want to kill me?"

"Who would want to kill Mom?" asked Judy Jr.

"Those are both very good questions. How do we find out?" said Celeste.

CHAPTER TWENTY-SEVEN

"Do something psychic," said Judy. "Isn't that what I'm paying you to do?"

"Not exactly, but we'll let that slide for now. Joe, have you made anyone mad in the last year? Mad enough to want you dead?"

"I don't know of anyone. You know me, Celeste. I'm the fun guy. I don't make people mad."

"Well, neither did my mom," said Judy Jr.

"Well, Judy, your mom did have an affair…"

"So… you think someone would want to kill her for that, maybe some religious nut? It wouldn't have been my father. He's been gone for years. And it couldn't have been Uncle Hollis. He wouldn't have any reason. He still loved her. He told me so."

"There are so many people who seem to be leading us in so many different directions. It does appear that one or more people want us to look in all the wrong places," said Celeste. "I wonder what, if anything, this has to do with the overgrown path between Harper's and Holly Farms."

"Oh, I remember that. We would walk through to look at the cows when our dad's had to work on Saturday," said Judy.

"We?" asked Celeste. "Who is "we"?"

"Other kids that had to come in with their Dads. It wasn't always the same ones and sometimes I would be the only one there. Dad didn't let me go to the pasture on those days."

"Odd," said Celeste.

"Well, my dear. We're going to have to end this now. My next client will be here in a few minutes."

"You called me My Dear," said Joe

"You and I have things to discuss," Celeste said to Joe.

Celeste walked Judy to the door remaining on the phone with Joe to say goodbye and let him know that they needed to talk further on the subject.

Looking at her schedule she noticed too late that Emma had put Mel Turner in this slot as a weekly and the woman was a oncer. That's what Celeste called those who came once in a while without scheduling a next appointment.

Just then the doorbell rang. It was Mel. Celeste tried not to act surprised. But in truth she was. This was the woman who came last week with her pastor to vet Celeste for the church Arts & Crafts fair.

"Mel, come in, I'll join you in the reading room in just a minute."

"Paul? Are you still here?"

"Of course, and I have some information you will be interested in about that path through the woods."

"Can it wait until after Mel leaves? I was calling you to stay disappeared for this one. She's churchy."

Celeste joined Mel in the reading room. "Are you here to have your angel cards read again?

"Actually… I'm …. Curious about the runes," said Mel.

"The Runes are my personal favorite," said Celeste. "They are from the Celtic and Nordic people who lived before Christianity came to the British Isles."

"So they are ancient," said Mel. "I think that ancient things have a touch of magic to them."

"I feel the same way," said Celeste thinking that this was taking an unexpected turn.

"Tell me, Mel, did you make today's appointment with my apprentice, Emma?"

"I believe so. It was while you were out. You didn't know."

"Well, it was written in the book, but it wasn't specifically mentioned. It's all good. I might have stashed some of the pagan objects, had I known."

"You don't have to stash them for me, sweetie. I love this kind of thing. God works in mysterious ways, after all."

Celeste was beginning to like this woman. Possibly a lot of Lori's friends were going to be less inclined to use only the angel cards. They read Mel's Runes. Mel was delighted with the reading.

"Don't worry, Sweetie, I won't tell if you don't tell," she actually winked saying it.

They were finished by noon and the next appointment was at one with John Scott. Celeste thought that also was a mistake. Had Emma just gone through last week and moved every client forward? It sure was looking that way.

"Time for lunch, Chaos," There would be no time for a walk to the creek today. She wondered if Norman would be watching for her along with the horses and secretly hoped he would. He seemed such a gentle soul. There wasn't one spirit around him the whole day they had spent together. But he had said he would call Sunday and didn't.

"I'll bet you are ready for a can of cat food, aren't you?"

Chaos felt obliged to talk back and said, "Meow" in her kindest voice. The human probably didn't understand, but they say it's not what you say, it's how you say it, right?

Celeste decided to call John to confirm his appointment.

"Oh he's gone to lunch. He should be back by two-fifteen," said his secretary blandly.

"Did he mention having an after lunch appointment? Is that the reason for the long lunch?" Celeste asked.

"Not to me," Miss Personality responded.

"Well thank you for all your help," said Celeste sarcastically hanging up the phone. "I guess I'll just have to expect him, just in case."

Tidying up the reading room didn't take much. One o'clock came and went. "He's usually late. Give him five more minutes."

Paul popped in. "Did you forget about me? I told you I had some information about that path."

"I did forget. I'm sorry. My schedule is very confusing right now. And my appointment book is no help."

"Judy says that her husband is most likely behind some of this. He's been pretty mean to her and you know how those two get when they're mad and mean," said Paul.

"Thank you, Paul. That helps more than you know," said Celeste.

"You'd be amazed at what I know," said Paul sternly and disappeared.

Celeste was just about to walk back to her bedroom to grab a book to read when the doorbell rang. It was John.

"John, why did you make an appointment when we will see each other Friday?"

"That's not soon enough. I knew it wouldn't be. You're the psychic. Why didn't you know? All hell broke loose at the warehouse this weekend. Joe said he called you, but there was no answer. Do you really not have a cellphone? Who doesn't have a cell phone in this day and age?"

"Good day to you, too," responded Celeste. "I knew there was activity, but Joe sounded like he had the situation under control. And I do not have a cell phone. I go out so rarely and I do have an answer machine. Surely that is enough."

"No, it's not enough. Come with me. We're going cell phone shopping."

"Oh, I don't think we need to do that. I'll look at some next week."

"NOW," said John. "We will go to the ATT store and find you a nice up to date IPhone."

"I don't think I want a fancy iPhone," said Celeste. "I just need a phone that rings when I get a call."

"I'm going to drag you into the twenty first century, Celeste. I want to be able to text you. And leave you voicemails that you will see before you get home. The most important thing is that you don't give this new number out to everyone. Your psychic clients can still use your home phone. This phone is for people like me or personal friends. This is for people that you would want to be able to get in touch with you when they need you.

"When did it kill anyone not to be able to get hold of me instantly?" asked a flustered Celeste.

"This weekend when there was more activity at the warehouse and no one could find you and why does Joe have your number? Is he a client?"

"Heavens no!" exclaimed Celeste sounding just a bit flustered. "We're just friends."

"How long have you been friends with one of my employees?" snapped John Scott.

"I met him in your conference room at your behest. But we've been friends since he was trapped between a beast and a spirit in the loading area. He fancies ghost hunting which makes me kind of special."

"Be careful," said John.

They arrived at the phone store. In this town that meant the Walmart. They had the largest selection and no pressure from commissioned salesmen to buy features you would never use.

Celeste looked at prices and contracts and the phones themselves. It was complete confusion. "Will you please tell me the easiest thing to operate that will allow me to make and receive calls and texts?" questioned Celeste.

A salesman overheard her. "Have you never used a cell phone before?"

"I have not. I lead a very boring life," responded Celeste.

"Well, nothing could be further from the truth," said John laughing. "This is the most incredible psychic you will ever meet. Her ability to see ghosts almost everywhere is a bit frightening."

"Are there any here?" asked Richard, the sales associate who was truly curious.

"Do you really, **really** want to know?" asked Celeste seriously.

"Absolutely," said Richard.

"It would be difficult to count how many are here. Many of them are attached to shoppers. So they come and go. Others seem to just be wandering or standing around. There is one over by the largest TV. He's not looking at the TV. He's looking down an aisle. He looks like he's been here since before the store was built. He seems to have come with the land."

"So, you're saying that there could be one hundred or more ghosts in this store?" asked Richard.

"Yes."

"Okay, enough about that. We need for her to learn to use a phone. So nothing fancy. Eventually we'll teach her to use the camera. But we don't look for her to be skyping or going on twitter or anything," said John.

"The easiest thing is this Jitterbug. It makes calls. That's it. But that is for old people who have stopped learning about new technology. You are not old."

"What would you suggest then," said Celeste.

"This one right here," he showed her a low cost phone with a month to month contract and showed her how to make or take a call.

"What do I have to do? I buy the phone and then it just works?" said Celeste.

"I wish it was that easy, but it isn't. I will help you get it setup and useable," volunteered Richard.

"I'm feeling pretty useless here. I think I'll walk down to sporting goods." John wrote his phone number down on a piece of paper. "Call me when you have it working."

Richard was very helpful and Celeste was up and running in just a few minutes. She officially had two phone numbers. Richard called her from his personal phone. "There," he said. Now you have a number of a friend in the phone. I'll show you how to save it." He walked her through saving a number.

"Now," he said. "What about the man who came in with you? He gave you his number. Would you like me to help you enter it?"

"Let me try it, and you coach me?"

Catching on quickly, and calling John to let him know, had her walking out with a new phone and a new friend. And he was a friend who was already saving her number as Celeste walked away from the counter.

Danielle was her first call. Her number was memorized by heart.

The call went to voicemail. "Hello Danielle. This is my new cell phone number. You should be able to see it, right? Call me back. Oh, this is Celeste."

"That was fast," said John. "We're not even in the car yet."

"I'm just trying to use it, so I don't forget what he taught me. He said when I get good at calls and messages, I can come back and he'll teach me about the camera and a few other things."

"I'm not complaining. At least I'll be able to reach you when I need you. That's the whole point of this, you know. So that **I can get in touch with you!** Everybody else is just getting a bonus. The most important thing to remember is to bring your phone with you when you are out. That is why we bought the phone so that people, especially me, can get in touch when you are not at home."

The phone rang. It took Celeste a few anxious seconds to remember how to answer it.

"I can't believe you finally bought a phone," said Danielle. "Who convinced you? It was one of your new boyfriends, wasn't it?"

"Actually John's company bought it for me. They say it's not fancy, but it is. I can't wait to show it to you."

"I'm going to send you a text so you can practice," said Danielle.

"Okay," said Celeste and hung up."

A text came in it took some fumbling but Celeste opened it.

{Why did you hang up?}

{So that you could text me.}

{We can talk and text at the same time.}

The phone rang again. "We'll play around with it some more when I come over tonight," said Danielle. "What time is your last client?"

"I should be finished up by five-thirty," said Celeste.

"See you then," said Danielle.

It was perfect timing because they were almost at her house. "I sure hope Emma didn't have me set up for a two o'clock," said Celeste to John.

"I reserved your whole afternoon," said John. "Now you can play with your phone and learn to use it.

John dropped her at her house at three o'clock. What a fun new toy this was going to be.

Emma was there at three-thirty. There were messages from the land line to go through. It took about an hour just to get the schedule straightened out.

"I hope you enjoyed today because this is going to be your last afternoon off for at least three weeks," Emma told Celeste who was busy entering phone numbers into her new phone. "And there was a message from someone named Norman? It came in Sunday afternoon. It wasn't about psychic stuff. It sounded more personal."

"Oh no, I forgot he was going to call and turned the phone to silent," said Celeste.

"Well, he'll call back," said Emma.

"I went to Barnes and Noble on Saturday. They had the Rune pack. I've been reading it over all weekend."

"Let's see if you can do a reading for me," said Celeste.

"Oh no, I don't think I'm ready. That's like doing a reading for the president or something. I still need the book," babbled Emma.

"It's okay to use the book whenever you need to," said Celeste. "You will eventually do enough readings to need the book less and less. Now let's sit at the reading table and read my runes together."

Emma took a deep breath and let it out slowly looking in the book for a setup for the stones.

"Let's do a simple three stone draw first," said Celeste.

Emma took another long breath of relief.

"Now talk to me like I know nothing. Explain what the Runes are for in this draw and what each Rune means."

Emma did the reading using the book most of the time.

"Now tell me your interpretations of what you read as they relate to the past, present and future."

Emma did as instructed and gave a very good reading although the client, Celeste, was a little surprised by the potential future. Celeste gave Emma high marks for a first reading.

Emma left at five-thirty as Danielle was arriving.

"Let me see it," said Danielle walking right in.

Celeste produced the phone and they were off and running. "The secret to learning to use this is repetition. So we're going to sit here and text each other. Under lots of different circumstances and I'm going to teach you how to use voice to text."

"That sounds like a lot," said Celeste.

"It's going to be fun, you'll see."

"I feel like a…"

Danielle held up her hand and cut her off mid-sentence. "Text it."

Celeste had a little difficulty opening the text box, but Danielle let her struggle with it until she found it for herself. "How do I put in who I'm texting? Do I have to know their number?"

"Okay, I'll help you with this part. It's tricky and there's more than one way to get there," said Danielle.

Soon Celeste had mastered texting and was moving on to the address book. It had already received a few calls, so there were numbers in the phone ready to be added. Danielle also showed her how to take a picture and text it to someone.

"That's enough for one day," said Celeste. "I don't want to get so confused that I forget everything I've just learned."

"Okay, If you have any problems or questions, just call or text me," said Danielle.

Danielle left and Celeste looked at this new technology in the palm of her hands

Her first thought now was to call Joe. Or better yet, text him. Text him and ask him to call her when he was on a break. He texted back,

{Who is this?} Joe

{Celeste} Celeste

{You bought a cell phone?} Joe

{this afternoon} Celeste

{I'll be on break at ten will that be too late?} Joe

{perfect} Celeste

Celeste was so proud of herself having texted with no help. Danielle would be proud, too. Should she call Norman to give him her new number? *No, I'll wait for him to call me and then I'll give him the number.*

Who else was there to practice with? The cell phone rang and Celeste panicked having forgotten how to answer it.

Finally finding the right swipe to answer with, "Hello?"

"Hello Celeste," said Richard.

"Did I forget to sign something?" said Celeste assuming this had to be business about the new phone.

"No," said Richard. "I just wanted to see how you were doing with it. You obviously remembered how to answer it. Have you made a call yet?"

"Yes," said Celeste. "I called my friend Danielle and had to leave her a voicemail. Then she came over and taught me how to text and how to take a picture and text it."

"Sounds like you're doing great."

"I am and I can't believe Walmart has this kind of excellent service," said Celeste.

"We don't," said Richard. "I was using the phone as an excuse to call you."

"How nice of you," said Celeste.

"I'm fascinated with a woman who survives without a cell phone and even resists having one when the company is paying for it. I'd just like to get to know you better," said Richard.

"I don't know what to say," said Celeste who was not accustomed to flirting.

"What do you do for Harper's? We can start with that."

"I'm just a part time consultant," said Celeste not knowing any other way to put it that wouldn't have him hanging up.

"Wow, I wish I could get a gig like that; Part-time work with a free cell phone?"

"You know you're right. Why would they buy me a phone? I only work there one day a week and it's a half day at that."

"Really," said Richard in disbelief. "A half day and you get a cell phone? Are they hiring?"

"Actually, I believe they are. Would you like me to ask?"

"What kind of jobs do they have open?"

"Possibly clerical and loading and warehouse," said Celeste.

"Wait," said Richard. "I didn't call you to find a job. I wanted to get to know you better. What day do you work?"

"I work Monday through Thursday from nine to five-thirty and Friday is my half day," said Celeste.

"Where do you work Monday through Thursday?" he asked.

"In my home."

"What do you do?" There it was. THE question. The thing that would make the phone "click".

"I'm a psychic and I do readings with clients in my home on an appointment only basis."

There was a long silence.

"Are you still there?" asked Celeste.

"Yes, I just don't have a response to that. Is that why you didn't need a phone, because you're a psychic?" he said.

"I don't think so. I just never had the need of one. I work at home and I don't drive, so I don't go out much," said Celeste.

"Wait. Why don't you drive? You didn't seem handicapped in any way when I met you a few hours ago."

"Sometimes I channel spirits and it's not always at my convenience. It's very scary to be taken over while driving. I don't want to cause an accident."

"How often do you channel?" asked Richard obviously riveted to the conversation.

"It's probably been over a month since the last one."

"So it doesn't happen every day? That's good. Would you let me take you to dinner one evening?" he said.

"I think that would be nice," said Celeste.

"We have a new schedule out this week, so I can see when I'll be off in the evening then call you to set something up, okay?"

"Excellent," said Celeste and hung up.

Immediately there was a text from Danielle. {Take a pic and text it to me for practice.}

It took Celeste a few minutes to do it, but mission accomplished. All the fun things that were suddenly happening in her life felt so good.

The phone was her amusement all evening, taking pictures and putting names and numbers in it. There was even a place to put emails. It was an amazing little machine.

Joe called at ten p.m.. He called on her cell phone. "I'm sorry it didn't occur to me to tell you about the accident. I try to forget about the events of that night as much as I can."

"Joe, I've been thinking about this a lot."

"I'm in trouble, aren't I?" he said. Celeste could feel the true remorse in his voice.

"The truck involved in the accident was a Holly Farms truck."

"Yes."

"You worked for Holly Farms?"

"No."

"Are you really going to make this like pulling teeth?"

"They use the same trucking company. So driver's take loads from whichever warehouse needs them," he finally started talking. "But after the fatality I told them I didn't want to drive anymore, so they gave me a job in the loading area at Harper's."

"I don't understand," said Celeste. "You worked for an independent trucking company that got you a job at one of their customer's business when you decided to quit driving."

"Well, they're not exactly independent. I don't fully understand it either, but the only people we hauled for were Harper's and Holly Farms, and I was on Harper's payroll."

"I shouldn't have been upset with you, Joe. You barely knew me. Why would you tell a total stranger any of this?"

"That's what I was thinking, too. But you were too upset to argue with you," said Joe laughing.

The laughter was contagious and Celeste quickly joined in. Joe talked about his day and Celeste told him about getting the phone and how the phone salesman had even called her a little while ago to make sure it was working correctly and the features were becoming easier to use.

"I bet he offered to come over some time and teach you more about the special apps, didn't he?" said Joe with no hint of laughter.

"Actually he offered to take me to dinner sometime, but we didn't set a date," said Celeste wishing she hadn't. Celeste had a policy of honesty as a general rule. Her abilities made it difficult for people to lie to her and so her habit of being open and honest with everyone.

Joe did not seem to appreciate the honesty, at least not in this particular situation. There was a long silence.

"I thought you were mad at me, but I didn't think you were that mad," Joe finally said.

"I'm not mad at you Joe and I like you. I like talking with you and being with you…"

"But?" said Joe.

"But… We've been on one date. Do you think I don't have other people who take me out to dinner occasionally?"

"So, you're saying I have competition?" he asked.

'It's not a competition. I enjoy being single."

"I'm going to have to think about that," said Joe.

"I'm a psychic, Joe. That automatically makes me abnormal. I will be your friend and maybe more. We just have to play it by ear and give me room to breathe."

"Wow! You really are blunt."

"I'm not very good at flirting, I guess," said Celeste.

"Well, I hate to end this, but my break time is over. Can I call you tomorrow?"

"I certainly hope you do."

Celeste was getting ready for bed while they talked and was about to tuck herself in when Paul showed up.

"What did I tell you about my bedroom being off limits?"

"I'm technically not in your bedroom," said Paul.

"Watch it. I'll ban you from the hallway, too."

"Do you think the little girl was Holly?" asked Paul.

"You've been listening in on me? I think I warned you about that, too."

"You didn't answer the question. Do you think the little girl was Holly?" insisted Paul.

"That doesn't make any sense. Why on earth would Holly stand in the middle of the road at night?" said Celeste.

"Someone could have talked her into it. The girl's very gullible. You see how Judy has her globetrotting these days."

"What do you have against Judy all of a sudden?" asked Celeste.

"I don't have anything against her except that part about turning into a red eyed monster! Or did you forget about that?" said Paul.

"No, Paul. I didn't forget about it. You won't let me. Judy seems fine now. I don't think there'll be any more problems."

"It's already causing problems with poor little Holly. Do you think Holly is meant to be here?"

"Why not?" said Celeste. "She seems to be enjoying it here."

"That's because you are still alive. You don't know anything about the afterlife. You think you do because you can see us and hear some of us, but you are only getting a glimpse of the fringes. Don't you think an innocent like Holly deserves more than the fringes?"

"What do you mean? What are the fringes? Do you know where they go when they cross over?"

"Of course I do, but I can't tell you something like that unless I want to go back to being stuck to a piece of paper in a locked cabinet or worse."

"Do you want me to call a spirit rescuer to help her cross over?"

"Do you really think that the living have more power to help the dead than the dead have?" said Paul.

"I backed Judy Sr. down in the warehouse that night," said Celeste.

"Yes, you backed down a fringe spirit. Well done. Good job. Did you cross her over? No. You just brought her from the outer fringes back to where we all are stranded."

"I don't know how to cross them over, but there are people who do," said Celeste defensively.

"You're very powerful for a mortal. You won't understand the things of which I speak until you yourself are crossed over. That is just how it has to be.

That said; do you think Holly was the little girl."

"My head is still reeling from all this fringe talk. How would I know if it was Holly?

"Well, don't you think that might be important? The little girl caused the death of Judy Sr. Why? It's a cinch she didn't have a reason herself, but someone must have. Look for that person."

With those words Paul disappeared once again leaving more questions than answers. Celeste had a lot to think about, but it was becoming clear that Judy was the target that night, unless Judy and Joe had been seeing each other on the sly. But Judy was in her sixties. Joe was closer to Judy Jr than Judy Sr. in age. And yet, Joe had been paying attention to Celeste and she was older by ten years. Joe could be one of those men that really like older women.

No, Celeste just couldn't see the two of them together. It was just a coincidence. Even though Celeste didn't really believe in coincidences, maybe that's all this was.

Paul had hinted at someone talking Holly into doing this to Judy by telling her it was a game or something harmless. That was possible, but who would be capable of something like that except maybe Paul himself or Judy's husband.

It would make sense for her husband to do it. Even though it took years to accomplish Celeste had already learned that days, minutes, and even years were as if they were interchangeable components of the afterlife. If it was her husband, he may have felt like he did it as soon as he found out about Judy Sr and Mr. Hollis.

The afterlife must be a very confusing place, thought Celeste drifting off to sleep.

Her dreams that night were as confusing as the afterlife seemed to be. The fog invaded her dream. It was too thick to see your own feet. There was laughter coming from somewhere. Following the sound she came to a clearing in the fog.

Judy Sr. and Holly were sitting on a blanket in the sun. They had three string puppets. Judy was working two of them and Holly was working one. Looking closer Paul was one of the puppets and Mr. Wells was another and the third was Celeste.

Holly was controlling Celeste and Judy was controlling Paul and her husband. This didn't feel right. The fog came in and they were gone from sight. Then there was someone crying and Celeste followed this new sound.

There was a thunder storm. There was no sunshine here, just black clouds and rain and thunder and lightning. The crying was coming from a little girl that Celeste had never seen before. Walking over to comfort the child it turned into a beast with red eyes and a tail. Once again the scene disappeared into the fog.

Celeste awoke to see a beast in her own bedroom. Celeste stared it down until it turned into a human looking spirit. It looked like Mr. Wells. He grinned a toothy grin and faded into nothing.

Celeste looked at the clock. It was three a.m., the witching hour. Turning on a light and finding the phone, she sent a text to the only person that might be awake.

{I had a nightmare} Celeste

{Do you need me to come over?} Joe

{Aren't you at work?} Celeste

{Yes, but you know the boss. ☺} Joe

{I'll be okay. It was just more like a vision than a dream}

The phone rang.

"Hello beautiful," said Joe.

"Hi and thank you. I was dreaming of another beast like the one at the warehouse," said Celeste.

"Did you stare it down?"

"As a matter of fact… I did. But, then I woke up and it was here in my room at the foot of my bed and I had to stare it down again."

"That sounds pretty scary. Are you okay to be alone? I'm being serious and I won't make any moves on you. I'll just be there for you. I get off work soon anyway."

"That's really nice of you, but if I can't handle this, I don't deserve to charge for my services as a psychic."

'Don't say that. This is the very reason you can and do charge for your services. You're the real thing," said Joe.

"I feel very small right now, not physically obviously, but spiritually. I feel weak."

"Have you been doing too many readings?" said Joe earnestly.

"I don't think that's it, I think I'm on the verge of solving the biggest mystery I'm working on right now and someone doesn't want me to. Joe, could you describe the man you saw on the road that night?"

"Well, I could kind of see through him."

Celeste laughed. "Thanks I needed a laugh. Please, continue."

"He was tall and slim and had a fedora type hat. He was wearing a suit and tie and glasses."

"If you saw a picture of him, would you recognize him?"

"Probably," said Joe.

"I'll find a picture of him in the morning. Could you stop by on your way to work tomorrow?"

"Try and stop me."

"What time do you go to work?"

"Tomorrow I go in at seven p.m. I'll stop by around six p.m. with a bag lunch. We can eat together."

"That sounds great."

Celeste had calmed down falling uneasily back to sleep. The dreams were not finished with her.

CHAPTER TWENTY-EIGHT

Sleeping fitfully for the rest of the night the dreams tossed her around the fog like a rag doll. There was the key and the anchor and the ring and the path with the wagon and a truck that had the name Holly Farms on it. And there was Mr. Wells, whose first name wouldn't come to her. Then there was Paul and Mr. Wells scheming. Then it was Judy and Mr. Wells scheming. Then came the crying little girl again. But nothing came together. It was like none of these pieces went to this puzzle.

Waking up tired it showed in her eyes. There was a client coming at nine o'clock. She forced herself to get out of bed and get dressed. Dragging herself into the kitchen for breakfast and just going through the motions when it hit her. There was a spirit in the office. One of the one's at the desk. He had an anchor for a tie pin. What if he was part of the puzzle? *Or what if I'm just grasping at straws?*

There was thirty five minutes until her first client. Celeste prepared a complex casting using the special silver runes. It should bring all the elements together or at least most of them. It turned out that the anchor clue was only to lead her to John Scott, which it had. That clue was no longer relevant. The key was to lead her to the safe and allow her to help Judy Sr., which it had. That clue was no longer relevant. The ring was never a clue. A mystery? Yes. A clue? No.

The men in her life were showing up because she no longer needed a man, surrounding herself with the aura of a confident, strong woman. The men who were attracted to that were appearing. And there would be more. There was no need to choose one.

None of the clues were relevant to the true mystery of Judy Wells' death. The path was just a path. The trucking company might be suspicious to a tax man or an accountant. Wait! Mr. Wells was an accountant. Had he found something all those years ago? Had he brought it to the wrong person's attention? How had Mr. Wells died? Had anyone ever said?

The doorbell rang. It was Clara, her nine o'clock. Celeste slid her reading off to the side and started her session with Clara. Judy's appointment was today at eleven a.m. Celeste would ask then how her father had died and if she had a picture of him.

The rest of the day was booked tight. Celeste hadn't been to the creek since riding with Norman. Today would not be the day for it and Emma had warned her the week looked very busy. She needed the grounding that the creek gave her and the walk and just to visit with the horses. Seeing Norman West again would also be nice. He hadn't called so there was a strong possibility he was not really interested.

Or was that Richard? Oh my, having trouble keeping up wasn't good.

Judy was there five minutes early for her eleven o'clock appointment excited to hear if Celeste had anything new to offer.

"Indeed, I do."

Celeste told Judy about her dream visions.

"Can you get me a picture or two of your father, Judy?" asked Celeste.

"I keep one in my wallet. Let me find it… Here it is."

"May I keep this for the day? Or I can return it at our next appointment."

"You're not going to use it for a spell or anything that would damage it, are you?" asked Judy.

"Not at all," said Celeste who had chosen not to tell Judy that there may be an eye witness to her father's part in her mother's death. That news could wait until it was confirmed.

"Judy, how did your father die?" asked Celeste.

"They said it was a stress induced heart attack. Mom said accounting was much more stressful than people thought."

"Did he have any heart symptoms before?"

"Not that I know of," said Judy.

"Let's read your Runes with that question in mind," said Celeste.

"I'm game," said Judy.

The Runes were rather wishy washy on the subject. They were both disappointed, but Celeste suspected that Mr. Wells was there and trying to miss-guide them. Judy didn't need to know that either.

By the time the hour was up Judy was caught up on almost everything and Celeste had a picture to show and a cause of death. Well, maybe a cause of death.

Judy left and Celeste took her lunch as slowly as possible. Emma called her on her cell phone to ask to come at three o'clock instead of three-thirty. Celeste really liked this phone more and more.

The afternoon went quickly with appointments every hour. Emma sat in on a Rune casting and Celeste made sure to use the book to explain the process to the client hoping to ease Emma's fears about using the book during a reading.

Joe came at six p.m. with a sack of hamburgers and fries and two shakes. It was perfect comfort food after the day Celeste had had and the sleep that she had not had.

Joe saw her phone and how it could take pictures and send them by text and there was a place for music which would be nice for meditation once her own music was on it.

They talked about her dreams from the night before and they talked about the various clues and her Rune casting that morning. They talked about the red eyed monster.

"Are you positive it wasn't part of the dream?" asked Joe.

"It's hard to say. I was waking up from a dream or a vision. I'm not sure which. It was like it followed me out of the vision and stood at the end of my bed. I swear it looked like Mr. Wells."

"You know what Mr. Wells looks like?"

"How could I have forgotten? Judy brought this picture." It was like there was still some fog left over from the dream.

"That sure looks like the man I swerved to miss. He even has the Fedora," said Joe excitedly.

"And he appeared to me this morning as a red eyed beast." I don't understand what he's up to, but I think it involves more than just Judy. I think he wants us to find his own killer."

The crystal ball rolled straight to her as thoughts became words. Joe looked at the ball and looked at her in amazement.

"See what goes on around here? I need to stop and read this. The universe obviously thinks it's important."

Picking up the ball and gazing deeply almost in a trance state Celeste saw Mr. Wells lying in a hospital bed. Mr. Hollis was there. Judy was there. Judy Jr. was there.

Mr. Hollis seemed to be threatening them with something. Judy was holding onto Judy Jr. a little too tightly. Someone walked in and the scene disappeared.

"This ball was trying to tell me that this has as much to do with Mr. Wells' death as it does with Judy Sr."

"So we have some research to do. Let me show you something about your phone."

She handed him the phone and watched as he pulled up Google. He typed in a few key words and they were looking at Mr. Wells' obituary.

"My phone can go on the internet? That could be very handy."

"You'll have to learn to use the feature, but it's pretty easy," said Joe.

"This is awesome. Show me how you did it again?" When he went back to the home screen, It showed the time. "Joe, Its almost seven o'clock. You need to get to work."

"Dang," said Joe, "This was fun. Can we do it again sometime?"

"Of course," said Celeste.

"And if you have any more frightening visions, you'll call me. No matter what time it is."

"I promise," said Celeste walking him to the door. He lingered for a long kiss.

"Good night," he said.

"Good Morning."

Celeste went into the reading room and retrieved the hand drawn copy of the rune casting this morning.

"Was that only this morning? It seems like days ago."

Celeste continued where she had left off that morning. Mr. Wells was definitely going to need some more detailed research. His death was extremely suspicious.

Also Mr. Hollis seemed more like a business problem than a former lover problem. Was Mr. Hollis threatening Mr. Wells or was Mr. Wells threatening Mr. Hollis in that scene from the crystal ball? As if to answer, the crystal ball rolled around the table and stopped on her reading.

Picking it up carefully, once again she went into a trance by gazing into it. Mr. Wells was threatening both Mr. Hollis and Judy. They were arguing and Mr. Hollis was losing his temper.

Judy was nervous, But not about being caught for her affair. There was more. Her husband knew something because of auditing the Holly Farms books. He had uncovered something.

Mr. Hollis was yelling and pounding his fist. Celeste wished to be able to hear them. In popped Paul.

"Old Hollis there is threatening the whole family if Wells doesn't drop the thing. Just leave the numbers as they are and walk away."

"Wells is telling him to forget that. He has enough to put both companies out of business and possibly in jail."

"Judy is crying."

"Which Judy?"

"Both."

The scene faded and Celeste started to look away from the ball, when Judy reappeared at the bridge over the creek throwing her ring in the creek. It landed near Celeste's old stash location.

"Well, that's interesting. But, look at her clothes. They are the same ones that Judy the spirit wears. This must have happened the night of her death.

"Paul, is Judy saying anything?"

"Just telling her husband she's sorry. It was the biggest mistake of her life."

"You have to believe me, though. Judy was always yours."

"Sounds like someone who's ready to do something stupid," said Paul.

"You make it sound like Judy and her dead husband conspired together to help her commit suicide," said Celeste. "I don't believe it. If anything like that happened it was Mr. Wells who drove her to it. He may have made her think it was her idea. But…"

"You realize you don't even know her, right? She was a ghost when you met her. You don't know her at all."

"I feel like I know her through her daughter," said Celeste.

"You don't," with that he disappeared.

Celeste sat there for a few minutes taking it all in. Judy may have committed suicide with the help of her late husband who knew there had been cheating on him with his cousin. Worse, they had been cheating since before Judy Jr. was born.

It was plausible.

The Runes pointed to it, as well. Paul still knew more, but Paul didn't just tell her what was needed. He made her dig for it. And he was very good at telling her she was wrong.

After all Celeste had done for him, too. Who had released him from that office even though he claimed that the dead have more power to do that sort of thing than humans do? Had he really been stuck or was he acting? Was he part of the conspiracy between Mr. Wells and Judy and possibly Holly? No, not Holly. Holly was not the little girl.

The little girl had to be the one that was crying in Celeste's vision. Or was that meant to throw her off the track, too?

Tonight Celeste would take a sleeping pill. There would be neither dreams nor visions this night: Only sleep, the kind of deep sleep that leaves you not remembering your dreams.

The phone rang. It was Joe. He must be on his break.

"Hello beautiful!" he said.

"Are you on a break?"

"Yes, did I wake you?"

"No, but I have taken a sleeping pill so I won't have a repeat of last night," said Celeste.

"I don't blame you there," said Joe. "I was just calling to check on you. But it sounds like you have a good plan for the night. Sleep well."

"Thank you. I will. And thank you for checking up on me. I appreciate it."

"Good night."

"Good morning," said Celeste.

The phone rang again. This time it was Richard, "Will you have dinner with me Friday night? Around seven p.m."

"That sounds lovely," she said in a sleepy stupor. "I just took a sleeping pill. Will you call me tomorrow and remind me? I often forget things that happen right before I fall asleep from these pills."

"I'll call you and text message you, as well," said Richard.

"Goodnight, Richard."

The next morning there were no memorable dreams. It was refreshing.

It was Wednesday and the schedule looked good today. There was extra time built in between some of the appointments. There might be time to walk to the creek.

That thought made her feel even better. Looking at her phone there was a message.

{Don't forget. Dinner Friday @ seven} Richard.

{Thank you for the reminder} Celeste

Only vaguely remembering having made a dinner date with Richard for Friday it was still a pleasant surprise. That was the one problem with taking these sleeping pills. You were subject to forget most of what happened in the half hour before actually falling asleep.

It was good to know that the phone could be a reminder, too.

Her first client was a new one from the restaurant incident. Celeste had seen her last week and signed her up for weekly appointments. Better yet, the woman paid a month in advance. It was Celeste's favorite kind of client.

By eleven-thirty there was no one until two o'clock. Bringing a sandwich she set out for the creek. The horses were out and there was a carrot for each of them. Belle seemed to remember being ridden Saturday. Norman came out of the house and greeted her.

"I was beginning to think you were never coming back," he said.

"I've had a very busy schedule," said Celeste. "I don't have a lot of time today, but I have missed my walks. I was afraid you had lost my number."

"Touché, except I actually did lose your number."

"Well that's a good excuse for not calling, I guess. And I have a new number for you anyway"

"Okay," he said as he pulled out his cell phone. "You call out the number and I'll put it straight into my phone this time."

Celeste gave him the number and he said, "I'm going to call you right now."

Her phone rang.

"Now you have my number, too," he said.

"Do you know how to text?" asked Celeste.

"Of course," said Norman.

"Oh good, I can text you when I'm going for a walk. If you're around you can come out and see me."

"I'll do it."

"I want to go down to the creek and do some grounding. It's been good to see you. I look forward to getting a call some evening."

Celeste walked on down to the creek checking first on her new stash hidey hole. It was just the way it had been left. Life just kept getting better and better. There was a rock for her to sit on and do some grounding meditation before walking back to the house for her two o'clock appointment. The rest of the day was relatively quiet. It was amazing what a good night's sleep could do for a person.

CHAPTER TWENTY-NINE

Thursday was less hectic but still exciting. There was no one at nine a.m. and her ten a.m. was Judy Wells. Celeste made a note to check her balance remaining on the retainer. It was likely that Judy was getting close to the limit.

"Judy, what would you like to do today? Tarot, Angel cards, Runes, crystal ball?"

"Are you any closer to finding my mother's real cause of death?"

"Yes, I think so, but you're not going to like it."

Mr. Wells appeared behind Judy and shook his head violently.

"Judy, your father is here with us," said Celeste as Mr. Wells continued to shake his head and started waving his arms. "He seems very adamant that I not share this information with you."

"Why?" asked Judy.

"Probably because you're not going to like it," said Celeste watching Mr Wells expand in size and transform into the beast. "There is a possibility that your father convinced your mother to…"

Mr. Wells' eyes flashed and he reached for Celeste's neck. He started to choke her. He took her breath. He wasn't flesh and bones, so there was no way to grab his arms or fight back. Celeste locked eyes with him. His eyes blazed brighter. Judy was now screaming as Celeste lay on the floor apparently having a seizure.

"I'm calling 911," said Judy pulling her phone from her purse.

"NO!" yelled Celeste managing to catch just enough of a breath to get that word out of her mouth before the beast clamped down again.

Celeste struggled to stay alive. A second later something in her snapped. She pushed the beast away without moving at all. As if willing it to back off. They locked eyes again. "I know Mr. Wells is in there," said Celeste in her head. "What have you done with him?"

The beast started to get smaller. Judy wasn't hearing anything except that Celeste was breathing again.

"How can I help you?" Judy said to Celeste.

"Talk to your father. We need to speak with your father."

"Daddy? If you're here, I love you and I miss you. Can you let me see you? I know other people have seen you."

It was perfect. Manifesting for mortals took a lot of energy. Celeste could feel his grip weakening as he made himself visible to his daughter but, he forgot that what she would see was a beast trying to choke Celeste. Judy's reaction was to begin screaming again. The beast immediately turned back into her father.

"Daddy? Is that really you?"

Mr. Wells nodded.

"Why was that monster taking you over?"

Celeste was recovered and back in her chair. Out came the spirit board.

"He can't actually talk to us without using more energy than he has. He's using up a lot making himself visible to you."

He pointed to the talking board. Then he pointed to the letters

N O T A M O N S T E R M E

"That was not you, Daddy. That was a monster. Why is the monster taking you over?"

I H A V E D O N E T H I N G S P L E A S E S T O P W O R R Y I N G A B O U T T H E P A S T S T O P L O O K I N G

Mr. Wells disappeared.

"Okay. What the HELL was that about?" said Judy to Celeste.

"I believe your father has been involved in getting your mother to commit suicide. He used that monster to drive her crazy enough to veer into the truck that day. He had some others that helped. He might have found out about something illegal going on at Harper's that may have involved your Uncle Hollis."

"Stop calling him my uncle. We both know that he isn't my uncle. He was just a man having an affair with my mother behind my poor father's back."

"Well, I believe that your father may have found out after he died and wanted a little revenge. That's why he made sure that it was a Holly Farms truck that your mother ran into."

"I believe that he had been driving her crazy for some time by appearing to her as a beast sometimes & himself at other times. I believe that that is only the tip of the iceberg. There is a lot more to find out, but your mother's death needs to be left alone. I believe he drove her to suicide."

"That's my mother and father you are talking about. Where do you come up with these ideas?" said Judy.

"They are more than just ideas. I have had a lot of visions about this. I don't have all the facts yet, but I will. Your father was an accountant at Harper's, right?"

"Yes."

"That's where this started. He found something in the books that made him suspicious."

"Did he tell you that?" asked Judy.

"No, I saw it in a vision," said Celeste.

"He went to someone with the information and probably the proof. I don't know who he took it to yet. But I will find out. Hopefully I will be able to get your father to just tell me. But that person was most likely involved in the books that were falsified."

"Your father conveniently had a fatal heart attack days later. Convenient for whoever was cooking the books, anyway."

"So, you're saying that my mother's death was suicide and my father's death was murder. A few days ago you were sure that my mother's death was murder," said Judy.

"I know. The more visions I get, the clearer it becomes."

"But you talked with my mother who said that it was not an accident."

"And it wasn't. It was intentional. Judy didn't know it was a Holly Farms truck. Only that it was a big enough truck to kill herself without hurting the other vehicle."

"I still can't believe that my mother would do that. And now you want me to believe my father was murdered and was involved in my mother's suicide."

"He was upset with her about Hollis. He couldn't kill her. He was a ghost.

He had to trick her into thinking it was what she wanted."

"But it was my mom who turned into a beast at the warehouse," said Judy

"I don't have that one completely figured out," admitted Celeste. "It's possible that they can all do that. Or it is possible that your dad did that so that no one would listen to your mom's version of events, but I know for a fact that your father is capable of turning into a beast."

"This is all just so hard to believe," said Judy. "I came here to get rid of a ghost and a shadow man and now… It's like my whole life has been a lie."

"Getting involved with the other side can change your life. You will never look at people the same way again. You will always know that there **is** an afterlife and you will wonder about it. That is the price of knowing it is there," said Celeste.

"I think we've had quite a reading today. But, our time is almost up," said Celeste. "Is there anything else you want to ask?"

"Is my mother here?"

"I don't see her, but we can ask," said Celeste. "Judy? Are you where you can hear us?"

Judy did not appear, but a pen slid across the table.

"That's probably a yes," said Celeste.

"Did you swerve into that truck on purpose?"

There was no answer of any kind.

"Your mother obviously doesn't want to talk about it, Judy."

"I need to hear it from her," cried Judy. "I won't believe it until I hear it from her."

"Then accept it as an accident," said Celeste. "But there was no conspiracy killing unless it involved your father. And very few people are going to believe that."

"Do we need to set up a new appointment or do you have one set up?"

"I think I have one for Monday."

"Very good, I'll see you on Monday."

"Wait! What about the picture? Why did you need it and what happened?"

"Your mother said she saw a little girl, but the truck driver saw your father in the road that night." The table started to vibrate. "I'd say your father is back. Why don't you go ahead and go home. We don't want to stir up the beast again."

Her next few clients were easy fortune telling. Dori was at her usual time. Her grand-cousin-nephew etc. was not coming back, but he was not trying to have her declared insane anymore either. That was a win.

There were a lot of questions still nagging Celeste about the relationship between Harper's and Holly Farms. Maybe there would be some answers tomorrow at Harper's. There had been no word from John, but she assumed he would be picking her up in the morning.

Emma was right on time at three-thirty. Coming in quietly and going straight to work cleaning up Celeste's office. There were unopened letters all over the desk. Most were bills. Some were payments. And there were a few letters of praise for her work. Emma felt those should be framed and displayed in the entry. Making a mental note to take them with her on her next trip to Denton, she put them in a special folder. There was a frame shop in Denton that would do a nice job.

"You went through my mail?" said Celeste with a look of horrified surprise. "You went through my personal mail?"

"I was trying to clean your desk and organize it better. Do you know how many checks you have here? You could go on a shopping spree in Paris with this much money!" pleaded Emma.

"I will get used to this, I'm sure. It's just all very new to me, having someone in my house and going through my personal letters is difficult."

"I'll ask before I do anything like this again. But there is a lot of money laying here. Do you want me to make a deposit for you?"

"That would be a good idea. Most of the clients either pay by credit card or often cash. The checks are just a bother."

"Now that you have a smart phone, you can also deposit them by phone. But there are so many here right now, it would be easier to take them to the bank," said Emma.

"I wonder why my four o'clock hasn't called yet. Or is it her off week? I have too many to keep up with."

"That's why I'm trying to get it all organized. May I practice reading runes with you today?" asked Emma.

"Okay, let's do it now."

"We'll do a simple three stone layout," Emma said as drawing the stones from the bag. "This is your past, this is your present and this is your future."

Gasping as she looked at the first stone. "You have had a horrific time in the last few days. Have you had to battle another beast?"

"How did you get that from that stone?"

"It spoke to me when I touched it. It showed me a vision of you battling another beast," said Emma

"You are going to do very well at this if the stones offer you visions."

"Your present has had a beast around you, but it is quiet now and at least for the remainder of the day."

"That sounds wonderful," said Celeste.

"But your future…" Emma paused.

"Oh, Gods, what? What do you see?"

"There is a bigger demon waiting for you."

"Demon?" yelled Celeste. "Who said anything about demons? These are spirits losing control, nothing like demons," said Celeste.

"I see what I see," said Emma.

CHAPTER THIRTY

Despite Emma's innate talent, there was still training needed and Celeste was happy to have such an eager student. It occurred to her to give Emma one client. It would have to be someone who would let Celeste know how it was going. She would not be able to charge as much as Celeste until there was more training, but her visions were incredible.

"I want you to familiarize yourself with the angel cards, Emma. I want to find out if they will give you visions when you are familiar with them," said Celeste. "If you can learn to read them, you can help me at that church bazar that Lori has roped me into. It's on a Saturday. Would you be able to do that?"

"OMG!!!" yelled Emma. "Do you mean it? I would get to do readings with real clients?"

"That would be the plan," said Celeste delighted with Emma's spontaneous reaction.

Emma hugged her. "This is going to be exciting."

"The only catch," said Celeste "is that you can only use Angel cards. No Tarot, no runes, no pendulums, only Angel Cards. I have an extra set that you can use, but if it works out you will want to buy your own set. You can probably find them online if not at the book store."

"I will order some tonight," said Emma. "Can I borrow yours until tomorrow so I can get familiar with them?"

"That's a great idea. Order some and use mine until yours come in."

"Okay, that's enough training. Go work on organizing my desk and papers. By the way, tomorrow is Friday. I won't have appointments, right?"

Emma giggled, "No, Ma'am. No appointments on Friday from now on."

"Have you been keeping track of your hours? I do intend to pay you for your time. You'll be contract at first."

"Two hours a day, four days a week," said Emma.

"What about that night at the warehouse?" said Celeste.

"Are you kidding? I should pay you for that! That was sheer entertainment. I watched you take a demon down."

"That was not a demon. Never call a spirit a demon. If they can still take human form, they are not a demon," said Celeste very seriously. "That was the beast that resides in all of us. For some it is more like a lamb. For others it is a full blown beast, but if the person can retake control, it is **not** a demon. If I can defeat it, it is **not** a demon. This is important. What you name a thing, it can and most likely **will** become. Do you understand?" said Celeste firmly.

"Yes, Ma'am, I'm sorry. I didn't know," said Emma.

"I hate to jump on you so hard, but you are on a spiritual journey now. Your words have power. Never doubt that and never forget that. I do not stare beings down. I bring them up."

"Will you still work with me?" said Emma.

"What a silly question. Of course I will work with you. You are my apprentice. I am responsible for you."

"Thank you. I'm sorry I took it so lightly," said Emma.

Celeste smiled. It was not a huge toothy smile. It was a contented smile that shone in her eyes. Her apprentice would learn more than she could yet imagine.

"You will do, my dear. You will be far more powerful than I am now or ever will be. You will learn the responsibilities that come with the gift."

Emma had been working on the desk while they talked. There were so many bills and checks and letters and random pieces of paper with poetry written on them and lists and recipes. It was a puzzle how to organize it all.

How would I do this on a computer? There was a three ring binder and a three holed punch on the desk, but it became apparent that it wouldn't work for her purpose. The sizes of paper made that impossible. Then she noticed some clear pockets in the back of the binder. Putting all the recipes in one pocket and the poetry in another and so on would work. It was at least getting organized.

Emma showed the binder to Celeste to get her thoughts

"This is marvelous! It had been my intention to do something like this. There is a box of the plastic pockets somewhere in my office. Did you find them?"

Emma shook her head. Celeste went in to look for them and saw her desk.

"I knew there was a desk under all that mess. I'm so happy you found it!"

Celeste opened a drawer and found the box of plastic sleeves and two more binders.

"If you use these then you can have a binder for each of these sleeves and a separate page for every two pieces of paper. Let me show you," said Celeste and proceeded to set up a few pages in the "recipes" binder.

"Perfect," said Emma. "It's almost time for me to leave. This will be my first project on Monday."

"I like it. This will make life so much easier."

Emma smiled and was happy to be back in Celeste's good graces vowing to stay there from now on.

"Listen. Make sure you have those Angel cards when you leave," said Celeste. "It's important to be able to use them. Call me if you run into any problems with them, okay?"

Emma left and Celeste pulled out her phone texting Danielle;

{Have you had dinner?} Celeste

{Not yet. U?} Danielle

{Starving. Where do you want to go?} Celeste

{China Star Buffet?} Danielle

{YES} Celeste

{B there in ten} Danielle

"I can see I'm going to have to learn a whole new language just to be able to text," said Celeste.

Chaos agreed that it was a travesty.

Paul appeared. "There's a desk there," he said.

"Very funny," said Celeste sarcastically even though she had just used the line herself. "What's up?"

"Holly and the other girl are the same girl."

"Is that possible? And if so, how is it possible? Ghosts don't change that much unless…"

"Ummmm Hummm," said Paul with a knowing, sarcastic tone.

"Her beast is a crying child?" guessed Celeste.

"Give that woman a cupie doll," said Paul in his best imitation of a Carnie voice.

"So.... Holly isn't running around the world with Judy Sr., they've been getting her riled up and using her inner beast when they need her," said Celeste. "That's brilliant, but poor Holly. What can we do to help her?"

"Try to summon her," said Paul. "Whichever version of her shows up, you might be able to help her."

Celeste tried summoning her. Nothing happened.

"Desperate times call for desperate measures," said Celeste.

Walking to the cupboard she withdrew her crystal wand. Channeling all her power and energy through the wand she said an incantation:

Wherever you are

By the name of Holly

Put down your toys

And come to me.

Swirling the beautiful crystal wand and repeating the incantation three times the crying girl started to appear. Celeste looked her straight in the eyes and said, "You have nothing to fear Holly. I will never hurt you and I will do my best to protect you."

The little girl stopped crying but still didn't look like Holly. In fact it looked like the girl was ready to start crying again.

"Holly, listen to me. I know your Daddy and I know he misses you. Do you miss him, too?"

The little girl tilted her head but nodded acting like she didn't trust Celeste, but was willing to listen.

"Would you like to visit him?"

Holly appeared where the crying little girl had stood. "How can I do that?" said Holly and Celeste could hear her.

"I can take you to him," said Celeste. "But I think you know where he is and I think you know deep down inside that you can get to him just by thinking of him. You may scare him at first. Has that already happened?"

"Yes," said Holly. "When I try to talk to him he gets all scared and tells me to go back to Satan, but I've never seen Satan."

"I know you haven't, sweetie. Your Daddy doesn't understand how it works. Is that when you start crying?"

Holly nodded and said, "I don't know what to do. A man tried to help me. He had me stand in the road one night. We played a game. He said the cars would go right through us, so we played chicken. My car lost. Then we went to a building I'd never seen before. There were lots of adults there, but no kids. Then I saw the kids outside and I went to play with them. Not all of them could see me, but most of them could. We played with some wagons in the woods, but when it was my turn to pull the wagon I couldn't. So they wouldn't let me play anymore and they started screaming and I started crying and I didn't like it."

"Maybe we could go see your Daddy together. I can explain it to him. Would you like to try that?"

"Yes."

My friend is coming over to go to dinner with me. Can you come with us and then we will find your Daddy together?"

"Yes."

"And can you stay like you are and not become the crying little girl?"

"I'll try," said Holly.

Paul had already disappeared and Danielle was at the door. Celeste let her in and explained what was going on.

"Why can't we take her to meet her father first?" said Danielle. "That's more important than some boring old dinner isn't it?" she said nonchalantly.

"Can you see her?" Celeste asked Danielle.

"Yes, she's a sweet little thing. Why wouldn't I be able to see her?"

"Danielle, I just told you it's a spirit."

"Like a ghost?" said Danielle, her eyes getting wider.

"Some people would say that, yes. But they are spirits. I don't like the other name and I don't think they do either."

"Why can I see her?" asked Danielle.

"You know, I'm still trying to figure that out. You're not the first one to see her and I suspect you won't be the last."

"Just for grins, can you tell me who her father is and where we're going to take her in **my** car?" asked Danielle.

"We can use my car if it's a problem. I'd be happier if you would drive, though," said Celeste.

"No, we can take my car, just joking. Can't you take a little joke?" said Danielle trying to act calmer on the outside than her nervousness let on and not doing a very good job of it.

"Do we know where her father is?" asked Danielle out of the side of her mouth and whispering to Celeste.

"Not sure," said Celeste. "Holly, do you know where your daddy is? Can you feel him? Maybe at the farm."

"Don't take me to the farm!" cried Holly turning back into the crying beast.

"No, Holly, not that farm. Your Daddy's farm," said Danielle.

"Oh, Daddy's farm, is he there?"

"Let's go find out," said Danielle and did a U-turn on a double highway to get going in the right direction to get to Holly Farms.

When they arrived, they noticed a house in front of the farm. The lights were on in a couple of rooms. They decided to try there first.

"Holly, will you stay here in the car with Danielle while I go see if he's here?" said Celeste.

"Okay," said Holly.

Celeste rang the bell and Mr. Hollis came to the door. He was surprised to see her but invited her in.

"What can I do for you, miss...."

"Just call me Celeste. We met here the other day when Judy Wells brought me here only to discover that her Uncle Hollis worked here. You remember?"

"I do. That girl needs help," said Mr. Hollis.

"That may be, but tonight there is someone closer to you who needs help. I have her waiting in the car. Apparently she has visited you before and scared you which scared her and then things got out of hand. May I bring her in?"

"Who are we talking about?" asked Mr. Hollis.

"Her name is Holly."

Mr. Hollis turned white as the glass of milk he was holding right before he dropped it spilling milk everywhere.

"I'll help you clean that up in a few minutes," said Celeste. "First I need you to say hi to a little girl that needs to know you are not afraid of her. Can you do that? Can you see her and not be afraid?"

"You are crazy. You are crazier than Judy. I don't know what you want, but if you think I'm going to pay you for some illusion that Judy cooked up, think again!" yelled Mr. Hollis.

"Mr. Hollis, This will cost you nothing. We are trying to help your daughter. Don't you want her to rest in peace?"

"That sounded a little out there even to me," said Celeste.

"Look, just talk to her. I know you've seen her before. She told me about it. I can't guarantee she'll rest in peace, but at least talk to her without freaking out," said Celeste.

"Bring her in," he said as calmly as any man could in the situation.

Celeste went to the door and waved Holly in. Holly appeared instantly beside Celeste beaming with joy to see her daddy. Which startled Mr. Hollis for a second, but he recovered well.

"Holly," he said. Then he opened his arms to her. Running to him she ran right through him. This was going to take some work.

Celeste waved Danielle in and let the father and daughter reunion take place while she cleaned up the spilled milk.

"Daddy, can I stay here with you?" Celeste heard her say.

"Yes."

"Mr. Hollis, we're going to leave you two now. Would that be okay with you?" said Celeste.

He waved them off.

CHAPTER THIRTY-ONE

Celeste and Danielle went to dinner. Danielle was beside herself over the supernatural experience. Celeste had them all the time and sometimes would share details with Danielle. But Danielle always believed that Celeste embellished the stories. Now it was clear that that wasn't the case at all. Danielle had chauffeured a ghost around in her car!

When they finished dinner Danielle wanted to go for drinks, still a little "high" on her first ghostly experience. But Celeste had to work at Harper's in the morning. Not wanting to be the party pooper, but needing to get home and relax a little before bed, she begged out.

"Dang, girl," said Danielle. "You have no idea what this is like for me. Am I going to have nightmares or dreams or will I even be able to sleep tonight? Is that girl going to haunt my car? This is just too much for me."

"You can handle it, Danielle. I have faith in you."

Danielle calmed down a bit, and said, "You do? Honestly?"

"Yes, I do. I wouldn't have put you in the situation if I didn't think you could handle it."

"Okay, I'll drop you off."

"Don't tell anyone about this, Danielle. In the first place, they won't believe you. In the second place they will think you have a few screws loose. Don't talk about it unless you say you saw it on TV."

"I won't. I'm probably just going home, myself," said Danielle.

Celeste wasn't too worried. But did feel the need to at least warn Danielle about how people would react.

Celeste got ready for bed, but decided to watch a little TV tonight. She turned it on only to find it was News time. Something caught her attention. A Mr. Kirkland was being arrested for embezzlement. They were standing outside HARPER'S front door.

All this time Celeste had thought of Mr. Scott as the head honcho at Harper's because he seemed to be able to do as he pleased having forgotten that he was only head of HR. This man they were arresting was the VP in charge of Finance. Apparently he had been there for decades and had accumulated a lot more money than could be explained by his salary and bonuses.

Police were crediting an employee of Harper's for finding the second set of books. There was Carol on the TV. They said she was a part time clerical worker who had discovered an old safe in the warehouse office. They were saying she had managed to get it open and had found a set of books from the nineteen nineties that had been prepared by Mr.Kirkland when he was a clerical worker.

These lead to an internal audit and investigation by an undercover agent of the IRS. His name and picture were being withheld for obvious reasons.

Carol had brought her finding to the head of HR months ago and the investigation was launched immediately.

"We were business as usual as far as Mr. Kirkland knew," quoted Mr. John Scott who oversaw the investigation. "We even brought in a well-known local psychic towards the end to cover our need to spend so much time near the downstairs office and files."

"We planted a story about boxes flying off the shelves and much more to enhance the illusion that the warehouse was haunted. Everyone bought the story."

"I'd especially like to thank Celeste, the psychic we hired, for going along with us on it. A true psychic she was a great help in a number of ways."

The business phone started ringing almost instantly. *Let them all go to voicemail.*

So John thought he had duped me? He didn't think there was any real paranormal activity? But Celeste knew the truth.

Celeste's cell phone started to ring. It was John. "So I guess you need me tomorrow to **pretend** to be a psychic?"

"Why did you think I bought you this phone? I knew when this came out that your listed number was going to be ringing constantly. I wanted a few people of your choosing to be able to get through. This isn't over."

"So you already know that Kirkland killed Mr. Wells?"

"What? Are you serious? We can get this man on murder charges? How do you know? Is there any evidence at all or is it all psychic?" said John talking a mile a minute.

"John, you have no idea what I have been through. I have wrestled with spirit beasts. I have dealt with Mr. Wells and his now dead widow. I have gone out of my way to help solve the murder you didn't even know about."

"I understand and we all appreciate it. You have kept people distracted while we went over the numbers and they were huge. But why did he kill Wells?"

"Wells found discrepancies in the books. He took it to the VP. Within days he suffered a "fatal heart attack". That means he was poisoned, but there was no reason to suspect foul play. They probably didn't even run any tests. I don't know if you can find evidence of any of this or not. But it's what happened."

"Celeste, I'm going to tell you something. You can't come into Harper's tomorrow. That would raise suspicions, but we still need your help. We think there was a payoff coming from higher up and now we have a murder to look into. We already have someone coming to see you as a client. They will be your contact now. You probably remember him. His name is Dean."

"Oh my Goddess, you have got to be kidding. That buffoon is an investigator?" said Celeste.

"Good cover, eh?" laughed John.

"Is there anyone else I need to know about?"

"Yes, but I can't tell you yet. Just know that your business is going to boom from the publicity and we know that you are a true psychic. We have all seen too much to believe otherwise. We have a team of people watching out for you. We're going to keep you as safe as we can. You and I won't be communicating after this because we have no legitimate reason to. If you need to contact me then you can do it through Dean."

"You understand that putting up with Dean will be above and beyond, right?" said Celeste.

"Celeste, one more thing, you should probably stay away from the creek until you've talked to Dean. Bye for now." John ended the call.

"Well if that doesn't beat all," Celeste said stroking Chaos on the neck.

The cell phone rang again, "Hi, Joe. Are you at work?"

"Yes, but the news is spreading everywhere. And you are on YouTube. How does it feel to be a celebrity?" he asked.

"I feel like I'm going to need to put in another line and hire a sister psychic, 'til everything dies down."

"So… You're enjoying the spotlight," said Joe. "I hope it brings some great clients. I'll bet you haven't even answered the landline since the News broke at six p.m."

"Six p.m.!" said Celeste. "I only saw it at ten o'clock. It was on at six o'clock, too?"

"Yep, all three stations."

"So my recorder is probably full and they are getting a full mailbox message," said Celeste. "Could be worse, I guess."

"Joe, I'm going out to dinner with someone tomorrow night. I just wanted you to know. It's a first date and it's nothing serious. He's just fascinated with being around a psychic who can see ghosts."

There was a long silence.

"You know I can't stop you and you know that I would be with you every night if I didn't work nights, but I understand. May I know his name?"

"Richard."

"That sounds okay I guess."

"He's harmless. Like I said he's just hoping to hear some ghost stories. He'll be a great friend, I think."

"The poor guy, he hasn't even had the date yet and he's already ejected to the friend zone."

"You make me sound like a gold-digger. I think I'll enjoy his company or I would never have said yes to dinner. He's the tech guy that set up my phone for me."

"Ooooh…. A tech guy…. That's special."

"You are just jealous."

"Of you or him? That's the question."

"Now you're just being mean. So when are we having dinner again?"

"I brought last time," said Joe. "It's your turn."

"Do you like pot roast?" said Celeste.

"I do," said Joe. "When did you have in mind?"

"How does Saturday look for you?"

"It's looking better and better. What time?"

"That's up to your schedule," said Celeste.

"Can you have it ready by four p.m.?"

"Absolutely I can. I'll see you then."

The phone had been beeping during her conversation with Joe. Apparently there were a few messages. It took her some minutes to remember how to get to them.

{Did u see the News?} Danielle
{Yes I'm Famous} Celeste

{Just saw the news. U want me to come in tomorrow?} Emma
{Yes, the earlier the better.} Celeste

{Are we still on for tomorrow night now that you are famous?} Richard
{Yes} Celeste

{nine a.m.?} Emma
{ok} Celeste

{I need to see you in the a.m. eleven ok for u? This is Dean}
{ok my apprentice will be here ok?} Celeste

{Are you the Celeste on the news tonight?} Norman
{Yes} Celeste

{Want to have dinner tomorrow night} Norman
{Already have plans} Celeste

{Saturday?} Norman
{Plans} Celeste

{I'm turning the phone off. Long day. Talk tomorrow afternoon?}
{ok} Norman

{Goodnight} Joe
{Good Morning} Celeste

Admittedly no one could have talked to all those people in that short of time if they had to do it by calling. Texting was proving quite useful.

CHAPTER THIRTY-TWO

Emma arrived at nine a.m. and let herself in. Celeste was still asleep. Emma started clearing messages from the phone, so they could get more messages until she could actually start answering the phone which was still ringing almost constantly.

When Celeste woke up and saw the time, she gasped. "How did I sleep this late? And why is my door closed? Emma, of course, Emma is here working. Still I have to be ready for Dean by eleven o'clock."

After showering and getting dressed she opened the door to Emma walking into the kitchen. There in her hand was a sack breakfast of sausage and biscuits with egg. It smelled delicious and Celeste devoured two of them. Emma ate the third.

"Thank you so much," said Celeste. "This is wonderful!"

"My pleasure," said Emma. "I have gotten all the messages off the machine and started calling them back. You are not going to be able to handle this many people. We're going to have to set up a gallery reading on a Saturday or Sunday afternoon. How does this Sunday look for you?"

"This Sunday? As in day after tomorrow?! That's pretty fast," said Celeste.

"Strike while the iron is hot. Isn't that what your generation says," said Emma.

"That might have been my mother's generation," said Celeste with a smile. "I'm not sure what generation I'm in anymore."

"Did you hear what they said on the news about you? They acted like you were no help as a psychic and I know you were. I was there," protested Emma.

"And yet the phone won't stop ringing," said Celeste. "Notoriety will always bring people in."

"I have a client coming at eleven o'clock. We'll need privacy. He's kind of a loud person, so you will be the judge of whether you need to take an hour off or not."

"No problem. I need to pick up a couple of things from an office supply store. I can go at eleven o'clock as easily as any other time."

"Thank you, Emma."

"It's almost eleven o'clock now. I already made the deposit. Do you have any cash for the office supplies?"

"How much do you think you'll need?" asked Celeste.

"If you have forty or fifty, I'll bring back change."

"Here you go," Celeste just gave her a credit card. "Sign as yourself."

The doorbell rang and Emma went to let Dean in, "Well, aren't you just a pretty little thang? I'm here to see Miss Celeste. You can tell her Dean is here."

"She knows," said Emma leaving him in the waiting room. He had a strange aura. It was like he was wearing a mask.

"Dean, come on in," said Celeste.

Dean walked in and the minute they were alone his demeanor completely changed. He had an inside voice after all.

"I hear you called me a buffoon," he said. "I appreciate that assessment. It's what I was going for."

"Why are you here, Dean? It's my day off again. Since everything at Harper's has been handled."

"You may be in a position to ruin this investigation, or worse. You could be in danger. We have someone keeping an eye on you. In fact we have more than one. I am one. You can call me anytime. We have the excuse of you being not only my psychic, but also my Gramms's psychic."

"If anyone gives you bad vibes, or if you pick up something psychically, or if you just want to talk to someone, you give me a call. You have my number. You got it last night when I texted you."

"Why would I be in danger?" asked Celeste.

We announced to the whole world yesterday that we have been involved with an investigation of Harper's accounting. There is still one bigger fish to catch here. We don't know for sure who it is, but we have it narrowed down to a couple of people and you have met with both of them in the last week or two. See where I'm going with this?"

"Well, who are they?" demanded Celeste.

"We can't tell you just yet. If we tell you then you will treat them differently. Then they might get suspicious and that could put you in danger. Let me ask you. Who has called or texted you since the news broke yesterday?"

Celeste pulled out her phone and let him look. It felt like an invasion of her privacy, but it wasn't really her phone and she did want his protection.

"This feels like you and your cohort set me up. You knowingly put me and Emma and all my clients at risk."

"Really, it was only you that was placed in a little bit of potential jeopardy. No one else was named. And all we did to you was praise you for your help and swamp your business to the point that you couldn't squeeze in any more boyfriends. You are one active woman."

"It seems to me that I've been used," said Celeste.

"In fact, did you dangle me out there as bait?" asked Celeste. "You did, didn't you?"

"Not intentionally," said Dean. "But it looks like we got ourselves a nibble."

CHAPTER THIRTY-THREE

"A nibble? A nibble?" shouted Celeste. "You've put me in danger and now what am I supposed to do? Treat everyone I meet as a big fish?" she said sarcastically. Celeste was not happy.

"Little lady, you just keep doing exactly what you've been doing exactly like you've been doing it. You treat everyone exactly the way you've been treating them. That's your best bet."

"John told me to stay away from the creek for a few days. What does that have to do with this?" asked Celeste.

"I don't really know, Ma'am. Unless he saw the heavy rains being forecast. That creek will flood or come close and there won't be much warning. Yep, bet he saw a weather forecast. I reckon you should stay away from the creek. Don't you worry about rattlesnakes down there, anyway?"

"I'd never thought about it. Are you trying to scare me away from everything?"

"No, I'm not trying to scare you at all. I'm trying to reassure you."

"You're failing," said Celeste.

"You can't blame a man for trying." Dean gave her a wink and a smile.

He really could be a charming man when he wasn't trying to be a buffoon and a big fish in a small pond.

"I guess my hour's about up," he said going back into character. He was so loud people outside could probably hear him. "Thank you. I'll be seeing you next week."

Dean left and Emma came back in. "That was perfect timing," said Celeste. "Were you sitting on the porch waiting for him to leave?"

"I swear, I just drove up," said Emma.

"How did it go? I know you don't like him."

"He was much better today. It turns out that if you hit him over the head with a baseball bat he can remember to use his inside voice," Celeste said as they laughed about it together.

"I've been studying with your Angel cards. Would you like to let me do a reading?" asked Emma anxiously.

"Sure. Why not? I don't have anything planned until seven p.m."

They walked into the reading room and Celeste sat in the client chair. Emma was nervous, but excited to show off.

The reading was conducted with flying colors. All the information was printed on the cards, so there was no book to refer to. It made it look easy. However it was anything but easy to pretend to be using the cards when you were really using your own psychic abilities.

The day sped by and Emma got all messages caught up and had a list of fifty people for the gallery reading. That meant they would have twenty five to thirty actually show up. That tied Celeste's Sunday up completely.

Dinner with Richard was less enjoyable not knowing which of the people she knew might be the big fish. Although a tech guy at Walmart hardly seemed likely. You just never knew.

Richard walked her to the door and he was ready to kiss her goodnight when Celeste noticed a strange car parked two doors down. John said people were keeping an eye on her? Had he meant it literally? She decided not to risk it explaining that a psychic had to be very careful about who they touched. She had been right, though. Richard was interested in the ghost stories. He was on a paranormal investigation team.

Satisfied that he was not the big fish she texted as much to Dean then called Danielle to talk about the date. They laughed and Danielle made her feel better as always.

Joe texted at ten p.m..

{Are you still on your date?} Joe

{No, I'm home. He just wanted ghost stories.} Celeste

{I miss you.} Joe
{That's so sweet. Just think tomorrow is pot roast} Celeste
{How could I forget?} Joe
{I miss you, too} Celeste
{Good night} Joe
{Good morning} Celeste

Celeste woke up early Saturday to get the roast started wanting it to cook all day. Everything was prepped. All that was needed was to seer the meat and add everything to the crock pot.

The cell phone rang at two p.m. It was Norman. She had forgotten that he was going to call.

"You're a hard woman to reach these days. So, you didn't tell me you were a psychic. What's that like?" he said.

"Some days it can be exciting and some days it's pretty boring. These days it's just extremely busy. My apprentice had to set up a gallery reading for Sunday because we've had so many phone calls we couldn't schedule them all. Do you believe that? It's just crazy," said Celeste.

"To tell you the truth, I'd rather go horseback riding on a Sunday," she said flirting just a little. She really liked Norman. He was such a gentleman.

"Then let's go horseback riding," he said. "You don't have to have whatever you called it to make people happy. Come ride with me instead. I'll bet I can take you someplace else you've never seen."

"I wish I could, but Emma has already scheduled it. It sounds like a wonderful afternoon."

"We could go in the morning..." teased Norman. "What do you say?"

"I couldn't in the morning either. I have things I need to get done. Things are going to be very busy for me in the next few weeks. Then the news thing will die down and I'll be more available."

"Can I at least call you again?"

"Of course you can. And I promise I won't be as busy in a couple of weeks. I'm training another psychic to help me and she is coming along really fast."

"Well, I'll give you a call later in the week," said Norman and they hung up.

"If I didn't know better I would call that a little pushy, suggesting I go out the morning of a big Gallery reading. He doesn't take me seriously."

Chaos wandered in, jumped up on the counter and sniffed the crock pot. Tonight's leftovers were going to be very good.

Joe rang the bell at exactly four p.m. "I could smell that cooking from the porch," he said. "I brought the desert, an apple pie and vanilla ice cream. I hope you like apple pie."

"Who doesn't?" she called from the kitchen, putting the ice cream in the freezer. "Are you ready to eat or would you like to visit a little first."

"I think I'd like to visit a lot," said Joe pulling her in for a kiss. "You are so tasty. I don't know how to describe it."

"Joe, let's not get too friendly here."

"Would you rather get friendly in the living room?" he asked still holding her he twirled her towards the sofa in the living room.

"You are a hard man to resist. But so is my pot roast and I do not intend to get sidetracked from it for long. I've smelled it cook all day. What time do you have to be at work today or tonight?"

"You think you're changing the mood, but you're not. I don't have to be there until midnight."

"So you should still be home sleeping."

"I thought I might take a nap here after dinner. What do you think?"

"I don't see why not. This is a very comfortable sofa."

"Woman, you tease me mercilessly."

"I'm going to serve up the pot roast," said Celeste. "I should have made quiche or something "breakfastier". I wasn't thinking about what time it was for you."

"I love a good pot roast any time of the day," said Joe. "And this one smells better than I can tell you."

"Well, come and get it. I hope it tastes as good as it smells," said Celeste.

It did and they both fell asleep sitting on the sofa before they even had any pie and ice cream. They may have squeezed in a kiss or two. Celeste woke long before Joe, cleaning up and then just watching him sleep.

Celeste would probably have slept with Joe if it hadn't been for the fact that someone was watching her.

But what little physical contact they had was enjoyable.

He left for work and she went to bed a little frustrated. It bothered her not knowing all the facts. Who did they suspect? Was she being watched even now laying here in bed? It wasn't easy to fall asleep that night.

Sleeping in Sunday morning to recharge her batteries for the beating she would take at the Gallery that afternoon was a gift.

Emma was there two hours before hand. Setting up folding chairs that had been rented Friday, there were seats for thirty. Emma had everything organized flawlessly. Each person was given a ticket as they paid for entry. In order to get a reading they had to give Celeste the ticket.

Celeste explained to the group that there were more spirits here today than there were living. Celeste would skip over certain people that either had no spirits with them or had too many. Those people were not to worry. Celeste would come back to them.

Celeste had a large vase full of red and white carnations. Finishing with each person she would give them a carnation. Emma had worked out a system; red meant they had good potential as a client. White meant sign them up if they asked, but don't push it.

As Celeste went from person to person delivering messages from the spirits that had accompanied them in, Emma escorted each one after their reading into the office to set up a future appointment. All but six of the thirty seven who showed up made appointments.

By the end of the day Celeste was completely drained. She could hardly move. It took so much out of her to connect with that many spirits at once. Emma finally understood as she was also being bombarded with messages. But Emma wasn't the one having to deliver them. When everyone was gone the two ladies collapsed on the sofa.

"How much did we bring in?"

"I don't know. I haven't counted it yet."

They both burst out laughing. They laughed for five minutes. It seemed to recharge their souls a bit.

When they had run out of laughter... Emma said, "I could do this, you know. I could help with galleries. I can see them and hear them."

"But can you deliver the message in such a way that the client is happy and the spirit is happy? Are you seasoned enough to do that?"

"I never thought about that. I don't know if I am or not."

"There will be plenty of time to explore it," said Celeste. "Take your time. You are young. Hone your skills so that you always help people and spirits alike."

"You are the best teacher I could imagine," said Emma.

The doorbell rang. Emma went to answer it. It was Dean.

She showed him into the waiting room and ran to get Celeste. "Dean is in the waiting room."

"What does he want?" moaned Celeste.

"You," he said in a deep soft voice.

He had broken character in front of Emma, so Celeste knew it must be serious. She just couldn't bring herself to care.

"I'm too tired for this, Dean. What exactly do you want?"

"Tell Emma its okay to leave now. I'll take care of the folding chairs and even return them to the rental house tomorrow. But Emma needs to go home."

"You heard him Emma. Go ahead and go home. I trust Dean. I've read him. He's actually good people. Shake her hand, Dean. Read him."

Emma was shocked. "He is good people. I would have never guessed it. Okay I'm outie. I'll be here tomorrow at three-thirty."

"I'll see you then," said Celeste.

After Emma was gone, Dean locked the door and checked the windows.

"He's on the run. Something or someone tipped him off. Did you ever read Norman?"

"No, I was wearing riding gloves that day," said Celeste.

"Have you talked to him in the last couple of days?"

"Yes, he called yesterday. He wanted me to go riding with him again, but I've been so busy. I had to put him off for a couple of weeks."

"A couple of WEEKS? I think I know what tipped him off. He has to be on foot. Wait? Did you say riding? He could be on horseback, except someone would have seen him leave."

"Not if he used the creek," said Celeste. "Last weekend he took me all the way to Holly Farms and the only time we were visible was when we had to cross the expressway. We had to ride up the service road and cross under and then turn back south to get in the woods again."

"Did you get that?" said Dean. "Good I'll stay here with Celeste just in case." Dean had an earwig to stay connected to the team.

"It was Norman? The big fish was Norman?"

"Yep, we had it narrowed down to Norman or old man Hollis. Hollis didn't contact you after the news. Norman West did."

"We did some digging and found what we needed to put it squarely on him. He made more from the deal than Kirkland did. And you were right about Wells. We found some papers in his home file that proved the embezzlement scheme was going on and implicated both Kirkland and West. Once we have him in custody we'll be out of your hair for good."

"Who is "we" exactly?" asked Celeste.

"Well, you won't remember him, but he was the first man you interviewed at Harper's. He's been watching you nights and I've been watching you days. You've been under surveillance since the first time you walked into Harper's."

"For a psychic you don't notice a lot of details, do you?"

"I knew I was under surveillance, but I didn't know by whom. And I knew that John Scott was hiding something, but I didn't know what. I pay more attention to the spirits than I do to the physical universe. For instance, did you know that you have about six spirits following you around?"

"I do not."

"Everywhere you go. I promise. I wouldn't lie about something like that. There are four men and two women. One woman is older and one is a child. The men are all in their twenties. If I had to guess, I'd say you were in a war together. They didn't make it. You did."

"Okay that could all be true, but you need to pay more attention to the real world."

"It's all real, Dean. You may not want to confront the Spiritual universe, but it's just as real as this one."

"I try not to get into philosophical discussions at work," said Dean closing the conversation.

"Got it. All units rally at Holly Farms," barked Dean. It looked as though he was giving orders to the chair.

He turned back to Celeste, "We've got him in custody. You should be safe now."

"Are you really related to Dori?"

"Yes."

"What about Joe?"

"What about him?"

"Was he involved in any of this?" asked Celeste.

"No. You pulled him in on your own. He seems very protective of you though."

"So…. What about Emma? Does she work for you or was that just a coincidence?"

"Do you believe in coincidence?"

"No."

"No, she's not with us, but seems to be a really good fit for you. I would keep her if she was on my team," said Dean. "But I would say the same thing about you. What do you think? Would you and Emma be available if we ever needed your help here in Texas again?"

"I think we would."

"Then I guess you'd better hang on to that cell phone."

THE END

View other Black Rose Writing titles at <u>www.blackrosewriting.com/books</u> and
use promo code **PRINT** to receive a **20% discount** when purchasing.

BLACK🌹ROSE
writing™

CPSIA information can be obtained
at www.ICGtesting.com
Printed in the USA
FSOW01n1846141117
41110FS